One Day to Live

One Day Trilogy, Volume 1

Brendan Kage

Published by Piskie Publishing, 2025.

ONE DAY TO LIVE

First edition. August 1, 2025.

Copyright © 2025 Brendan Kage.

ISBN: 978-1068283314

Written by Brendan Kage.

Kate

Thanks for
your Support

22:00

Dark. It felt cold. Stone cold. Almost wet, but not. Like the feeling of laying on a tiled floor naked. He lay on his back. Why can he not move? Thoughts rattle around in his mind. Something was stopping him. *What is this? Am I stuck, trapped maybe? I can't see a thing.* Never had he experienced blackness like this before. Total blackness, no sign of any light at all. Panic had set in, and his heartbeat started to rise. It pounded in his ears and pulsed at his temples. There was an itch across his chest as he took each breath. With every rise and fall, he could feel it; moving. The sensation reminded him of a poor quality t-shirt, the harsh fibres scratching at his skin. *What the hell is this? Where am I?' This thing, this, this.... sheet; it's a sheet.* Like hospital linen he thought, thick, hard, course, like no fabric softener was used to wash this. But was that it, was he in a hospital? Why was it so dark? Had he gone blind? Confusion did not begin to express what he was feeling. Fear arrested him.

Was it the grip of fear, or something more that held him there, motionless, grasping his very soul.

Cold. Why did it feel cold? Something else alerted him. It felt close. Something about this just felt close he thought. The warmth of his breath lingered, trapped almost; within inches of his face. Close.

He could see nothing. There was no smell, no sound at all? *Have I been drugged?* he thought, although his mind seemed to have clarity, free of the groggy awakening from chemical unconsciousness. *Have I lost my senses? No, wait; cold; itchy sheet; warmth of breath. I am still alive at least. But what is this?* Was it the fear that was suppressing his regular functions? Terror now nibbled at the edges of panic, chewing its way through his thoughts.

He tried to focus, to gain some form of perspective to at least understand if his other senses remained functioning, or if there was simply nothing to detect. No sight, no sound, no smell, no taste. He drew a deep breath through his nostrils causing his chest to rise. At least he could feel; this sheet, hard, coarse, scratching at his skin.

Within his fingertips there was a sensation of pins and needles, but he could detect movement there also. Were they moving? Was he imagining this? Dreaming perhaps? No, he could definitely move them. His mind was losing control of thought with the myriad of things that could be. He could feel the roughness of his fingertips rubbing together, as the print from each digit slowly moved in circles as he passed his thumb across his forefinger and middle finger on each hand. The sensation was relief, to know that he was alive, he could move. But something was preventing him from moving. 'What?' He could now feel each of his fingers move more freely, he drummed them from little finger inwards, and now there was the feeling the tapping of each movement against his thighs. This did little to ease his torment, and terror was still lurking in the corners of his mind.

Toes. In the movies, it's always "can you wiggle your toes?" He could, but his feet, ankles at least, felt stiff, frozen, as if encased in ice, no movement at all. His hands were the same. His entire body even. Something had happened to him. *Am I paralyzed?* he thought. He tried to speak aloud. *'Hello'.* In his head it sounded like he spoke, but he knew that he made no sound. There was no sensation of motion in his face, no jaw movement, nothing of the tongue striking his teeth to create the 'L' sound, nor the lips contracting into the circular formation to annunciate the word. Nothing. Panic continued to rise. Distress now seemed to weigh heavily upon him.

He wondered were his eyes even open? Was this the reason for the darkness? But he could feel that they were. The fold of the skin as his eyes opened from a blink was evident enough to know his eyes were indeed open. He was able to blink. But he could focus on nothing. He could see nothing. His mind raced.

Something gripped his attention; in a unanimous fashion. There was a movement; a gentle dull sensation to his left wrist, though he could not fathom what that was; but at the same time there was light. A dim, soft light, as though it was the glow from a screen of a phone, but covered over. In the light he could see, but whilst his eyes fought to focus, the light faded and was gone. He reeled over the sight. Indeed it was close. Very close. The light had allowed him to see that he was contained in some form of box, metallic in appearance, steel perhaps. He was unsure. He had only caught a glimpse through the faint light that had only momentarily allowed him the opportunity to know that his eyes at least were not betraying him; that he could in fact see; there was just nothing to see. Once more, all he could see was black.

Panic became petrified, seeming to have suddenly leapfrogged several stages at the realisation that he was entombed within some form of box. The fading of the light only seemed to make the walls close in further still.

He could feel that slowly, sensations were returning to him, his arms were able to move just a little, at the elbows at first; he felt like a bird that had been dazed from crashing into a window but trying still to flap its wings. His legs, he became aware that they too were recovering from whatever state of suspense it was that captured his body. He hoped, longed that he would be able to get up, but where could he go? There was no room to move, not even sit up. The enclosure felt like being woken in a coffin, only it seemed as though it was slightly larger. From his fleeting glance in the subdued momentary light, he thought it was no more than six inches from his nose to the fortifications that seemed to entomb him. As feeling slowly returned to skin, he gathered that his body was naked, covered by this sheet. There was something on his wrist. It felt like the plastic type paper wristbands that he remembered from theme parks in his childhood, or the music festivals he went to in his carefree days. Could this be some form of hospital tag he wondered?

He could hear the beating of his heart in his chest. The pace had been rising, now it felt like excitement, or worry; faster than a normal rate, but not so fast that there was exertion. His breathing rate had risen too. Was this a restarting of his entire autonomic system, or just his anticipation of his surroundings and what awaited him? Terror had now taken over. He had never considered himself to be claustrophobic, but this box was restraining his very existence. *How did I get here?* his mind raced.

Before this box, this darkness; she was there. A park; which one? The thoughts danced in his mind. They were walking, it was Autumn, the air had been crisp, the colours were exquisite, the river had looked still and calm. And her, there by his side, with her usual casual appearance. They had walked together, her arm linking his, replaying the events of their week to one another. They had laughed; they had been serious; they had talked about the plans for the coming weeks, about too fast approaching Christmas get together with the families, and where they wanted to spend New Year. Then there was nothing. Just this box. How?

The ability to move had progressed from wing flapping to nearly full function, but there was no space to move. He could wriggle his body, and was able to turn onto his side somewhat, where he again felt the biting cold sensation. Whatever this prison was made of, he was laying on it. Cold, metallic, smooth.

Once more, his senses were overcome as he felt a vibration on his wrist and light seemed to flood the place. A mixture of emotions flooded his thoughts.

He brought his arm up towards his face and watched as the light again faded to blackness. This band, it had lit up. At least part of it had. It looked like a screen from a smart watch, but he had never seen one like this. There was no shape, no form, only that same plastic type of paper band. The lighted section had been rectangular and seemed to display "22:20" and beneath it, a familiar looking message bubble with the number "2" inside. With little room to manoeuvre, he pressed on the band, but nothing happened. He pressed again, held his finger on it, and shook it but nothing.

As he was now at a point of full sensation and ability to move, he began to press against the walls of his prison. He could detect a slight movement, but he knew that he had neither the strength nor leverage to have done anything more. Still, that didn't stop him from trying. He lay on his back and pressed upwards, then outwards to either side. He almost exhausted himself in pushing with all his might. He banged, as hard as he could, would anyone be able to hear him? He tried to shout again, but only managed a mangled sound of half chocking and half speaking. After clearing his throat, he tried again. He knew this time that it was much louder and clear. He listened intently for any sounds around him, yet the silence was deafening. The box only seemed to kill the sound. No echo, no reverberation, just a hollowness. He called out once more, but still there was nothing in return. Only silence. Could anyone even hear him from inside this tomb? Did anyone even care? Was he being held, against his will, by some tormentor that would only ignore his pleas for help? He concluded that he had watched too many movies, and that real life was something different.

His sarcophagus was still in complete darkness. He felt around, touching the edges and corners of the walls that surrounded him. By his estimation, this crypt was nothing more than 24 inches in height and width.

There it was again!!

Light.

Nothing more than a soft glow, but it seemed to illuminate the darkest secrets of his innermost being. Oh, how his eyes had longed for something other than blackness. "22:24" and "2" the display read.

Over and over, he pressed the band in some mad ditched effort to make the thing light up. It was futile. But what was this thing? Trying to get a better understanding of what was his only possession other than the sheet, which itself was now somewhat entwined in his legs from the wreathing inside this coffin like prison; he twisted and turned his fingers around the thing, feeling around for some form of button, catch or other such method of making it do something, anything.

It lit again "22:27" and "2" said the display. With his right hand already poking around at the band, he was perfectly poised for 'doing' something as it came to life this time, though he could not account for why.

With his finger on the display, he poked, pushed and moved it around. Upwards! His face alighted with excitement that the thing responded to an upwards sliding gesture. The display changed to one typical of a smart watch, but this thing, this plastic paper band, was still something out of a science fiction story to him. Flexible, yet seemingly versatile and durable. Like the similar felling bands of his past, he knew this thing would likely be difficult to damage without a direct attack.

The display gave a number of options, the first of which was the message bubble that he had seen beneath what he assumed to be the time display on the initial screen he had witnessed. Inside the bubble remained the number "2". He pressed the bubble and as he now expected, it responded to open the messages. The two messages were displayed in a manner familiar to all. The first had been received at 22:10.

"ONE DAY TO LIVE"

What did this mean? His pulse and respiration rate increased suddenly, and the trepidation began towering over his existence. His mind was already exhausted from the awakening, and being trapped in only God knows where. One day to live? What was this? His very being became agitated with anxiety.

The second message, received at 22:20 read "Task 1 – Get Out!". This was not what he had expected. He didn't even know what he expected, but this was not it.

Was this a sick and twisted game?

Was he with her last?

He remembered being at a party with friends, they had drank a lot, he was a little worse for wear. He tried to convince himself, surely this was a prank from his friends? A lurid half smile pursed at the corners of his mouth, until he realised they were not that gifted or cunning.

Whatever was happening, he needed to get out of this box.

He once more reverted to his vain attempts to push against the sides of this box. Over and over, he pushed with all he could muster, but he only succeeded in expending his energy, as he had minutes earlier. He rolled over and pushed against the end section that had been above his head.

Movement!! The panel had not given way, in fact, it held firm. But he had moved, he felt it, heard it even. His arms had been able to extend some minute amount, whilst still being bent, he figured he had moved about an inch or two. There had been a sound of drawer runners, before the inevitable thud as his movement halted.

Whatever this surface he was lying upon was, it had moved. He pressed with his feet against the bottom, but that only served to slide the surface back to where it had been. He pushed again with his arms, only repeating what he had before. This thing was definitely sliding, not by much, but it was. He kicked down hard at the bottom, but again it only moved him back to the original position. Stretching his arms up, and pressing his feet against the bottom, he pushed as though to extend his body to its maximum reach and could feel the give under foot. He pushed and pushed, the pressure felt so great that he was sure his back would ache and become stiff as soon as he released. Two new emotions now seemed to balance on scales, an equalising dose of relief that there was some form of movement, against the frustration of his feebleness.

As he continued, he could feel the movement continue under his feet. He knew he was going to succeed in Task 1. As long as he continued to push, he was sure he could 'get out'. But pain wreathed through him from the force of his pressing. His body could only cope with so much at a time. He stopped, hoping to take a moment to recompose. Under the mental stress of the situation, and the physical exertion he had put into his fruitless efforts to escape this cage, he was drifting along the edge of consciousness, in the zone of not realizing you're actually dozing off. He rested his forehead on the cold steel on which he now lay face down.

He thought of her, where she was now, what was she doing? Her face was the only picture he could see. Her head tilted slightly to the right, and a cheeky smile that slowly broke into a laugh as he had tried intently to stare into her eyes, which had now closed over as she chuckled, her hair loosely falling by her face. She ran her finger through it, tucking it behind her ear.

But she was not here, not now. He was alone. Time had passed, he knew it had, but unable to get this infernal wrist strap to work on command, he did not know how much. It had felt like seconds, but he knew it was longer. Surely not hours. He recomposed his position to push once more, above and below; beginning slowly at first, easing up the pressure. He could feel the give beneath his feet, but still there was nothing but a slight movement. He tried to stamp at it, but over again, the slab on which he lay, just moved in the opposite direction.

As he proceeded to push, hands and feet, there was something to give, he could feel it. A bending almost. With the sliding slab pushed up as far as he could, he began again to stamp at base of this box, this time knowing that the slab had nowhere to go. He kicked with his heel, but this only sent a shock though his leg that he knew he would later regret. Turning onto his back, he was able to clasp his fingers around the edges of the sliding slab on which he lay, and with as much leverage as he could manage in the 24 inches of space to bend his legs, he kicked out hard at the foot of this crypt.

It gave.

Light burst in from around the seams. This was the entry; this was the exit. He kicked once more, causing the door to swing open towards his left-hand side. He could see there was a room out there. A clinical, clean white light seemed to flood the place. He was free. Reaching his hands above him, he pushed, causing the slab to partially slide out of the opening. Pressing his hands against the sides of the now broken cell, he pushed the slab further out and then wriggled his body the rest of the way.

As his eyes began adjusting to the light, he could smell the pungent chemical cleaning products. Something of that smell reminded him of his high school biology lessons. As he sat on this virtually floating slab, suspended several feet from the floor, he recognised the room, but only from what he had seen on TV. He knew this was a morgue.

Once more his thoughts raged, and he wondered for a moment whether he had come back from the dead. Nonsense, how could any rational human consider such as a reality? But why was he in a morgue, naked, covered by a sheet, with a band around his wrist. In the cold clinical light, he looked at the band in more detail. It was white, with a green stripe running most of the way around it, slightly off centred. The only place the stripe did not feature, was where he thought the 'screen' had been located. Confused, he saw there was just a white expanse in its place, about an inch and a half long, and a number printed in small red numerals "36".

With eyes darting around the room, he took stock of the place. Around 160 square feet, this room was painted an uninspiring grey on what he assumed was already grey breeze block. There was no need for fancy decorations in this place; its usual occupants had never complained. The clinical lighting emanated from typical strip lights, sunken into a suspended ceiling commonly found in office places. The floor was covered in some rubberised fashion; this must be a hospital he thought.

The room had two sets of double doors, pale green in colour, each with partial glazing, the kind with wire mesh running through it. There was sheet aluminium across the middle of the doors, which had obviously taken persistent impacts over a prolonged period, he assumed from porters' trolleys. It was evident that there was no lighting on the other side of either door.

One such porter's trolley sat across the room, in the space between the two doors; one opposite him; and the other to his right, at the end of the room. The trolley stood, in vacant occupation, the bed bound in black leatherette, with only a pile of folded clothes and a pair of cheap pumps on top. As he lowered himself from the extending bed of the mortuary cabinet, the feel of the floor on his feet was relief that he was free. There was no sign of life in this place. Despite this, his nakedness created a sensation of vulnerability. He called out again, hoping that someone would respond, a nurse attend to him maybe; what was happening? The remainder of the room was empty. No desk, no chair, no filing drawers or anything else to speak of.

As he turned, he could see that he had emerged from a middle stowage section of a cabinet three tiers high, which was located in a bank of eight such units. He noticed that each of the doors had a padlock fitted to the bottom of a pin that seemed to drop through cylindrical sections, two mounted to the door, and three to the front casing in an alternate layout. Though the door to *his* unit had the same cylindrical fittings, he could see no signs of any pin or lock that may have come off of the door from whence he had escaped.

In his escape, he had evidently had to forcibly overcome the handle of the pod, which from the outside, seemed to require only a squeezing action to release the latches of the door. Wondering if any of the other units were occupied, whether some other poor soul may be trapped inside as he had been; he began shouting and banging at each of the doors. It struck him however, that although he had felt cold in there, it was the cold of the metal against his skin; he had not been in a cold environment. This mortuary cabinet was not 'on'; at least it was not set to a 'chill' temperature. Surely there could not be bodies inside, or the smell would be rancid.

He turned to the trolley and paced across the room; the pain of striking the door with his heel now showed itself and caused him to limp. Moving the shoes from on top of the clothing, he sifted through the neatly posed items, that appeared to have been carefully placed, prepared even. There was a plain white polo shirt, 'Medium' was printed in a black ink on the inside of the fabric, just below the collar. It had no labels of any kind; they had clearly been removed. A pair of dark blue trousers, of thick cotton material; once more, the labels had been removed. Below there were underwear. Plain, black, elastic at the waist, the kind that were a close fit; but again, there were no labels. He put them on covering his manhood for the first time since his awakening. Beneath the pants were socks. Plain and black, but oddly folded, as though they had been ironed. He got dressed.

Twice he noticed as he was clothing himself that the 'screen' of this wrist strap had illuminated. "22:51" and "22:52" it had read as he glanced at it. He had not lost as much time as he thought he had from dozing in his tomb. It occurred to him that movement had 'activated' the band. He moved his arm, wrist and hand in different directions, trying to replicate the illumination of the screen to work out quite how this thing operated. Twice more he had made the screen illuminate, each time it faded within seconds; "22:52". The third time it lit, he was aware of what motion was required to make this thing spring to life; a flick of the wrist, rotating the hand outwards and quickly in towards himself. The screen came on but would fade quickly. At least he had finally figured it out.

Now fully clothed, it was time to leave this room. The first set of doors was clearly locked, though he knew that with a little brute force, he could push the two doors hard enough, so that the lock would be overcome. He peered through the glass, and with the light casting through from behind him, he could see that this was not a hospital. This was a real morgue. The room he now faced was clearly where bodies were prepared for burial. He could see another empty trolley, similar to the one from which he had just dressed. There were various 'tools' on a steel table to the side. A shiver passed through his spine, and a wave of disgust and horror washed through him. He gathered there were high level windows to this room, though they were covered from the inside, painted over almost. If necessary, he could use these to escape to the outside world. But he first resolved to check the other door. It was open.

Pressing against the right-hand leaf, he hesitated as it moved a few inches. Peering through the glass of the door, he could see a corridor ahead that turned to the left some 12 feet onwards, clearly around the side of the room he had inspected through the other doors. A smell was creeping in through the open crack of the door and lingering in his nostrils; musty, stale, unused and abandoned. There was an orange spill of light across the floor, and he knew that there was an exit at the end of this corridor. As he pushed open the door further, he could hear the outside world. The dull sound of passing vehicles. He knew he was close to being free.

As he rounded the corner, he was faced with glass double doors. It was streetlight that was spilling in, creating an orange glow. There was something covering the middle section of the doors, casting a shadow in the shape of a thinned torso; no head, no legs. An eery apparition of a floating body seemed to be all that stood between him and his escape.

A coat. It was hanging from the latch of the door. Black, heavy, a short overcoat type with a fleece lined collar. Just hanging there, inviting him to take it. He lifted the jacket and twisted the latch. To his amazement, it was open.

He stepped outside and was overcome by the elation of being out of this hell. It was cold, typical early December temperatures. He looked at the coat in his hand, as though it was too good to be true, and put it on.

It was clean smelling, freshly washed, but was not new. It had clearly been used before. He started to walk, to where, he did not know. He just walked. With the pain in his heel, and the ache of his body from forcing his way out of his prison, he was not sure how far he could get. Whilst the imminence of danger had been left behind in the metal casket, turmoil of emotions continued to pursue him, and the necessity to know just what the hell was going on, ran ahead of him.

There was a road some 300 yards away with intermittent passing traffic. If he could make it to the road, someone could help. He checked the pockets of the coat and clothing as he walked, he found nothing but lint and fluff. He had always hated that feeling. It repulsed him more that this was not *his* lint and fluff, who knows what else had been in there. As he approached a streetlight, he saw that the jacket had an embroidered insignia on the left breast. Looking at this from upside down, he realized it was a number.

"36" it said.

This had been the number on his wrist band, he was sure of it. He stood, under the streetlight, and lifted his arm to look more closely, being careful not to flick his wrist to 'activate' the screen. "36" he was right. And as he stood, with confusion across his face, knowing not where he was, nor what was happening, as it had earlier when he had been confined in that infernal borstal; trepidation engulfed, and there was a unanimous vibration as the screen came to life.

23:00

————

The display showed the time, it was 11pm, and below it was now that familiar message bubble; "1". In light of the happenings of this strange contraption less than an hour ago, he came to know that the vibration alerted him to the receipt of a new message. Pressing his finger to the screen and swiping upwards, he found within the message menu a new communication from whoever this anonymous sender was.

"The significance of 23:00 is more than just coincidence. The clock is ticking..... tick tock".

Confused by the message, he had no knowledge, no reference as to what exactly it meant, but it was becoming clear, this was no prank. Someone, somewhere, intended for him to do something. What?

It seemed that he had less than 24 hours to complete this task. Task? Yes, he remembered the first messages. *"Task 1"* one of them had read. Surely there would be a Task 2? It had not come, as yet at least.

He slumped to the floor, leaning against the lamppost, to take better stock of this contraption on his wrist. He quickly learned to navigate around the menu with swiping gestures. Whatever this thing was, it seemed that although it had the ability to receive information, it was unable to send anything. He noted that one of the icons was a timer, a countdown, "22:51:53". The time was now 23:08, this was counting down in synchronisation, 23 hours from the time of the message. He now knew at least what was ticking, and just exactly how long he had. By his reckoning, the countdown would expire at 10pm the following day, 24 hours after he had first woken encapsulated in the morgue.

He searched through the functions of the band and he found there was a map, which was able to determine his current location. The roads were not named, too much detail for such a small screen. He could not recognise the area. He was able to move the map around, to orientate it, searching in hope for some point of reference that was familiar to him, though there was nothing that he remarked. However, he then noticed two blue dots, similar to that which marked his own location, yet smaller, less luminous. They were close to one another, but not so close that they were together.

There remained the intermittent cacophony of passing cars, now only a hundred yards away, but he sat, motionless, staring with intent at the tiny screen on his wrist, watching the movement of these two blue dots, which he knew, like his own representation on this map, must represent other people. One was approaching the other, gaining on it as they moved in the same direction. He had no way of judging the distance between them, but it was getting smaller by the second.

The screen faded and went off.

He flicked his wrist back and forth quickly, and sliding upwards once more, it had returned to the initial main menu function. It had taken him a few seconds since the fading screen to find the map, and once it loaded, it was back to default, showing his location. Frantically he searched around for sight of the other two dots. He found them; together. He had missed the interaction, the arrival of one dot to another. But the two seemed to move together now, much slower than before. They stopped.

He wondered who they were? What were they doing? Where they had paused?

He was hungry. The beginnings of pain in the stomach that spoke before a strong desire to eat. He needed food. He needed coffee. Perhaps this was what the dots were doing. He imagined a cafe, dingy, greasy, a narrow street hidden from the majority footfall. The kind of place where an 'all day breakfast' was about the only thing on the menu, and the coffee was stale from being left on the warming plate for too long. They sat, he imagined, discussing a great adventure. Who were they he wondered?

The thought occurred to him that there seemed no other signs of life around this pair. Or was it that he could only see these two, and if so, why them. What was so special about the dots that he could see where they were, yet no one else? Perhaps they could see where he was. A thousand possibilities played out in his mind, of who these dots could be, or what they were. Time had passed as he sat there. He had poised his finger over the display of his band, and each time the light started to dim, he had quickly pressed it, bringing it back to full light and thus avoiding the 'return to main screen default' if the screen went off. The top of the display exhibited the time, he had not noticed this before, too intent on searching the content of this device, or watching the dots as some voyeur of the unknown. 23:19.

He became curious of the band once more and began to study the other features. It was rather basic, though considering its uniqueness, seemingly some future technology, it was an extravagant piece of technical engineering. Aside from the 'messages', 'countdown timer' and the map, it had some form of compass. The direction of what he assumed to be north floated in an arrow around the edge, and there was a number in the middle of the dial, '1,361m'.

The night was dry, cloudy but not overcast. The stars were visible in patches, but mostly drowned out by the light above his head. He stood and walked towards the road, where he knew there were signs of life. It seemed that a vehicle passed roughly once every few seconds. At this time of night, that meant it was definitely some form of main carriageway. He startled at the striking sound of sirens only a short distance from him. A police car had seemingly been called with some urgency, as he heard the roar of the engine meet the demand of the driver, but the sound was all too familiar of a vehicle moving away from him. Through a gap in a hedgerow, he could see the vehicles as they passed.

Having moved a sufficient distance away from the streetlight, he observed the sky once more. He studied the visible stars in the vain hope that he could identify something to help him navigate; but he had never paid much attention to that sort of thing, and as he scrutinized the glistening pinpricks in the black veil that was surrounded by patches of purpled velvet cloud, he knew that it was stupidity to believe he could make any informed decision of his location based on the night sky. He continued towards the road. Progress was slow, his leg hurt, but he knew that with some over-the-counter-meds, he could easily take care of this.

Passing through the gap in the hedgerow, through which he had observed the passing vehicles, he emerged at a dual-carriageway. The relief of seeing people, even as they hurtled by, giving no regard to a jaywalker; brought a feeling of exultation to his chest. A weight had lifted. But as soon as his spirit had enlightened, it was crushed with the sentiment of doom, as he felt another 'buzz' to his wrist. A sinking feeling set in, pulling in the pit of his stomach as he knew this was another cryptic communiqué from his tormentor. Even though the buzz gripped him like a hand wrapped around his heart, his curiosity was stimulated and he knew it was impossible to not give this his full and immediate attention.

He lifted his wrist, shook it in the now familiar fashion to once more illuminate the display. 23:30, one new message. He opened it. At first glance he knew this was significant, he had almost expected as much was to come.

"*Task 2*" - his fear had been realized.

Whatever had happened to him, whatever was happening to him, it seemed as though it was the perverted game of some distant persecutor, who was evidently intent on plaguing his future, at least for the next twenty-two and a half hours.

" – *find 35*" it continued.

Gathering himself among the question of what or who 35 is or was, a sobering realisation befell him; this was not a dream.

In a daze, he stood at the roadside, staring at this message, unable to compose his thoughts. The screen faded, went off, but still he stood with his arm in front of his chest, wrist exposed, head tilted down towards it though his eyes had completely lost focus in the way that things seem to become distant, an insignificant blur.

A lorry passed him. His bemusement had him so engrossed that he had failed to notice the approaching sound and lights. It had registered that his shadow was moving in a semi-circular motion, yet his bewilderment gave this no further attention. The rush of air as the wagon swooped by him, almost close enough to have scraped his arm, caused him to lose his balance somewhat and search for surer footing. The grit and debris brought up from the surface of the road by the passing lorry's length and multiple wheels, sandblasted against his exposed skin and entered his nostrils causing him to grimace.

He stepped back from the edge of the tarmac, and found a place to rest himself, slumped on top of the crash barrier. Perched there, whilst physically ruffled by the wind-rush and sandblasting of the HGV, his mental tranquillity of days gone by was now beaten to submission by the anguish that presented itself through the weighing of the state of affairs he was facing.

Now pondering whether to be compelled by the instructions from this unseen author, or to throw in the towel now and begin seeking the help of others, to tear off this infernal band and to hell with this game; his mind was dominated by a desire to know.

35? He was 36, so who is 35? Is it even a 'who'? Was there another, similar to him, wandering in the dark, not knowing what was happening to them? If it was his task to find this other, this '35', what tasks had been assigned to them? Was it even possible that there is a '34', and perhaps yet another 33 before them, all of whom potential victims to this deranged happening? Was he the last? What if there were more than 36? Oblivious, the remainder of society seemed to busy about with their regular schedules, cars continuing to pass him, merrily on their way to whatever had taken them on their voyage, no thought for him, or anyone else wrapped in the odd events he had experienced.

The gravity of the situation began to pull him back to the reality of his surroundings. He now found himself at the side of a road, he did not know where. He knew not why. But there was a sense of urgency, that gave him to know that he must act, and fast. Whatever this was, the clock was indeed ticking. 23:37. He checked the timer again, "22:22:19", as he had suspected, the clock was reducing by the second. Becoming conscious once more of the two dots he had witnessed a short while ago; he searched the map for them, knowing roughly where to look this time. After what seemed like an age, he found the location they had been, but now there was only one dot, with no sign of the other.

The one he could see was still, motionless, a little further on from where they had earlier been, but only by a miniscule amount. Was the size of this screen problematic to his perception of distance he wondered? As he gazed with intent at the beacon of another being, probably trapped in this same nightmare, he once more considered the possibility that 'others' may also be able to see him. They needed a collective, a gathering, a coming together of each of them to reach a communal understanding of what, why.

But how daunting it was to think, the harrowing thought; what if they were to find him? What if that meant to him harm? A million possibilities played out before him in an instant. Still, he needed resolve. He needed to know.

A task had been set of him. He must find 35, whoever this was, wherever they were. He imagined the possibility of finding another also enslaved to a wristband which, like with him, was now taking control of their very existence. But again, he considered this person would not be all that he may hope for. In that moment, he was sure that finding 35 was not the end of this madness. He rose from the crash barrier, and like a child struggling with a paper maze, he studied a way back towards his own location from the position of the other dot, which remained fixed some distance away; he resolved to find them, if nothing more, to find this one, and workout the riddle of his current status.

With the map as his guide, he would find them, and together they could seek out others. Together they could make sense of their place in this monstrous predicament.

23:40

As he paced along the embankment at the side of the carriageway, he saw the inevitable encounter in his mind, playing over the initial meeting and discussions. He did not know what he expected to find, though the mere presence of the dot on *his* map caused him to consider it most likely that whomever this dot turned out to be, they would be dancing under the strings of their own wristband and the puppet master. He wondered how this other, towards whom he was heading, had come to realise themselves, their band, were they too awoken from some mystical slumber? Had they also been captive in a temporary resting place of the dead?

With each step, still feeling the intense pain in his heel, he played over the events of his escape. Why had he been trapped inside a body cooler? He again considered the possibility that he had died and had somehow been resurrected. Were it not for this bizarre game to which he was now a pawn, he would have thought it too absurd. But now anything was possible, wasn't it? He rationalised his thought, and he knew that it could not be so.

Save for the aching of his body from the exertion of his escape, and the pain in his heel now shooting with each step, as far as he could fathom, he was otherwise uninjured. Before his awakening, he had been a man of reasonable health and had kept himself in shape through his passion for cycling. As he had gotten older, despite his system slowing down, the rate of metabolism plummeting from that of his earlier years; exercise was something of a must rather than simply for enjoyment of the sport. It seemed like fate was a twisted notion; as the body grows older and becomes more worn, less able to exert itself as it had in youth; it now needed a greater level of use to keep that 'middle age spread' at bay.

His level of fitness, whilst certainly nowhere near its peak, was reasonable enough that he was relatively 'fit and healthy', as he had checked on so many forms and documents.

There was no sign of significant injury to his body that he had noticed thus far, and he could not comprehend why his awakening had found him captured within that corpse fridge. The door had been closed, but it was not locked, as the other doors had been. Why? The padlock and the pin had clearly been removed prior to his awakening and his was the only compartment that seemed to be occupied. He could not have been there for long, nothing more than a few hours. Whoever put him there, had either failed to secure the door with the pin and lock, or deliberately removed these protections in order that he would be able to free himself from within. He remembered 'Task 1', and immediately knew that his escape had been allowed to occur; this was all by design.

Having travelled a distance of several hundred yards, he came to an intersection and made sense of his position on the wristband map. A few hundred more until the next cross-roads, where he figured that according to the map, he needed to make a turn. Plodding on, his sore heel and subsequent limp was slowing his progress and the pain seemed to rise upwards, creeping higher up each time his leg was forced to bear weight. His knee now throbbed with a deep aching pain. Could this be an infectious pain, spreading from the initial injury below it; or had the limp caused him to carry his leg differently, that before long would present as a further problem? The traffic was thinning now. A vehicle passed only now and then. The side of the carriageway along which he moved, facing the oncoming vehicles, was seemingly busier than the other. Only a small volume of traffic travelled in the same direction as him. Was the more heavily travelled route as a result of people moving towards the city nightlife, or heading home to the suburbs?

The last he could remember before the sepulchre box in which he had found himself, it had been a Saturday. Was this still the same day? There was no immediate way to know how much time had elapsed. As an adolescent he had seen films where the protagonist had found themselves thrust into some unknown place or time; they would always check the date on discarded newspapers, but daily printed media had become a thing of the past. He must find some other way to know what day it was and how long he has been away. Had it been days, weeks, months, or God forbid, even years? And with that thought, came a gut-wrenching feeling, the pit of his stomach turned as he realised the grip on reality that was lost. Not knowing how much time had passed since he was last with her, caused him to feel, in the deepest sense of the term; lost.

23:49 as he approached the next corner and raised his wrist to check the map once more. He was relieved to see that there was still no movement of this mystifying blue dot.

The cold was biting hard. Grimacing at the thought of the lint and leftovers, he stuffed his fists into the jacket pockets to add some protection to the bare skin. At least there was no wind to speak of that would multiply the chill factor.

The road was quiet, but considering the speed at which the traffic seemed to fly by he knew it would be madness to attempt to cross with the sluggish hobble he carried. It would be a much safer option to use the pedestrian crossing at the signal lamps. The anticipation of reaching the control button welled in him like a child running ahead of their parents to 'get there first'; his gait had lengthened, and his pace increased, but as the button sank in and the 'wait' light illuminated, the excitement subsided immediately. He watched intently, staring at the recognizable red figure anticipating the change to green. Impatience tiptoed in and he urged to just start trundling across the tarmac. Turning his gaze to the lights that control the traffic, he was pleased to see amber and considered it safe enough to commence his crossing.

There was an uneasiness that befell him as he moved across the hard surface of the road, a knot in his stomach. As he approached the midway point, there was a car approaching at speed on the other side with no signs of slowing. The driver had clearly failed to notice the red light towards which they advanced, until such a time as the only manner by which they could ensure they did not breach the crossroads, was to perform an emergency stop. The tyres screeched as they struggled to find grip, the sound blended into the ABS system fighting to maintain composure. Stepping out from the central divide, his eyes caught those of the driver, who was obviously shaken by the manoeuvre. As she looked at him, her face was a picture of her startled expression, as though she was the proverbial deer in the headlights, a role reversal for a driver. This woman was clearly distressed by her late perception of the right of way being removed through the imposing rouge luminescence of the floating boxes over the road. She stared at him intently, unsure whether to be thankful she had not continued through the red light to save herself from the embarrassment she now felt, or worse.

The pungent smell of the burning rubber slapped his nostrils and was then interrupted by the stench of the overheated brake pads. Passing in front of the vehicle with his eyes locked on hers, it became clear to him that this was the first person he had shared any interaction with since his awakening. So drawn to her he felt, that he was unable to release his gaze from her, and turned his body to face her, whilst continuing across the road, walking backwards. He must have appeared as some drunk with his sagging form as a result of the pain crippling his leg from any regular movement. She must wonder why on earth this stumbling figure was intently watching her. Perhaps she thought that her ridiculously late halt at the lights was the reason he peered harshly into her skull, looking right through her eyes and into her soul. She moved on. Evidently, her light had changed and her car sprung into life, lurching forward like a prey that just escaped the clutches of a predator.

He turned back to the direction of his travel, and looked ahead down the road on which he now found himself. The warm glow of the streetlights afforded him sight for some distance but eliminated the possibility of observing greater details, particularly colour. A blanket of orange was draped across the scene, only permitting the observation of shade for every other object in his field of vision. He was entering an urban area, passing through the fringe from unoccupied ground, to scattered residential. As he continued, there were parked cars, houses in silence with no signs of life other than the odd a faint radiance of a bathroom light that had been left on through the night. His progress was much slower than he would hope for and knew that he would need to resolve the pain soon. Surely there would be a pharmacy around here before long. He would rather deal with this sooner than later, and concluded that he would plead for help from the first person he encountered.

Midnight approached as he checked his position on the map. Quickly finding the other, there was still no movement and he seemed to be getting more proficient at the limited features of this mysterious band. Considering the hour, it was likely that they were asleep he thought. Perhaps this dot had not been, like him, entombed only a little over an hour earlier, perhaps they had found a much different set of circumstances, and were not plagued with turmoil as he currently found himself to be. Determined that he would find them, he cared not about the politeness or decorum in not waking them, how could they sleep at in a situation like this anyhow? The previous interaction this dot had shared with the now absent other, continued to vex his emotions. How could they not have rallied together? If they were also hostage to the instructions of a distant persecutor, what tasks had they been instructed to do, and why would this cause them to separate from their union?

Swiftly now approaching his destination, after making several turns, he perceived he was only a half mile or so away from the dot. He became more anxious, knowing not whether this was in anticipation of the impending encounter, or impatience at not being able to move faster. So far on his voyage, he had not passed another soul save for the startled driver at the crossing. He had witnessed the odd person, walking, crossing in the distance, but they were too far away to have given any coherent response had he tried to seek their attention. He had passed a few houses where the curtains were closed to the lower level, but lights were on behind them. Shadows had danced with a bluish tinge presumably emanating from television sets. He knew that he could call upon the assistance of the occupants, but this would only prevent his engagement with the dot, or jeopardize this crazy quest. And what could such people do to help beyond his physical ailment?

Would the Police be able to assist him? Would they give him the time of day considering the ridiculousness of his story? Who would ever believe that he had emerged from a cadaver cooler. The predicament of his circumstances was nothing short of a fiction novel. But whoever this dot was, surely they would believe him; surely they too would have a band, like him, and be manoeuvred by the hidden puppeteer to complete their bidding, whatever it was that they wished for them to do. Hoping that he would soon find out what had been asked of this other. He was minutes away from discovering who they were, what they knew, and what undertaking they had been instructed to complete.

00:00

———

The chill in the air grew stronger as midnight passed. It was crisp but not cold enough for ice to start forming. Regardless, a night outside in this cold would not be good for anyone. The suburban streets had developed into a more commercialised area, with rows of houses intermittently interrupted by groups of retail shops. One shop he approached, on the other side of the road, was projecting light from within that spilled out onto the footpath. As he drew closer, he could see that there was some signage written across the windowpane by clear elements of glass in the midst of a satin finish around it; *Peggy's* it read. There were signs of life within; silhouettes and shadows danced with determination at the glass.

Standing across the road, less than 30 feet from the place, he observed a man inside, scurrying around as he went about his business. Mid-20's, tall but thin, a man of little frame, with dark hair and a face that looked unshaven and roughened by early aging. Evidently, 'Peggy's' was a bar, now closed for business. The occupant was cleaning up, moving glasses, lifting chairs onto the tabletops. Fixed there, watching, unsure how to approach this unknown bar keep for help, he stared into the window as the man looked up to see him. This gave him enough start to advance towards the establishment, his mind too hazed with tiredness from the pain in his heel and its constant overworked, over-stressed state of the last two hours. A momentary slip in his resolve, that perhaps also came with a drink.

He crossed the road, resolutely heading directly for the door, his body, wrought with pain, exhausted from the physical and mental anguish was simultaneously drooping in places but stiff in others. He must look like a zombie to the eyes of this barman as he slowly wilted across the road. The man turned his attention back to his tasks; apparently, he cared not about this figure of inebriation looming outside. On reaching the door, he grabbed at the handle and was bemused that the door did not open. 'We're closed' he heard as the tapster pressed glasses into an automated washer and slammed the door shut.

'*I need to ask you something*' he responded, sounding as hoarse as someone dehydrated and scorched, the projection of his voice was weak and unassuming. '*I need to ask you something*' he called out again, louder and stronger than before, and he rattled the door handle. 'Piss off, we're closed' retorted the other, slipping out into the back rooms, leaving only a momentary portrait of a man shaped outline in a doorway that swiftly closed. Darkness befell the bar, descending the entire place into obscurity. Whoever this bartender was, he was not intent on offering any assistance to the vagabond at the foyer.

It was time to move on. He needed to find 'dot', and when he found them, together they could seek out help. 00:09. The melancholy of a group of spirited men being ejected from another establishment seemed to fill the air with sound, though it was distant enough that he could not make out the annunciation of their bawling. They were not to be seen, perhaps a street or two away from him, their muffled hollers dampened by the buildings that separated them from where he walked.

He could hear his pulse, throbbing in his ears and at his temples. He was fatigued and needed rest, but that would have to wait.

Having navigated down several smaller side streets, he grew ever nearer to the position of this other. There remained no sign of movement on the map from where they had now spent the best part of an hour. He soldiered on as the sounds of the night began to grow; he perceived he was heading towards a busier area. Soon enough there would be a thick of people, the streets awash with the loutish crowds enjoying their evening 'on the town'. If this was, as he hoped, only hours from his memories of the Saturday morning, it was now the beginnings of a new day. Should he not find some other mystery of his awakening, it was a Sunday, 'the Lord's day'. What on earth would God make of this mess.

He had never considered himself a religious man, but in light of the current predicament, he prayed as he walked, asking God for forgiveness of whatever wrongs he had committed that may have led to this strange awakening and all that it brought. He replayed the details of all his bad decisions and poor choices, reeling to know if any could have resulted in this torment. There were a few that stood out to him; wrongs he hadn't righted; sins he hadn't repented. Perhaps he was deserving of this after all.

It was only a few hundred feet by his estimation to where 'dot' was shored up. One more corner. At the next left turn he would find them. The excitement and anticipation swelled within him as he envisaged the unfolding of their meeting.

As he rounded the building at the corner of the street there was a convenience store, now closed for business; but he was too transfixed with finding this other than searching the shop windows for any signs of his place, both in location and in time. The street he now faced was narrow, only wide enough for one vehicle to pass down at a time. The scene reminded him of images of yesteryear, when towns and cities were still in development, the early creations of a modern civilized society, but were now surpassed by advancements from a horse drawn cart making deliveries. This road was of little use to modern haulage machines.

There were several industrial bins lining the footpath, many of which had clearly been overfilled by their users, the lids of which being propped open by collection of refuse sacks piled within. There was no one in sight. Having expected to be greeted by the face of this other, he was now nothing short of deflated. He checked the map, he was close, as close as the now absent other had earlier appeared when there had been two of these dots at this location. Wherever had this missing dot disappeared to, and why?

He moved along the narrow street and noted a number of doorways. Evidently these were the rear access of commercial premises that fronted on to other roads. There was still no sign of 'dot'. Perhaps they were behind one of these doors? How ever would he seek them out, without appearing as some desperate vagrant knocking at the back-alley doors of whatever trade outlets were to be found here? The street was short, no more than four or five buildings on either side. Somewhere within this infinitesimal spot, there was something he was supposed to find. For the first time, he considered the possibility that this dot was not another person. Perhaps that was why the other, now missing dot, had left this place.

What could be of importance and why would it be here? He moved along the street, searching the ground, looking for anything that may be of interest. Several times, by the sides of the large bins, he had believed there to be something of importance, but on further review there was nothing that would be considered of use.

Each of these industrial sized bins now appeared to be a possible container of whatever he was to find. Gathering himself, he pondered over delving into each of them, riffling through the contents in search of whatever he was to find. And then it struck him; when he had initially viewed the two dots, watching from above and captivated by their presence, they were moving. This was not where he had first seen them. They were not even together at the onset of his voyeurism.

They had moved to this location, one behind the other. The mere fact of their independent movement made him realise that these dots were not simply an inanimate object. One had clearly caught the other. Had they been in chase? Was one trying to flee, to evade the possibility of capture? A myriad of possibilities consumed him in an instant. Which of them was still here, the pursuer or the escapologist? He must find them, but now he began to wonder whether he really wanted to. There was no knowing what may have occurred when the pair interacted.

Recalling that they had clearly spent some time together before the other had vanished, he was satisfied that the duo had not had quarrel with each other, lest they would unlikely have entertained one another for such a period. Checking the map once more, he gathered from the position of the two dots now present, that he had passed wherever this other was waiting. Walking back along the street, he studied each doorway intently for any sign of light emanating from around the edges that would speak of there being someone behind.

One door seemed out of place. At first glance, it appeared to be closed. But on closer inspection, there was a miniscule gap between the panel and the lipped edge of the frame that suggested that the latch had not engaged. There was darkness behind this door, but intrigue about what was behind and the likelihood that he may find 'dot', spurred him to push the door open. Slowly and with minimal force, he pressed his hand against the cold harsh metal exterior of the door and pushed with increasing force until the thing started to move slowly open.

Peering around the edge of the door, darkness continued to befall the hallway he now faced, though he could still make out an obstacle on the floor. Pushing the door open further still, the flood of emotion he felt in an instant, was perhaps the singular most horrific experience he had ever felt. Light had sprung the hallway having been tripped by a motion sensor, but the luminescence had cast onto the 'obstacle' behind the door. A lifeless body lay there in a pool of blood, collected around the abdomen. The face of the man was pale, bluish, and held the expression of pain and suffering, the brow was furrowed and the lips taught. A stench of iron filled the hallway, a smell of rust that seems common of fresh blood.

So horrified was he by the sight, that in the very instant of the illumination of the scene, he had stumbled backwards and the door had begun to close. Turning on his heel, he broke into a sprint, giving no regard to the pain in his leg. Leaving the street, he turned and continued to run. Despite his modest fitness, under ordinary circumstances, he could only keep up that pace for a quarter mile at best. But now his system was filled with adrenaline as he fled from the scene of some horrendous murder and he thought only of escaping the nightmare he had encountered. Fight or flight had jolted him once more, as it had in his tomb only hours before.

He knew not how far he had travelled by the time that exhaustion engulfed him. He slowed his pace and could feel the pain in his leg once more, now stronger than ever. He was out of breath and could no longer continue to run. Drawing to a complete stop, bending at the waist with his hands on his knees, he lent against a wall to prevent him from falling over; he tried to compose himself.

He vomited, knowing not if it was in shock of the hideousness of what had surprised him in that hallway, or from the weakness and pain that now riddled his body.

Turning his back to the building that was supporting his very being, he slumped to the floor, with his head in his hands, and he closed his eyes. The sight of the dead plagued his mind and though he had glimpsed this inert shell of a man for only a fraction of time, it seemed that every minutiae of the sickening vista had ingrained itself in his memory. This man had been early to mid-30's, average height and build, his dark hair, though cut for a common style, was scuffled and unkempt; his face had a 12 o'clock shadow and his eye sockets were sunken, drawn, darkened as though he too was in some terrible nightmare even before his demise. There were indentations of glasses to the bridge of his nose and the sides of his face, though there was no sign of spectacles present.

The puddle of near black blood seemed to bridge the entire width of the some four-foot hallway, the figure doubled over on the floor in the foetal position, with the hands clasped to the stomach which spoke of the fatal wound. His shirt had been white at one time, but had now more closely resembled a 'tie-dye' with various shades of red and pink in an expanding circular motion.

In all his years, he had never encountered a dead body, and was surprised at his own reaction. Though he had been appalled at the sight of a gruesome figure, there had been something more of that image that had filled him with dread. Something beyond the pale corpse and treacle that had leaked from within it. This carcass was clothed in identical attire to himself. The shirt, though soaked in blood had been previously a plain, white, uninspiring polo-shirt. The pants were the same dark blue, and the pumps on his feet were of the same kind.

The jacket the man wore was the very image of his own; a black short overcoat with a fleece lined collar. It too had had an insignia embroidered onto the left breast. 29.

The fate to which this unlucky soul had fallen foul, was evidently connected to the mis-happenings of his own existence. This person, this 29, whoever he was; had also been a pawn in this game in which he was caught. Frightful that a similar demise awaited him, he was concerned for his safety; his life may be at stake as had been that of '29'. The last three hours had been enough to consume a man's thoughts for a lifetime, but as he sat there reviewing this predicament, he was overcome by the remembrance of the first message he had received from the nameless author of his fate.

"One day to live". What on earth did this mean?

With sudden clarity of thought, he checked his wristband. The timer read 21:18:57, and continued to reduce by the second. One day to live. Evidently, this timer was counting down the seconds until 24 hours after he had woken. This 24 hours must be his 'day'.

But why, and what? Who – who was doing this to him? To them!

He was tasked with finding '35'. He knew now that this was indeed likely some other person also captive to this tormented reality. He knew now that there were others, like he, called to do the bidding of the unidentified dealer of doom that instructed their life, at least for 24 hours, but who knew what was beyond this.

Time was slipping away. He had now a little more than 21 hours to find '35' not knowing where to begin. This map on his wristband seemed the obvious place. Clearly this had been able to show him the position of 29, and therefore 35 must also be visible somewhere. Navigating his way to the map, he began to search his immediate surroundings, hoping to view the area around his current location for any evidence of another part in this sorry tale. He found one. He was fairly close to one more dot, but as he stood to proceed towards them, his leg buckled beneath him and he knew that movement would now become a chore.

Setting off in the direction of this new other, his mind still consumed with the sight of 29, his thoughts were interrupted by a loud crack, and in that instant he believed it to be gunfire. His heartbeat had instantaneously doubled and he felt a surge of adrenaline which caused his pain to subdue for a short while, but the sound had only been that of a motorcycle firing into life. He could now hear the thud of each cylinder as the thing warmed up, the rev's slowly decreasing as it settled to its normal range. A 'hog' of some kind, close but not visible, ahead of him. Light emerged from behind a parked car being cast from the front of the bike; as the rider snapped the throttle and he could hear the thing knock into gear. The thud of the pistons rose in pace as the light began to move, and the machine emerged straddled by a burley man in a denim jacket covered in a leather waistcoat.

As it roared up the street, the rider's eyes caught his, and he felt as though this man could read his every thought. He remembered a comic book from his youth and the 'penitence stare' given by 'the rider'. It felt like his soul was being drawn out of him. Was this the author of his fate, keeping a close eye, watching the pawns play out this game from among them. As the rider passed and thundered on into the distance, he broke down. The emotions he was trying to control and make sense of, now erupted like the contents of a carbonated drinks bottle that had seen as much action as he had. Sobbing, struggling for breath once more but this time from fighting back the mental torment of his situation, she came into his thoughts.

He longed for her presence and companionship. He needed her right now, more than he had ever realised he had needed her before. It had been some years since they had first met, yet the initial encounter was as clear as if it had been only yesterday. She had captivated him with the beauty of the smile in her eyes. He had charmed her with stories from his life, with his comical and anecdotal charisma that had previously allowed him to 'punch above his weight'. He had always been grounded by the fact that she was a far greater catch than he was, and had often wondered what it was in him that she had admired so much as to stick around.

Dates had turned into weekends, and weekends into cohabiting; and now they were to be married in only a few short months. He continued to sob as he thought of her, unable to move onwards through being too distraught to walk. Would he see the end of this madness? Would he see her again? There was no sense to life without her now, she had become his world. Life had changed when they became serious. Until that time, he had pursued his own goals, followed his own dreams; but something about her had changed his viewpoint incredibly. His focus had been shifted from self-indulgence and self-importance, to the needs of others, the importance of others. His care and love for her had altered his reality, he had become a better man for it and was enjoying life in a drastically different way.

But now his reality had been plundered by the upshot of his slavery to the strange occurrence that had presently been bequeathed to him from a hidden tyrant. Continuing to cry, he wiped his face with his hands and began to move on again. 1am was looming and he wondered about the likelihood of receiving another coded clue from his wristband at the turn of the hour? The map showed he was closer than he had imagined to the position of this other. He could see at a corner ahead, there were several people stood on the street corner, all gawping in the same direction.

As he moved on, he could see the echo of blue lights from the buildings surrounding the crossroads. Police were present. People were watching. As he approached the small crowd, he saw two police cars and officers stood with their weapons drawn, pointed at some miscreant being pressed headfirst to the bonnet of one if their vehicles, a large bodybuilding champion of an officer putting handcuffs around dainty wrists, the hands seemingly stained dark red with dried blood. Being pulled up by her collar, he watched as her hair, curly and golden brown in the headlights, swung as she was dragged back to standing and spun around to be frog marched to the rear of the vehicle.

Fear gripped him as he witnessed familiar clothing. The jacket, polo-shirt, pants all matched his, only in female form. Without any care for the fact she was less than half the body mass of the officer who was manhandling her, she was pushed into the back of the squad car and the door was slammed shut. The other officers replaced their weapons in their holsters, and two got into the vehicle now containing the criminal who bore the same garments as him. In watching the unfolding of the arrest, he had not been able to see if this delinquent had any number on their jacket, as did he, and '29' had.

As the car now moved away she peered out of the window, her eyes darting around the crowd, reading the faces of the spattering of onlookers. The vehicle disappeared, and the two remaining officers slipped into an 'all hours' café across the road, with purposeful intent on speaking with those inside. As the crowd started to disperse, he caught the attention of a couple as they turned to walk away. '*What happened?*' he asked as they set off from the scene. 'She just sat in the café crying and covered in blood' one of them responded. 'She had a knife' called out another from the swallow of people that moved away from the corner.

A car raced towards the junction, and pulled up only yards from the police car that remained. The driver jumped out in a hurry, and pulled a large SLR type camera out of a bag slung over his shoulder and pointed it forwards with intent, but as he approached the window of the café, he dropped it back to his side. He had missed his big scoop. Having watched for a few seconds, the guy went in and approached the cops. Watching this character go about 'interviewing the witnesses', he realised he was alone once more. In light of the arrest, there was nothing of significance for anyone to find interesting enough to stick around. Just he, stood there watching, too engrossed to have realised all others had gone.

The men in uniform emerged from the place, with a Greek looking man in tow, who had an apron of sorts, folded over and around his lower half. He must be from the cafe, perhaps off to give a statement at the police station. They got into the squad car and the broken blue echo of light ceased as the vehicle moved away. The man with the camera left, he had what he needed, but it wasn't much. It was unlikely this story would get any significant coverage, but what had she done?

It occurred to him that this female figure in a costume similar to his, may very well have been the perpetrator of the carnage he had witnessed in the hallway where 29 had met his end. She had blood on her hands. She had a knife so say others. And now this unidentified number in garments the picture of his own, was at the mercy of the authorities. Would she have really been the one who had murdered 29, and if so, what deranged torment may have driven her to do so? The game to which he was but one of the many contestants was developing into something far worse than he had anticipated. Morgues, pursuits, death, murder, assassins; this was becoming a sick joke.

Intent on discovering what the patrons of the cafe may know of the unidentified woman, he began to move, but as his body leaned forwards and his foot raised from the ground to take his first step, someone grabbed hold of him.

01:00

───

A hand had taken grip around his right arm. From the impression of the grasp he knew this hand was large, sizable, much bigger than his own. The authority of the arresting nature of the hold gave him to know that the man behind this hand was powerful, strong and intent on preventing him from his mission towards the cafe. As he turned to inspect his apprehender, he was greeted by a powerhouse of a man, at least seven or eight inches taller than he and built like a brick wall. His blond hair had a military crew cut look to it, his blue eyes were hollow and lacked any empathy. A rather square cut beard surrounded the lower facial features, which had a familiar reddish tinge to it. The same black jacket with a fleece collar, '31' on his chest.

'You don't want to do that' they spoke in a voice which matched perfectly with his appearance; deep, bold, certain. The accent was foreign, European, this man was likely Nordic; Aryan even. 'Come with me' they instructed with conviction that would make any man respond in submission to this towering figure.

'*Who are you?*' emerged as he was pulled from his stride in the opposite direction from the cafe. The man remained silent, but continued to move him onwards and rounded a corner, still with a tight grip around his arm. This was a familiar image of a hostage and captor.

Taking another left turn, the picture in front of him now was one of a town centre. A pedestrianised area not accessible to vehicles, bollards set in place to prevent unauthorised traffic from entering. Shops of all kinds lined either side of the street, and there were several collections of people moving about ahead. This man, 31 as they were, made no attempt to speak or engage him in anyway. With all that had happened in the last few hours, and with the image of 29 freshly imprinted in his memory, there was now a clear and present danger that had manifested. What did this man want of him? Where were they heading, and for what purpose?

As they approached a fast-food branch, it was clear they were heading inside, still ushered with the grip around his bicep. This place was open, and there were several people within. The fear that arrested him began to subside as he came to know it was unlikely this monster of a man would do anything to harm him in the presence of these witnesses, who continued on with their lives, enjoying the freedom of being a citizen not bound by the twisted fate of one in these garments, and the peculiar band adorning his wrist.

For the first time since this character had appeared in his story, the clench of their grip subdued as they arrived at the doors. Taking hold of the door in their free hand, 31 yanked it open and by their demeanour invited him to enter. As they crossed the threshold, the warmth of the overhead heater gave him instant relief from his aches, which seemed to have worsened with the cold that edged its way into his body.

'Take a seat' came from 31, in a tone now more akin to a suggestion than a command. Taking the weight off his legs was a good idea about now, and he headed towards a booth along the inner wall of the place. Red leatherette bound the seats, tired and worn, and covered with a thousand stains from overzealous children with soda, shakes and sauces. He cared not for the state of the bench on which he near collapsed as he parked himself. Looking back, 31 was now at the counter with their hands thrust into the jacket pockets, standing like an oak tree, solid and unmovable. One of the staff held something out to them, as if for inspection, he could not hear the words they exchanged. 31 held out a hand and fumbling with the object for a few seconds, the employee handed something over.

Turning his attention and with intrigue as to whether he would find two dots representing both he and 31, now visible at this location on his wristband map, he raised his wrist to once again inspect this contraption. 01:17. As he expected, the presence of 31 was clearly marked by another dot on the map.

Approaching now with a stern stride, a cardboard cup held in each hand, the ogre set one down on the table as the lowered himself on to the bench opposite, with a grace like manner unbecoming of such a giant. Reaching into a pocket of the jacket, his shovel of a hand emerged with a clenched fist and extending his arm across the table, he opened it palm down, spilling two tablets onto the top. 'For the limp' they said. 'Ibuprofen was all she had. You may get a chance to get something stronger when the shops start to open'.

Bemused by this colossal character and the manner of the aid and respite he now bestowed that followed from the earlier aggression of their arrival a short while ago; he stared at the man, unsure of whether to speak. Inspecting him for some sign of intention, their face showed blended emotions of anger and intrigue, confusion and sadness. Raising the cup, the giant sipped at the lid and satisfied that the contents were of a drinkable temperature, proceeded to take a large swig. Watching them now, it was obvious that this man meant him no wrong and sliding his cup towards him, he removed the lid to check the contents, relieved to find a deep black with foam gathering around the edge. '*Coffee?*' he asked, and the man nodded. Collecting the pills, he threw them both into the back of his throat and swigged from the open topped cup. He nearly gagged, not from the tablets, not from the taste. The temperature was far greater than he had imagined having seen his neighbour gulp from theirs. His mouth pulsated, scalded by the heat of the liquid.

'Game over' spoke the other, with a sullenness that suggested they were talking to themself. Raising their left wrist, the ogre exposed his own wristband and placing his cup down, they proceeded to poke at the thing several times. 'Less than six hours', once more in a thinking out loud manner. The giant took a deep breath, then expelled it over a long few seconds that felt like it dragged to eternity as his huge form began to lose composure around the shoulders as though a sinking feeling had consumed him. 'How long you got? About 20 hours I guess?'

Checking his own timer, "*20:37*" he responded. '*How do you know?*' he asked.

'Basic maths. You're 36.' There was a pause before he continued 'I can't believe she just gave up? Why the hell would she do that?' Was this more thinking aloud; a rhetorical question, or did this Goliath need an answer?

'*I don't think I know what's going on*' 36 spoke after some silence. '*I'm.... I just.... I woke in a bloody morgue and.....*'

'Still new to this' interrupted Goliath. 'I know. It's the same for us all' they said in a way in which they had experienced the same. 'The first few hours are.... well.... actually, it doesn't get any better. And then she goes and gets herself arrested. For fucks sake' now more annoyed than anything else. Raising their cup the ogre took another oversize mouthful of the burning contents. Confusion was written all over the face of this '31'.

'*Who was she? I saw the clothes. They were the same as you and I. I saw the same clothes on another also. What the hell is going on?*'

'Who did you see? 35? Have you found 35?' Excitement sprang in his voice and the words seemed to bounce with joy as he spoke them, his face became animated and hopeful.

'*No, it was 29. Who is 35? Tell me what the hell this is*' he demanded, wanting to take charge whilst this giant had seemed to have dropped his guard.

'You sir are 36. I am 31.

'That woman back there was 30. Le'me guess, you've been given two instructions so far, right?' and the pair of them nodded their heads in unison. 'When you woke you were trapped and escaped from a body cooler in the morgue' once more they nodded in unison. 'After your escape you were told to 'find 35''.

So far so good, how did this man know everything unless he had experienced the same thing?

'Have you found them? 35?'

'35 is not for me my friend. That's your game. Mine was 30, but how I'm going to manage that now is beyond me. Its game over' and again his face and posture became riddled with sadness. 'What the hell was she thinking? She'd won. She did it, and then...... just...... gave up' and he let out a grunt, that sounded as though they were in pain.

'I know I sound like a broken record here, but can you please find it within yourself to explain to me quite simply, WHAT THE FUCK IS HAPPENING', the tone and volume of his voice caused every other face in the building to turn and stare at him. He could feel a dozen pairs of eyes watching but gave no regard to them, fixing his gaze on this Goliath, his face set with certainness. 31 let his eyes close over and took in a long nasal breath, then slowly releasing both breath and eyes, his entire composure became serious and solid.

Leaning forward, the goliath folded his arms on the table, and spoke with importance in his voice. 'What happened to you has happened to us all. So far as we know, we all share the same fate. It's now a case of "do or die". You have been given a poison and you will die. The only way to prevent this, is to find the antidote. You are 36, and so far as I have been able to gather, this started with 1 and 2. There is something of Chinese Whispers at play, as no one I have met has been instructed to do anything other than find their predecessor, and we gather they have your antidote'.

This entire situation seemed nonsense. The notion that someone would poison random strangers and force them to search for an antidote, with no apparent reason, just seemed absurd. But here he was, wearing the same costume as several others, who by the sounds of things, have all experienced the same maddened happenings as he. Had 31 also woken in the morgue? They were certainly wearing the same garb including the strange wristband, and making the same suggestions.

'But you said it, you knew, surely you've been in my shoes? I've not been told to find any antidote. What the hell? Poisoned? I was told to find 35 - nothing about poison and antidotes'.

'Chinese Whispers' said 31, 'It's all Chinese Whispers. 35 has your antidote. 30 has mine. She found hers, and then got locked up. How am I going to get it now?' Was this the same rhetorical question? 'Oh man am I screwed'.

The weight of the words rested heavy. Was it possible this was all true? Someone was clearly playing the role of puppet-master and controlling his life for at least 24 hours, and whoever this was, had seemingly plucked him from daily life, probably drugged him, and left him to wake within a locked box.

'So you are basically saying that we've been poisoned, that someone has the remedy, and all I need to do is find them, find this '35', and that will be it, done'.

'Yep, that about sums it up'

'But you're screwed as 30 has yours, and now you can't get it'

'You must have a degree' he responded in sarcasm.

'Except, that's not 'it' is it? If she found hers and you were still looking, it wasn't over for her was it?' There was a stunned silence for a period bordering on the awkward.

'What do you mean?' asked Goliath with a thousand questions written on his face.

'I mean that, you were pursuing her, she would have had to evade you. Maybe she got arrested on purpose? Maybe she knew that this was not over, she had not got out. Maybe she knew that she would still die, unless she was protected by the police.'

'What are you on about? Why would she die?'

'Perhaps you would kill her?'

Anger and disgust burst onto their face, and their voice became gruff and stern again, 'What do you take me for? I may look a little menacing, but I'm a gentle giant. Murder? That is far beyond my capabilities my friend, and I see no reason why I would have cause to do her any harm'

'She had your antidote right, perhaps you would kill for it, like she did'

'What? 29 is dead? How do you know?'

'I saw him. Stabbed it seemed, laying in a heap on the ground. I just ran. Did it never occur to you to consider why the police took her?'

'I don't know..... I just..... Well, I thought she just lost it, maybe went a little cuckoo from all this shit. I knew she had found 29 'cause I knew where he was heading. I was tracking her and I saw them interact' and the man looked at his wristband once more, poking at the screen. 'I caught up with her about a block away from where they had been. I followed her, about a half mile behind, right to that cafe. By the time I got there, the 'fuzz' were rolling in, and next thing I knew, she was being cuffed and taken away. That's when I spotted you'

'So you don't know about the knife, the bloody hands?' a blank expression faced him *'Chinese Whispers again, but I think she killed him'.*

'Why would she do that? He was a good guy!' He stroked his beard tugging slightly at the tips. 'His time was running out and so far as I know, he had not found 28'

'So what, he succumbed to the poison? I don't think so. I saw the body, he'd been stabbed. She had a knife. I may have a degree, but a child could do the math' he jostled, just to ensure Goliath knew he wasn't a dumb nobody.

'I just don't get why she would kill him. He was surely close to his time, he would just hand it over. It makes no sense that he wouldn't just give it up'.

Realising that somewhere on his person there was likely an antidote ready for 37 if this madness continued beyond him, he searched through his attire once more, intent on discovering everything that was on him. *'Where's yours'* he said to Goliath, as he went from padding himself down to deep searches of the pockets.

'Where's my what?' asked 31 as they aimlessly patted the pockets of their own jacket.

'You have an antidote for 32 right? Where is it?' and rising from the bench, he dug into the pockets of his trousers hoping to find some small vial, tablet or something. But there was nothing. Unable to find any sign of anything at all other than the lint and fluff which three hours ago had repulsed him, a sickening feeling grew as he came to know two things. He was not the first to wear these clothes, how many 36's had there been before he, how many 29's, 30's, 31's. Where did this cycle begin and end?

It also occurred that there was nothing on his person or in his belongings that appeared to be any form of magical 'antidote' to the poison he had supposedly been gifted by this unknown tormentor. 31 had nothing either. They pondered whether these strange bands they each wore had something to do with it? How could they get their antidotes if they could not even find the ones they carried. These bands were the key to it all.

Sitting again he drank from his cup, feeling the refreshing sensation of the taste and the aroma that blended to awaken his senses through the fill of caffeine. Had 29 been killed? Was this explosion of blood that filled the corridor caused by the hands of another, or was this 'poison' a literal ticking time bomb that erupted as the clock expired? Maybe the band of a predecessor would act as some remote switch to stop the timer? Who could really know? All he knew of anything so far was what had been handed down to him from 31, who in turn had clearly only heard tales from others before him. How long this had been ongoing was known only by the author of their fate, the curator of torment behind the veil of obscurity.

He continued to converse with 31, as they toiled over the crazed reality that forced their decisions for the following hours. This elephant of a man was now hunted by time, stalked with every passing second, and the crosshairs were beginning to draw in; a little over five hours to go. As the discussions continued, he came to hear of how 31 had discovered his knowledge of their poisoning through having been near ran over, just about able to evade certain significant injury had it not been for the bravery of a passer-by. The driver had been 26, desperate in his final two hours to capture his cure, hell-bent on ramming the next of the dots on their map and would deal with the carnage later. After hearing the tall tale of poison and potion from the man, 26 had set off once more to search for his predecessor, and was not seen or heard of again.

Of all the interactions he and 31 had between them shared with others involved in this sordid chronicle, they were able to gather that each new cycle, each release of another numbered victim whom had 24 hours to solve this ambiguous happening; they were all tasked with finding their predecessor, whom they were three hours behind. With every third hour that passed, there was a new player to this destitute dilemma that captured so many; but at the same time, someone else would end their torment if they had not already escaped from the venom within them. 24 hours, split into three-hour blocks, meant 8 players at any one time.

And there he sat, the two of them together, visible to anyone else that may peruse their location on the wristband map. His current presence with 31 left six others still active in this contest of wits, all searching for their cure, their forerunner, who was only three short hours ahead of them. 29 was dead, and of the six other active participants, he knew the location of 30, or at least that she was now incarcerated.

A realisation befell him. Three hours had passed since his awakening. Was 37 now a part of this tale?

Vexed by the arrest of 30, he was unable to shake the image of 29, the picture of pain that had etched onto his face as life had slipped from him. Wondering whether the grotesque scene had stemmed from succumbing to the passing of his time, or at the merciless will of the curly haired enchantress that was shown no leniency by the beast of a police officer that cuffed her; he decided to see whether 29 would still be present on the map? How long after his timer expired would his dot disappear?

Tracing back to where he had been part of the small crowd that watched the uniformed men capture the unknown woman at the cafe, and from there to the corner where he had wretched out the contents his stomach at the revulsion of a dead man; he made an educated guess how far he had ran from the place of horrors. Recognising the streets on which he had earlier travelled, the dot was gone. Was this as a result of the end of life? Perhaps the life of the wristband had not much more than 24 hours? Maybe someone else had discovered the body, called it in, and emergency services were now investigating the death?

31 was now at a point of mental processing, that he knew his future was doomed. This goliath was to be taken down by the proverbial stone that right now was sitting in a sling, about to be set loose. Death was only a matter of time. A certainty that could no longer be delayed. His remedy was now in a cell, if that is, she had it somewhere on her. Perhaps it was held by the police in her personal possessions. Maybe there was still an opportunity for release from the poison that spelled his end.

Resolving to find where she had been taken, 31 seemed to gain a sudden burst for action and finishing the coffee in a long swig, rose to his feet. 'Time to move on'.

The pills had taken the edge off the pain he noticed as he too rose to standing and slipped out from behind the table. Heading towards the door, he once more felt the rush of heat from overhead before the bite of the cold sunk its teeth as they crossed the threshold into the night. A plan had been formulated. The first point on the agenda was to see what they could determine of the demise of 29. Heading back towards the place where the lifeless corpse had been slumped in the hallway, there were now even fewer people on the streets. Traffic had all but dried up save for the odd taxi and various delivery vans.

There was a melody in the air, something he knew was familiar, faint but growing. An intrusion of drums and bass erupted from the ever-nearing origin, which seemed to echo from the buildings around him. For a moment, the pleasantry of the music seemed to surpass the simple sound waves and he could almost see the tune float in the breeze. But now the sounds were fading, drifting away from him.

He had walked alongside this oaf of a man for more than five minutes without sharing any dialogue. The intensity of their indwelling emotions was clearly being toiled by the giant as much as he. He became conscious of the expressions on his face. Anger, confusion, disgust. His brow pulled downwards and together, nostrils flared but drawn up at the edges and his lips were pursed in tightest fashion that was possible. He did not know what to say, nor whether his new associate wished to speak at all.

He glanced at him, this leviathan like figure, and considered it hard to believe that a man of this stature had been taken without any fight and thrust into the torment of the ticking timer. Thinking of his own capture, he could not recall his last moments before his awakening, aside from the park, the waterway, the canal boat that merrily chugged its way past them. The day had been young, an early morning walk before lunch with friends. She had been an encouragement to him; his colleagues, as great as they were, had played their share of office camaraderie in such a manner that had upset him. She had taught him to laugh it off as they walked beside the fields that were thick with people attending the weekend's children's sports.

Thoughts of her grew, and he wondered what had become of her. He had no recollection of anything beyond the sporadic patches of that walk, then only the box that had kept him captive for who knew how long. Had they made it to lunch? Was she safe? She must be going senseless with his disappearance. How long had it been? Surely, she would have alerted friends, family, the police? People must be looking for him? She must be looking for him. He must get word to her.

'*Do you have a phone?*' he mustered.

'A phone? What the hell would I have a phone for? Who the hell would I want to call? I have only a few hours to figure out what I am going to do, or else I die. I see no need for phone calls at a time like this.'

'*It's just.... my*', he was interrupted; 'Your girl, right?' He nodded. 'Do you think she could help? Seriously? Would you even want to involve her in this? I know I wouldn't, but then my girl left me 'bout six months ago'

'*I'm sorry, but I have to let her know I'm okay. I don't even know how long I've been gone, she'll be worried*'.

'Most likely so. It's been about three days for me. Gone I mean. From what I can gather anyway. But 29 seemed to think it was the same day for him'.

'*If we pass a payphone, I'll have to call her. Do a reverse charge or something*'

'Payphone?' and the ogre roared with laughter. 'When was the last time you saw a payphone? I don't even think they exist anymore'.

The monster was right. He couldn't remember when exactly the last time he had seen a payphone was. It certainly was not in recent times. Suburbia at least had been eradicated of these former call boxes and now they were a vision of the past, occupying only a place in history rather than progressive reality. Maybe there would be something at a major transportation hub, an airport, train or bus station. But they were not likely to be heading to such a destination in the immediate future. There would be more chance of flagging down a passer-by and using their cell phone.

As time passed, he and his companion slowly approached the block where 29 had met his end. Again, anticipation welled inside him, but now it was not as it had been before. No longer was he encapsulated by the thoughts of meeting another who was likely experiencing the same as he, but he knew he was heading towards the spectre of a dead man, whose destiny he was likely to share, unless he could solve the puzzle of the predicament. He had only 20 hours left to find 35, and somehow figure out the enigma of the countdown before his time elapsed.

02:00

———

Though the pain in his leg had subsided, the injury was more significant that he had considered. He continued to carry the limp, making the progress towards the temporary resting place of 29 slower than it ought to have been. He knew that 31 was not walking with the speed and intent that would have been preferential, but was deliberately shortening his gait so as to not leave him behind. He was grateful for the company, despite the lacking conversation.

The night was now well into the small hours. In not much more time than had passed since his awakening, daylight would be breaking. The cold of the night was slowly being fought back as his core temperature rose through the persistent movement; but he knew the air around him was icy. He could see his breath emerging before him, like a smoke that quickly disappeared. The tips of his ears tingled with pain from the temperatures that must now be approaching subzero, and fingers began to throb with each pulsation of blood rushing within them. In spite of the irrational phobia of pockets, he knew these were the best place for his hands right now even though they spoke of further horrors of previous participants in this melancholy madness. They provided minor immediate relief from the cold, but with a little time to get warm, he knew that it was a good thing to keep them there.

He checked the wristband again and saw that it was now past 2am. His timer continued to progress with every second towards the expiration of his life in less than 20 hours. There had been no further 'buzz' at his wrist, but he checked for messages all the same. There was nothing new. Searching through the previous communications, he was bemused and bewildered by them. One day to live, get out of the box, find 35. Whoever was directing his destiny, their messages were so to the point there was nothing further that could be interpreted from them.

Their position on the map was getting ever close to their destination and it would be only minutes until they arrived at the doorway from which he had earlier fled. '*It's not far now*' he said as they crossed a small intersection. There was a figure on the other side from them. A shadowy silhouette, half obscured in darkness, a lady of the night perhaps. Clearly these two men were on a mission, and would not be engaging her with custom. They pressed forward with an assuredness that was evident of their intent to meet some target or deadline. They were not to be interrupted from their quest. He wondered if it were likely that she would get any custom at this hour of the night? It was a little late, and both vehicular and foot traffic were almost non-existent.

It was 02:25 as they turned the corner of their destination, and immediately his attention was taken by the ambulance and a police car that between them seemed to fill the short, narrow street. The mass of the vehicles obscured his view of what would be certain commotion in the hallway. 29 was now in the hands of the emergency services.

The ambulance had reversed into the street and was parked adjacent to the doorway behind which the fallen contestant of calamity was laid, soaked in red and drained of life. Immediately he knew that they could not make themselves known to the authorities. The clothing they wore matched that of the dead man and undoubtedly people would start asking questions. If nothing else, this could significantly delay their progress. Any time at all that was lost to answering to the authorities, was time they could not afford, especially the beast who had become his companion.

He knew it was deranged to approach the police, especially as they dealt with a body in this unusual clothing. If he was just one of a series of competitors in this wickedness, how many other bodies had the police and paramedics tended to that were similarly attired? To come forward now would likely spell the end of his assignment to find 35, which would have grave consequences.

But, there was a remote possibility that the police would be able to offer him some assistance; that they may know something about what was happening to him; to them all. They may have some answers, perhaps even be working on an antidote to their poison if there were indeed many other participants of this game of doom that had sought out their help.

The risk was too great for the time being. Any side track to their progress would undoubtedly run down the clock on 31's remaining lifespan to the point of extinction. 'We need to find out what happened' said the ogre, 'But if we make ourselves known, as sure as there is hair on my face, they'll pull us in for questioning'. The words he spoke seemed to mirror the thoughts of beardless 36. There was a long pause as they stood, motionless, knowing not what to do next.

'She was in the same get-up. When they figure out a woman with blood on her hands was wearing the same odd clothing as the dead man in a pool of blood, anyone else in the same attire is likely a suspect'. After another pause, he continued 'We need to move to the shadows and gather what we can from watching them'.

He felt the thud of the giant's elbow, which disturbed his balance briefly as he nudged him. Turning to look at him, the oaf nodded his head in a direction across to their left. Swiftly and silently, they moved, crossing the road to a stoop that rose to a building almost immediately opposite the narrow street now occupied by a squad car and an ambulance. They turned and sat on the steps at their very top, resting against the brickwork, attempting to hide from as much streetlight as possible. Surely, they would seem only as shadowy figures amongst the fading light, nothing of importance, simple onlookers to the unfolding events, or vagabonds in a resting spot for the night.

At first, they could not see any signs of the emergency responders at this scene, save for the shadows on the floor outside that doorway, being cast from the lights and movements within. A vehicle approached and pulled up to the spot where he had been stood only moments earlier. A police vehicle, "Scientific Support". Out climbed a mid

30's woman. As she opened the side door of the van, the scraping of the sliding door on its runners was louder than the engine had been on its arrival. She retrieved a holdall from within and slid the door closed, more scraping, now accompanied by a loud thud as the door slammed home; a deafening sound for the dead of night it would otherwise be at this location.

The paramedics emerged from the doorway and stood back several feet, allowing her space to observe the body from outside, looking in. Two uniformed officers also exited the hallway, and the four of them formed an arc around it as the CSI went inside. Evidently, she was taking photographs. There were strong flashes of light several seconds apart as she catalogued the scene for forensic analysis. The persistent hum from the diesel engine of the ambulance, which was still running, drowned out any chance of them hearing the conversations as the others crowded around the doorway.

For what seemed like an age, there was nothing happening. One of the cops was drawing from a vape, plumes of vapour much thicker than his own breath in the cold air swirled around the policeman's presence as he exhaled; the other spoke into his radio several times, but still could not be heard. The paramedics went into the ambulance and were unseen for some time. 02:44 now showed on his wristband. It was unlikely they would learn anything from what was happening here. He looked over at 31 and was about to speak when the sound of a car approaching with some urgency surpassed the reverberating idle of the diesel engine across from them. He watched as the headlights approached from down the road on which he had now travelled in both directions.

A dark coloured hatchback slowed as it grew near to the CSI van and then crept slowly past the end of the street, where the driver was clearly taking a good look, before the vehicle parked up at the side of the road. The driver jumped out dragging something cumbersome in his hand. In the dim street lighting, he recognised this man from earlier. It was the same guy with the camera from the cafe, a Stringer, looking for the latest scoop to sell, now concerning a body found in a hallway. He lugged the camera out of his bag, pointed it ahead, and stepped off towards the doorway in search of his story.

Quite quickly he was accosted by the officers, and from the looks of it, had been instructed not to film either the body or the scene, but by that time, he had images enough to land him a few hundred for the exclusivity of the story. He dropped the camera to his side, pulled out a packet of cigarettes, offered them around, before putting one to his own mouth and replacing the carton to his jacket pocket, pulling out a lighter. The vape toting officer joined him, taking pleasure in a real honest to God cigarette, whilst his colleague now seemed to kill time scrolling on his phone. There was still no sign of the paramedics, shored within their vehicle from the cold of the night.

Several minutes later, there was some discussion with the CSI inside as they crowded around the doorway, leaning in. It was still impossible to hear the interaction for the sound of the engine ticking over. One of the officers turned around and banged twice on the side of the ambulance. Out came the paramedics, and following a brief exchange of words, they returned to their vehicle, but emerged moments later with a trolley stretcher. The CSI emerged from the doorway and stood talking with the officers as the paramedics went inside.

It was strange he thought, that even in this early hour of the morning, there was not more traffic in this moderately built-up area. The road on which he was now sitting was quite a major throughway, although clearly not a main road. He looked around, taking stock of the surroundings, trying to process the details of the architecture around him. Did he know this place he pondered? There was nothing that looked familiar, certainly not that 'stood out' in his memories. As he had perceived earlier, this place had the look of historic buildings amongst regenerated and redeveloped properties that spoke of the changing of the times.

The paramedics had now gone inside and were sure to be manoeuvring the body onto the portable stretcher they had removed from the rolling trolley. They were taking their time. He checked his wristband once more, 02:52. There had still been no new message for quite some time, and he wondered whether it was likely that he would ever hear from his tormentor again? Had 31 received any more messages? They had not discussed this it occurred to him; he would need to ask at some point.

Though he had no understanding of which direction was north, the compass type screen had changed since his last review. The arrow around the dial had turned to green and was pointing across to one side. The numerical readout now said "2". Another indicator had appeared, on the outside of the circular dial with a number floating above it, "2621". Whatever this thing was, it did not seem to be telling of true or magnetic North.

With the amount he had travelled on foot since his awakening, he was able to gain some form of perceivable distance on the map. Retracing the route they had taken since the coffee, he perceived that the width of the screen covered an area about an eighth of a mile. It must have been a little more than mile from the high street where the fast-food place had been. He was fondling the thing when he heard a click of fingers beside him. He looked over, and 31 motioned with his head as he had earlier.

Turning his attention to the scene across the road, he saw that the Stringer had seemingly fired up his camera again; the spotlight above the thing faced forwards and was casting light at the limbs and doorway that surrounded him, though was kept by his side in the most unusual attempt at being incognito that he had witnessed. But the officers paid no attention this time, as though they didn't care anymore; they watched the paramedics carry the stretcher with a body bag on top and place it on the trolley.

The officers returned to their vehicle, and the CSI to hers, as the paramedics loaded the trolley into the ambulance and closed the rear doors behind it. The cameraman lingered at the end of the road, talking on his phone, as one by one, the service vehicles drove away. As the sound of the last one faded, he could hear that the freelance filmmaker was trying to sell his story.

Murder. He definitely spoke of murder. He must find out what this man knew, and now that he was alone, it was the perfect time to ask without arousing suspicion. He would not have had chance to see the clothing being worn by the corpse, and he was too late on the scene to have seen 'curls' when she was stuffed into the cop car. The camera man would have no reason to think he was anything other than an interested passer-by. *'Stay here'* he said, *'I'm going to find out what happened'.*

As he rose to his feet, 31 neither spoke in return, nor showed any inclination of moving. Descending the stoop, he began slowly across the road as the man was wrapping up his call. Approaching, he had to linger for a few seconds as the man said his goodbyes to the one with whom he was speaking. Their eyes had locked as the phone call was concluding. Widening his eyes in a mannerism to suggest an interaction when the other was ready, the night-crawler hung up and returned an expectant expression.

'What happened over there?' and he motioned his head towards the alley.

The man turned around to face the doorway. 'Robbery gone wrong they say. I think there was more to it. Some poor schmuck got butchered pretty bad, but they wouldn't say more than that'.

'So, no ideas on a suspect then hey?'

The man turned back to face him and looked him up and down with questioning. 'Not yet. Do you know something about it?'

'Just walking by and I saw the commotion. CSI, cop car, ambulance. I figured it was something bad'.

'It didn't look great to be honest. There was quite a bit of blood in there. He's been cut up pretty bad around the middle. It was more than a simple stabbing in a 'robbery gone wrong', but that's what the cops are trying to spin. Sorry but I've got to go, story to sell and all that'.

The reporter set for his car and fired it into life, leaving the scene quite swiftly. Moving back across the road to the stoop, he reached the foot of the steps and beckoned to his companion, *'Come, there's nothing for us here'*. Whilst he did not know where they were, and despite his best efforts, he could not recall having ever set foot in this location previously; 31 seemed to know his way around. He knew which direction they must set off for next, as he pursued 30 who was now likely bound in a holding cell in the custody suite.

As they walked, he told his new friend of what he had learned from the journalist. The other was saddened by the demise of 29 who had been kind to him during their previous interaction, and from whom he had learned much of the tale he now paid forward.

'I just don't get it. Butchered? Geez. What the hell was she doing?' Yet another rhetorical question.

'It seems to me that she had taken to him pretty hard. Butchered! I mean, that doesn't sound great, does it?'

'She must have cut him up real bad' said the ogre.

'There was a fair bit of blood. It filled the hallway when I saw him there earlier. It looked like more than I would expect a human body could actually hold'.

'But he was a pretty big guy.... though she was a pretty small woman. She must have surprised him. Blindsided him in a blitz attack. There's no way she would have been able to take him down otherwise.'

'I wonder if she found it?' he said and it crossed his mind he was now offering rhetorical questions himself. *'The antidote I mean'.*

''I had just assumed...... I know they interacted. I didn't expect this'

'And it never occurred to you before that you must have an antidote on you somewhere, for your pursuer, for 32?'

'Well, it had, but not enough to think about what, where. Are you sure you have nothing? I can't find it on me.' The giant was patting himself down again with vain effort.

'What about other messages, on your band? Have you been given any other instruction, told what to do? How to get your antidote?' now posing deliberate questions requiring the colossus' response.

'Chinese Whispers. All I know is what I have told you, and I learned that from others, and they from those before them. It is possible of course that this is all an elaborate trick, a twisted game for some sicko to get their thrills from watching others run about causing carnage. I just don't get why she would kill him'.

And then it occurred to him, all these tales that he had heard, passed down through the players of this anarchy, which no one quite knows for sure; poison and cure, death and murder. What if there was just one cure? Perhaps just one bottle, one vial, a single jar of pills perhaps, to be passed from player to player? Who would have it? Maybe no one did. Maybe it was kept at a single location, the position of which only to be found through reaching your predecessor.

Too little was known. There was not enough data to make an educated guess, never mind drawing any logical conclusions through inductive reasoning, the way his favourite author had written about the world's first 'Consulting Detective'.

Did he simply fail to 'perceive'? Was there something so obvious about all of this that he had thus far failed to recognise? This was a constant drain on this mind as they walked along the roadside, perplexed by the endless possibilities that were ahead of him. 30 had some answers.

They must get to her, and somehow seek her audience. This was no mean feat considering that she was now subject to the authorities.

Perhaps they had nothing on her. Perhaps they would not be able to connect her to the death of 29. Without the involvement of the same officers in both cases, it would be likely that her unusual attire had been noted as anything out of the ordinary. Presently she was undoubtedly at some holding cell, and 31 seemingly had some idea of where this may be, given that he was so resolute on heading in a particular direction.

'I have an idea!'

03:00

———

The darkness was at its peak. It was now passing the dead of the night and dawn would be on its way. It would still be a number of hours until daylight came in full swing, and considering the thickness of the cold, it would be unlikely that the sunlight would offer any great warmth. Clouds were thinning and ice was forming on the pavement. Parked cars had been covered by dew and the chill was beginning to freeze.

'We need to get in there, right? Wherever she is. We need to speak with her; we need to find out whether she has it.'

'Has what?'

'The antidote, whatever it is. If it's even real. We need to know!' and he began to explain his plan.

If they were to consider her a suspect of some significant crime, with blood covered hands and possibly a knife in her possession, it was unlikely that she would be mixed with others in her detention. And if she had been put in an isolated cell, then her personal effects would likely have been taken from her and checked into a storage box.

This box would be much easier to access than the curly haired woman, who was unlikely able to meet with anyone other than the detectives that would be interviewing her as soon as they were able. If they could get access to the box, they could find out whether she had in fact been able to gain hold of the antidote from her encounter with 29, or whether there was anything of use to them; some clue of what it may be.

The clothing they wore, similar to that of hers, had a somewhat industrial look about it. He explained that the two of them could pose as employees of some fictitious corporation, and that they believed that the woman had stolen something before going crazy and ending up in police custody. The company needed to retrieve this item due to its importance to their business, a long process with it being in evidence, but they would be happy enough as long as they knew it was safe - if they could get access to her effects, they could see if she had it on her person when she had been arrested.

The story was plausible enough, only they lacked anything that would corroborate their tale. They had nothing that would identify themselves and give a perception of some authority over the woman. They needed to fabricate something more than just a cover story.

The giant seemed to have an epiphany. 'All night printers' he muttered. 'We could knock something together at an all-night printers. ID cards, laminated and everything'.

They worked out their plan as they meandered down the road. The progress was slow, the limp was persistently problematic and would need rest before long. The journey ahead was at least three miles, plus a visit to the printers.

This was going to cause great delays, and the loss of time was simply not a viable option for 31, who now had less than four hours remaining.

A sickening feeling came upon him that his compatriot may have thus far neglected to consider. Though the colossus had four hours left, if 30 had been unsuccessful in her quest at locating the antidote, she had less than 60 minutes. This may cause a domino effect and leave his new friend without hope.

They needed to move much swifter than they were. *We need a car'* he said *'Our progress is being hampered by my leg, and time is ticking away'.*

'And how do you suppose we get one? We have no money; we couldn't even take a bus.'

'The way I see it, we do what we must to survive. And if we do survive, we deal with the consequences later. We borrow one!'

'Borrow?' queried the giant in a tone that spoke of intrigue.

'Yes, we don't intend to keep it, therefore it's not stealing. We're just…. taking without consent'.

'Okay hotshot, where do we get this car?'

'We're heading out of town, into the suburbs, right? We get one from a driveway' he suggested, with a manner that juxtaposed the ogre's intrigue.

'What about security? Immobilisers, trackers?'

'*We need something old, that will be easy to get into, easy to hotwire*'.

They continued to discuss their plan as they moved onwards, now approaching an urban housing area. Home after home had nearly new cars, with nothing that would seem an easy target for their taking. They decided to turn from the main roads into the quieter streets that branched out into housing estates. Somewhere they would find something ripe for the picking.

They came across a late '70's American muscle car. It was in pristine condition and gleaming from the immaculate attention that had been given to the finish on the paint. This car was well looked after, preserved with utmost care. It must have been used within the last few hours. Surely this would normally be kept under some cover? There was no dew settled, no signs of ice forming. There was a faint warmth emanating from the engine bay.

Getting in would be easy as it had a soft-top. They circled the car with a mixture of envy at the prize this thing was and the joy at being able to take it without thought of repercussion, at least for the time being. The notion of such an historic and iconic collector's item not having modern security and alarm systems was obviously stupid when they thought further about it. This vehicle would simply not do.

It was after 03:30 by the time they found their victim. An old pickup, it wasn't even locked. However, neither of them had any idea what they were doing in trying to hotwire the thing.

His compatriot told him how he had once had a motorcycle stolen, and when it was recovered, despite being in otherwise good condition, the ignition barrel had been snapped off revealing a very simple switch beneath. 31 thought it was likely that the truck had a similar mechanism in view of its age, and that ramming a flat blade screwdriver down the barrel was likely to reach this switch.

At the end of the driveway was a simple garage, with a timber personnel door to the side. Through the glazed section, he could see plenty of hand tools and knew that they would find what they needed within. A basic latch lock secured the door that could probably be slipped with a credit card, but they had nothing of the sort on them. The only way in was to break the glass.

Using his elbow, the huge man had them inside within seconds, but not without a significant ruckus that would surely have disturbed people from their sleep within the houses around them. They grabbed a small toolbox and made way to the vehicle as quickly as possible. But before they could get in, a light came on within the house on whose driveway they found themselves.

Seconds later there was movement at the window, and ducking behind the vehicle, he saw a man of much older age peering out. His heart was pounding, and the feeling of an adrenaline rush took over as it had when he had fled from the sight of a dead man lying in a pool of blood. He did not know whether he should just 'run for it' as he had previously or hope that they would be unnoticed hidden beside the pickup. The face in the window watched intently towards the garage, and then searched around the neighbouring house. Seemingly satisfied that there was nothing noteworthy, he disappeared, and the blinds closed over the window again.

After several minutes had passed, they slipped into the unlocked vehicle as quietly as possible, and his companion had already retrieved a screwdriver from within the toolbox. With the ogre behind the wheel, he sat at the passenger side, staring up at the window for any sign of the man returning having possibly heard the truck's door open or close.

31 was fumbling with the ignition barrel. They needed to get away from this place quickly and quietly. Perhaps they should push the vehicle down the driveway and start it at the roadside. If the occupant of the house had not been disturbed by the smashing of the garage door glass, this may have been a good idea, but now it was likely that he was sat waiting to hear some other noise.

Out the corner of his eye he saw movement. Near the edge of the garage, the man had emerged from the back of the house clearly to check that all was okay. But all was not okay. He would surely find the window broken, the door ajar, and without doubt, he knew this person would check his truck and find two strangers there, within the cab. Their intentions would be pretty clear, and the man would without doubt raise the alarm with his neighbours and seize them before they could take flight from the place.

Wide eyed, heart racing, he knew his breathing was deep and fast. He looked over at 31 who gave him a wink, and turned the screwdriver that was buried in the ignition. The engine cranked, but did not immediately start. It took several seconds of turning over before the thing fired into life, and by this time, the owner was rounding the corner of the garage with haste at the sounds of the engine turning.

Gripping the door handle so tightly his knuckles would surely be pale, the anticipation and fear made him transfixed on the figure now pursuing them as they reversed from the driveway at pace. A man in his mid-60's, wearing nothing more than a white vest and striped boxer shorts. He ran for them in his bare feet. The driver turned slightly in their reverse from the driveway to the road, and before the truck could spring forward with the changing of the gears, he was now sat facing the old man who was as surprised as he at what was happening as he reached the end of his driveway, the horror of being robbed written on his face as their eyes met.

The vehicle lurched forwards and they sped towards the end of the road, thankful for their escape, and the emptiness of the road ahead of them. Their getaway had been fairly easy, but not without a large helping of fear, shock and excitement. They were on the move, and with the ability to make up for their lost time now that they had a vehicle. They could from now on cover greater distances with minimal effort and in little time; and his leg would have chance to rest. However, it would not be long before the police were looking for the stolen truck within which they were travelling, and which the owner would surely call in immediately.

Neither spoke as they fled from the scene of their crime. He wondered how he could have stooped to the point of becoming a felon, with disassociated delinquency. His reckless lawbreaking would possibly continue for the following 18 hours. Breaking and entering. Grand Theft Auto. What would be next? Was it possible that he could perhaps be dragged into this nightmare far enough to commit murder too? Would he become so desperate that he would take the life of another just to save his own?

'Do or die' his companion had earlier commented. Would this become his reality now?

As they left suburbia and entered an artery road, he realised that they were heading back towards the built-up area from which they had come. *'Are we going the wrong way?'* he asked.

'We need papers, ID, documents. I know a place in the city' muttered Goliath, with a shallow and hollow attitude that gave him to know that the ogre too was struggling with the moving morality meter they were riding.

The roads were dead, no traffic at all. He was grateful that 31 clearly knew where they were and where they were heading. Something about this area looked familiar to him although he could not work out where he was. Not that it mattered anymore. The priorities now were to find 30, retrieve the antidote for his friend, and then find 35. It occurred to him that with their intent on acquiring a vehicle and the commission of their crime, he had not checked his wristband in quite some time.

03:42 he saw as he swiped at the screen. Navigating the band had now become a task that was almost second nature. The map did seem to show that they were heading towards a built-up area. Ahead of them the roads became less spaced out, compacted, interconnecting like puzzle pieces linking together as part of a bigger picture. Expanding his search around the city, he caught sight of another blue dot and his pulse increased again at the sight of what he knew now would be another in this twisted tale. Watching intently, it was obviously moving, but at a slow pace, probably walking, as he had been until only minutes earlier.

The arrival of another player in this perversion gave him a mix of emotions. This person could be his saviour or his enemy. If this dot was 35, it was possible that they held the answer that could end his torment. But on the other hand, considering what he knew of the interaction between two sequential numbers in the doorway of doom; where a murder investigation was now underway - 30 had likely killed 29; would he also be drawn to some violence? Would this new character seek them out to harm he or his companion?

His mind raced through the possibilities of how his inevitable interaction with his predecessor might play out. If these whispers were true, 35 was possibly in possession of his potion. He would need to turn his intention to 35 as soon as they had found the cure for his friend. He had lost focus on the wristband, which had faded and reverted to its plain state. And there she was again, occupying his thoughts. He had become so engrossed in his own situation that he had not had thoughts of her in some time. What would she think of him now that he was a criminal? Would he ever make it out of this alive, and be able to hold her again, to tell her the tale of his captivity and escape, the horror he had found, the unfolding of the web in which his story was but one strand?

She would be grateful for his escape from this all, if indeed he was able to evade death from both poison and person; but at what cost must this come? Would she be able to live with a law breaker, a thief; and if it came to it, a murderer? It was madness to think that he would take a life; that he could take a life. If he was able to save 31, perhaps this monster with his huge form and significant strength, would be able to do such bidding for him; to take the life of another to save him? Better still, perhaps they could find this cure before anything so ridiculous would be needed.

He longed for her to embrace him now. His mind danced with thoughts of her, and he could feel the warmth of her body against his chest. It gave him such peace that he knew he would be fighting to stay awake if his eyes were closed for any longer. As he focussed on the dash ahead of him, he knew that the warmth of her embrace had sprung from the heaters in the truck. Although it was not his love, he was thankful that the cold of the night was no longer infecting his joints, that he was now in relief from it within this stolen carriage.

His fingers throbbed as the heat crept in. From the freezing temperatures outside, which he had been exposed to for over an hour since the warmth of the coffee he had held, his digits were now suffering from chilblains and gave him a pain he had not experienced since his teenage years. He could not remember what his mother had told him about keeping the pain at bay. Was it that he needed to warm them slowly or that the quicker they warmed the swifter the pain would pass? He tucked his hands inside the breast of his jacket and under his armpits, trapping them with his arms against the sides of his chest.

After only a short time, they arrived at their destination. The truck slowed as they approached what was clearly the only establishment open for business on this street. The place was illuminated like something from Vegas, neon lights, LED signs; it was clearly trying to draw attention. They passed the building moving slowly, and they both stared intently into the place, where aside from the employee behind the counter, there was one other person inside, by the looks of it, copying documents.

Parking the stolen vehicle immediately outside the place would be madness and inviting trouble. The driver continued to roll forwards at a steady pace, and his eyes searched around the place for a side road or alley way. 'We're best leaving it some distance from here' uttered his companion. Turning into a side road that would surely be a few minutes' walk back to the copy shop, 31 pulled up at the curb and let the thing idle for a while before he turned back the screwdriver and killed the engine. 'You ready?' he said with a tone that invited no response, only action; and he sprang open the door and slipped out onto the asphalt. 36 popped open the door on his side of the pickup and swung his legs out and over the foot path and dropped on to his feet. His knee was immediately in pain as soon as he made it bare weight and his heel more so which was now sheer agony. It was intense enough to grimace and he would need better pain killers before long.

His companion was looking into the loading space at the back of the truck. Something must have attracted him, or maybe there was an idea under construction within the brute. Though he routed around the small cache of belongings, he arose with nothing. 'Check the glove box' spouted from him with another instructive tone.

'*What for?*' he responded with a bewildered expression evident through both his verbal and facial response.

'Anything of use. We need to hide the vehicle's ID number'

Leaning back into the vehicle he opened the glove box to see only an array of papers. Old receipts so it seemed. A ballpoint pen, black ink, possibly of use, but it would be difficult to make significant marks with such a small nib. A marker pen would be preferable. The ogre ripped open the driver's door and leaned in taking hold of the toolbox they had liberated from the old man's garage. Pulling it out and into the streetlight, he rummaged around the contents and discovered something that apparently offered him some delight. Black insulation tape.

Using the screwdriver that moments ago had acted as a makeshift key, the giant scored marks across the tape, and he ripped off a few strips and delicately placed them on to the rear number plate. Once satisfied with his work, he moved to the front of the vehicle, completing the same process.

'It won't stand up to scrutiny, but you've changed enough to not draw immediate attention if a cop drives by'.

His friend considered that a compliment.

Walking again, they were approaching their intermediate destination, which was only minutes away. Where was this new player he wondered now and raised his wrist to check his map. They were heading towards him, or so he thought; perhaps it was just that they were heading in the general direction, but now he was becoming paranoid, so self-involved in this predicament that everything seemed to be of significance, even if there was really nothing to it. At any rate, their progress, whoever this was, was slow enough that it would be some time before they came upon him, if indeed they were wishing to seek him out.

Perhaps this was 32 in search of Goliath; in search of their cure, their escape of this terrible torment. What did they know about this ordeal? What had they learnt in their pursuit of others? Maybe whoever this new dot was, they could shed more light on this unfortunate episode. But for now, that would have to wait. They had a job at hand. His friend had little more than three hours left to figure out what exactly he was looking for, and to lay hands on it.

The clock was ticking down for more than the two of them; 30, though incarcerated, may well be in her final seconds. Whilst the leviathan believed that she had found her antidote, 36 was not so sure. They would no doubt come to discover her fate once they arrived at the custody suite. But at this moment, she may be approaching the end of her life. It was the turn of the hour.

04:00

———

The cold seemed worse than he remembered. Perhaps he was just used to the temperature of the truck's heaters now that he had been warmed; though the sensation of blades cutting at his fingertips had not yet subsided, the pain in his heel was becoming more tolerable with every step, or at least he was becoming more used to its presence. Only seconds away from the door of the printers, a lone car was approaching from behind, the headlights casting long shadows that grew ever smaller as the vehicle neared. Turning to observe the passing motor, 31's attention had also been taken by this, and they seemed to have moved in tandem as their heads and upper torsos swung round to inspect it, like synchronised dancers in unison. It was a police cruiser.

It felt as though his heart had stopped and his breathing ceased. Shock grabbed hold and engulfed him like a fire, consuming every morsel of his being. It was tense. But the vehicle didn't even slow as it passed, and together they turned in tandem again as it glided by and continued up the road as they arrived at the door to the place where their criminality would continue.

Identity fraud, false representations, things that would ultimately be used at a police station no less, where they would doubtless look to arrive in a stolen vehicle! This was spiralling to a place he would under any other circumstances, never fall so far, never stoop so low. He was a good man, above reproach. Sure, there had been times in his life where he had done things that were 'not entirely lawful', but speeding, or using company materials for personal purposes, even buying a replica watch were about as far from the line as he had ever stepped before.

There was a sound of an electronic bell that would alert the attention of the shop clerk, as his companion opened the door and they entered. The employee, still behind the counter, observed them for a moment, waiting for the door to close before speaking and querying their needs. They requested the use of the computers to edit documents before printing, and would require the use of their ID photograph booth, and laminator. The man was fairly young, probably inexperienced, but his suspicions had certainly been roused by their request, his expression said as much.

Nevertheless, he was satisfied that whatever their story, it was nothing to him what their reason would be with false identities. Were they that obvious he thought? They were legal age for everything and there was no need for creating convincing identity documents for drinking purposes; so as unusual as they may seem to the graveyard shift worker, they were free to go about their business. They set for a bank of monitors and keyboards along the window at the shop front; from here they could keep watch of anyone approaching, though the map on his band would serve as the best viewpoint of anyone who was of importance to them. All others were simply insignificant.

The plan needed fine tuning. They needed a name for the fictitious company, names for themselves. They needed some back story. Considering their clothing, some form of industrial work would be a good call. Factory workers, part of a construction or production line maybe. But they needed to appear to have superiority to the curly haired woman, management types, after the rogue employee. But what about the item they would be looking for? They had no idea if it was a pill, a bottle, a small vial, a hypodermic syringe. How could they concoct a story for something they knew nothing about? They searched the Net for 'poison cure' and several variations, planning to create the story of their search around whatever was the most likely item.

The common response seemed to relate to venomous creatures and the remedies to bites and stings, most of which were to be administered by medical professionals via injection. It seemed unlikely that the woman would have such equipment in her possession unless she had come to inherit it from her interaction with other players of this twisted tale. He knew that neither he nor 31 had anything of the sort on their person.

What did they have? Aside from the bands on their wrists and the clothing they wore, they had nothing.

He wondered then was it likely that the band *was* the item? Was it possible that the band itself is the item of concern; perhaps serving both as their cruelty and cure. Did this thing have more functions, beyond that which he could see? Perhaps this was the device that would kill him, yet the same item on another participant, 35, could be that which saved him? Perhaps during interaction with one's predecessor, the band would be able to deactivate some device that would otherwise bring about his end? This thing, this band, whatever it was, wherever it came from, was riddled with some micro-technologies that seemed to be a far way off from the present. Surely it was possible that the band could have such capabilities?

What then if the band was simply to be removed? Would that end his involvement in this affliction, or would it simply remove the possibilities of him being in contact, viewing others, and possibly even from saving his life? Would removing this band even spell an immediate end by triggering whatever it would be that would kill him? Poison may be a misnomer. There could be a time release device within him, or the band itself could give some discharge that would kill, through shock, or maybe even poison after all. He considered this seemed unlikely as the wearer would simply remove it in the final seconds and thus avoid their demise. There must be something more to it than that; but there was simply not enough data to make any kind of educated guess. Their quest must continue for now. It was imperative that he and his friend get access to the possessions of the mysterious maiden now in the care of the authorities and discover what they could through enquiry and investigation.

There was little noise in the print shop, other than the continual hum of the copy machine being used by the other patron, which would intermittently be paused for several seconds as documents were changed in the scanner. There was a smell of the heat and ink slowly filling the room that reminded him of the laser printer at his office desk in the years gone by. The clerk was still behind the counter and his attention was taken by something underneath. It seemed he was watching a movie or TV show on his computer as the pimple faced youngster just stared with an expressionless face.

His comrade was fairly au fait with computers, but his own skills far outweighed the other. Using a number of programs, he had quickly put together a pair of identity cards that now only required an image.

Whilst he proceeded to piece together some fabricated letterhead paper of their fabricated company, which may serve them a purpose later, 31 went to speak with the clerk who remained engrossed in the movement on his monitor. In the several minutes it took to make the document look convincing, his companion had discovered that the ID photographing services at this establishment, were no more complicated than the counter man pointing an archaic web-camera device in the direction of a white background marked out on a wall.

This could produce for them a digital image that could be accessed from the network of computers, before being sent to a printing machine, from where they could give the final touches to their identification documents. This place had the ability to print good quality cards and the employee had offered his 'reserved, special service' for them, which would make the documents more authentic looking. He could reel off a couple of phony security access cards, and throw in some lanyards with the company logo on too. God only knew what the ogre had promised the man to have him offer to aide in the creation of falsified documents, but as long as he had not compromised their mission, it would be of little consequence.

'Compromise our mission' he thought. 'Dear Lord, I watch too much television'.

In turn they each stood in front of the white patch on the wall, on top of stickers of footprints on the ground so the spacing could be uniform. Watching the monster of a man attempt this was actually quite comical to him, as the beast stooped to lower his towering height, and then tried to readjust the angle of his lean to not appear awkward on his photograph. This isn't a publicity shot for Man of the Year he thought as the oaf stood with gracelessness and a half smile pursed at the lips.

Taking his turn to be imaged, he set place on the footprints, took a deep breath and raising his chest and shoulders, stared into the camera with what he hoped was a purposeful look. The employee seemed satisfied that he had captured what they needed, and they returned to the machine at which they had been working, now accompanied by the clerk, who took the pilot seat at the machine and imported the images to the fake identity cards they had created. Seeing his 'purposeful' look, he was embarrassed at how ridiculous his pout appeared; taut like an arsehole he thought.

The other man there, who had been at the copier, had now finished their printing and was gathering their documents into bundles, preparing to leave. The clerk had to leave the task at hand for a few minutes to return to his proper post and process the order of the copyist.

Why had he not thought earlier..... they have no means to pay! With the shop keeper away to handle the transaction, he turned to his companion knowing that that had no more than a minute or so to talk privately until the other man returned to their station.

'We have no money! How are we going to pay?'

'Leave it to me, I have it all under control' retorted the other.

'Have it under control? What have you told him? How on earth did you convince him to help us?' he resounded with less hush than he would have preferred, but his emotions were raging now. He could feel the rush of blood had caused his face to flush with a crimson colour. His jaw set tight as he concluded his interrogative questions, and his brow furrowed as he stared with intent at the man who would have the power to smite him in an instant if he chose to.

The ogre took a deep breath, which he held for a few seconds before speaking. 'Just let me handle this. When it's time to go, follow my lead. Okay?' he spouted in a commanding manner that reminded him of the first moments of his interaction with this giant, the accent pervading, the authority assuming. This tank of muscle and brawn had something not so 'citizen like' up his sleeve. Were they simply going to run for it; or something worse? The copyist was leaving, and the clerk was returning; whatever it would be, it would have to wait for now.

Within not much time at all, their documents were ready, and the man set to using some form of laser technology to etch onto plastic and cord. He created something that without intense scrutiny, would stand up to inspection, and would give them an appearance they were hoping to achieve.

But then his new friend made an odd request. He asked the young lackey if he had any box tape. 'Sure' the guy responded and went off towards the stock room down a narrow corridor. 31 set after him and immediately he knew this was it; the mammoth was intent on securing that they got away with their loot, unpaid and without repercussions. Whatever did the giant intend to do to the man? Should he follow, or hold steadfast and behave like there was nothing happening? Could he hold clear conscience knowing that the colossus meant the clerk certain harm?

Tiptoeing down the corridor, he could hear the kerfuffle, something was going down in that stockroom. Whatever the beast was doing, as long as he did not leave the man with any permanent scars other than to his psyche, it was okay. To become physically violent to save your own life from the poison within, was just about tolerable as it was; but to intend harm to an innocent bystander, was simply not acceptable. As he approached the door, he heard the sound of a reel of tape being pulled apart, the distinct ripping sound as the outer layer peeled away from the roll with speed to the required length.

On peering in the doorway, the brute had the other parked on a disused, damaged and torn typical office chair that had clearly been discarded in the back rooms when newer furniture had arrived. There were several other such chairs also present. The man seemed wilted, flaccid, lifeless almost; though he was conscious, and 31 was kneeling behind him, binding his hands behind the seat back. Watching as the menace made use of a roll of box tape to bind the man to the chair, he was mesmerised at the sight, which seemed so surreal. He observed the scene as though he were watching something from Hollywood, it looked real, but surely it was not.

The limp man's eyes stole a glance at him, which grounded him back to the room. This was real. This was happening. Despite what he would rather, there was no making this undone. Even if he tried to release the man, the leviathan had the force to overcome them both simultaneously. And worse, if he were able to free the shopkeeper, what would be next? The police would no doubt be on him in no time, and that would destroy his possibilities of getting to the end of this torment. He looked right back in the man's eyes, with no empathy in his gaze, just a cold and calculated face observing him being bound by brown tape, as the constant rip continued with the reel being pulled over and under, round and around.

31 bit through the edge of the tape and snapped it, releasing the roll from the piñata like figure in front of him. The tape ripped again as the giant pulled out another section which he placed over the mouth of the captive, and ran the roll twice around his head, ensuring that though his mouth was firmly covered, he could still breathe through his nose. Snapping the tape again, he proceeded to place another double loop this time under the prisoner's chin and over the top of his head. This would prevent his jaw from opening enough to wiggle out of the other mouth covering.

Stepping back to observe his work, he seemed satisfied that the man would not be moving until morning when his colleagues would come to relieve him of his shift. And then the bell rang. That distinctive electronic 'ding dong' of the door alarm, alerting them that someone had just entered the place. They both froze. His heart sank, this was becoming a frequent feature of this night. Now he felt like a rabbit in the headlights, not knowing which way to run, what to do. They fixed their gaze on each other, and he could feel his eyes widening. From staring deeply at him, 31 shot his eyes towards the shop front and back several times. He took that as his suggestion that he should go and check it out.

The horror of dealing with whoever had just entered the place, while his colleague was confined to the stockroom taking charge of their captive, was just one more stress on the nightmare he had already found himself in. Would Zit-Face stay quiet? 31 would surely see to that, but could the Goliath remain quiet in doing so, should the need arise? Silently, he slipped out of the room backwards, and pulled the door closed behind him. Making his way towards the shop floor, he slid off his jacket and let it fall to the floor behind him. It would be better for him to be seen in a plain white shirt that would go unnoticed, rather than in the coat that was being worn by the unfortunate ones caught in this cunning contest.

His band. The map. He had been so engrossed in his act of creating false identities that he had given no attention to the position of any others in quite some time. 04:44. Was this new arrival the blue dot that had been heading their way less than an hour ago? Relief washed over him like a wave as his map showed no other dots in immediate vicinity, but then the fear engulfed him once more as he realised that if the dot had arrived at his location, their proximity might be masked by the presence of his own, and his companion's markers on his wristband's map.

He needed to face them, whoever it was now awaiting the tending of a copy clerk. If it was another contestant of this madness, they might think nothing of the man in a plain white shirt behind the counter. He stepped out of the corridor with purpose, with a smile at his mouth and his eyes, as his sight caught that of the other, instantaneously alleviating his heaviness as he saw a random night worker, who was clearly after the facilities of the place. He took position behind the counter, fixing his seat, and engaging the new arrival with a warm welcome and an offer of assistance.

'You're new here' said the other, 'you'll get used to me, I'm a regular at this hour. Not that you lot are. Seems like every other week they have someone new working the graveyard. There's something about the dead of night that people find uneasy and just can't take the unusual hours'.

'*Not for me*' he responded with a bounce in his voice, '*I've been working nights as long as I can remember. The only problem with them is...... the weirdo's you get at nearly 5am*' and they smiled together.

Tilting her head towards the bank of computers, she informed him that she wouldn't be long this time, 15-20 minutes tops. He watched her intently as she went about photo editing on one of the machines. She knew what she was doing and before long had moved to the high-definition printing machine on the far side of the room. The presence of this woman drove his thoughts back to his love. By now she would surely be going insane trying to figure out what had happened to him. The phone. There was a phone right in front of him, on the counter, perfectly placed for his use.

He picked up the handset and began to punch in the numbers but stopped before fully dialling. They had a hostage in this place. By the time the man is discovered come the day shift, there will be all manner of investigations. An outgoing phone call at this hour would surely attract attention, and the number would be traced and would lead back to her, and ultimately to him. But that was only if he ever found his way out of this snare that presently controlled his destiny. Was it worth the risk?

He decided it was, and as he placed the handset to his head, there was a repeat of the ringing tone through the earpiece, that continued until it reached an automated response; 'You cannot leave a message. This mailbox is full. Please try again later'. '*Shit*' emerged from him, and the woman across the room turned to look at him. He just smiled sweetly back and dipped his head to look down beneath the counter.

Her mailbox was full. Most likely from spreading the news about his disappearance. People had surely been trying to get in contact and had clogged the thing up. Why did she not answer? She must be too busy searching for him, engaged in something, possibly driving, scouring the streets for any sign of him. But where was she? Where was he? He still had no idea of his location. Nothing had looked familiar enough to him that gave him to know he had been here before as he travelled with his companion both on foot and by truck over the last few hours.

There were too many things going on for his brain to handle. Poison; antidote; the woman in police custody; their prisoner in the back rooms; his fiancée; death and horror of the gory scene; murder and butchery; theft; the vision of the old man giving chase down the driveway. He was tired, he needed to rest his mind, but this was not a likely prospect for the next 18 hours. The passing of time since his awakening had felt like an age; days not hours. The details remained with him, the initial feeling of cold as he woke on the icy steel surface of a cadaver cooler; the pungent wash of chemicals stinging his nostrils; the stippled rubbery surface of the floor on which he had ultimately rested his feet having made his escape.

Then the door chime went off again. Another 'bing bong.' Another new arrival.

A cop!

05:00

'Holy shit' was about the only thing that went through his mind before he completely blanked. Of the infinite possibilities that could have led to an officer arriving at that doorway, there was nothing but emptiness in the thoughts as he stared at the uniformed man. The cop returned the look also with inquisitive eyes as he stared back at the man behind the counter before his head turned his field of vision to inspect the shop floor for other occupants, then reverting his attention to the man at the desk.

'Where's the other guy?' he enquired with some positivity in his voice. The mannerism of his body language and the tone of his question had not indicated any hostility. Who was the 'other guy' he was asking after? Certainly not his companion in the back rooms, currently holding hostage the true nightshift worker of this establishment? Perhaps he meant the employee himself? That was most likely, but he decided to be vague in his reply.

'*I'm not sure who you mean? I'm just an agency worker brought in to cover a shift on short notice.*' That was sufficient to cover his being there if the cop had personal knowledge of whoever the captive bound to the chair out back was, and he hoped that it would satisfy the officer and that no further questions cropped up.

His thoughts turned to the ogre in the stockroom, who might emerge at any moment to survey the scene. If he presented himself whilst this officer was still here, there would no doubt be further questions. Despite his cover story, it would be improbable that they could explain away the presence of this ogre if he were just 'covering'.

The sound of the door chime as the lawman had entered may have been taken by his companion to be the sound of the woman leaving. At any moment, the massive man may emerge from the corridor and be confronted by more than was perhaps expected, and then have to think quickly for some kind of response that would not only fit being here, and in the back rooms; but 31 would have no idea what he had already said.

Worse than this, what if there was some ruckus, the bound man trying to call for help, the giant raining down a blow or two to keep him from doing so? Would the officer be able to hear such from here on the shop floor? The noise of the printer to his right would surely compensate for some muffled sound that may emanate from the back rooms, but would it likely drown anything out?

'Don't worry' said the cop, 'I was just calling in for a social really. He must have called in sick', again his tone was anything but threatening. The man was clearly here for more than he suggested; he advanced towards the counter as he looked over at the woman operating a printing machine. 'There have been a few strange happenings around here over the last few weeks, at all kinds of ungodly hours. We're dropping in on anywhere that is open all night just to check on them, and if they've seen anything'

'What kind of stuff is going on?' he asked the officer, trying to seem inquisitive and engaging, rather than arousing suspicion by having any urgency for the man to leave, despite the worry that his friend may alight the stock room at any moment and be confronted by him engaged with an officer of the law. The response of the cop was similarly vague, but enough to ignite in him feelings of remorse, fear, anticipation and anger at his own involvement in these peculiar happenings.

Multiple missing persons. Murders, robberies, assault. Thefts of all kinds. The worst of it seemed to be that all of these things, though otherwise everyday dealings of police, were considered unusual by virtue of all of the reports they had received indicating the offender to have been a sole individual. Always a lone assailant, but believed to be part of a group, each with a rather nondescript account of their appearance; a person in a black jacket with a fleece lined collar.

How far back did this madness stretch he wondered?

This was all becoming out of hand. He knew of, or at least suspected, that Curlylocks had murdered 29, but the uniformed man spoke of multiple murders and assaults. He had struggled to listen to the rest of what the cop said, feeling a little queasy at his own involvement.

CCTV recordings of multiple incidents had failed to identify anything other than a vague black jacket wearing individual. No hits on facial recognition for any of the perpetrators on any of their criminal databases. It was as if these people were all otherwise regular members of society, not lowlife scumbags with a record, just your average Joe, but something had flipped their switch. Several of the murder victims had been wearing the same black jacket when their corpse had been discovered.

He learned how they had found another that very night, and that the officer's colleagues had arrested a woman that they believed may be able to give them some answers. It was the first break in the investigation they'd had. Until now, no one could figure it out and all of the city's servicemen had been continually briefed on the developments. This was quite a persistent issue for them. But this woman was the key to bringing down what was considered to be a small band of radical activists with some unknown agenda.

This cop really needed to unload he thought, but he lapped it up all the same. More detail meant he would be better prepared.

Eventually the officer thanked him for his ear and instructed him to be extra vigilant before leaving. He was quickly accosted by the woman who had overheard a little of the officer's account and wanted to know all of the details. Neither of them could understand why they had seen or heard nothing of this on the news, though it was possible that the police wanted to keep the people from panicking.

Sure, there were robberies all the time, home invasions, burglary, and even murders hitting the public eye through the media every now and then. They wondered how many murders go unreported on a daily or weekly basis.

She had finished her tasks and presented him with an account card of sorts for this printing place. He scanned the card and the details of her tasks that night were already loaded into the computer, which made it easy for him to process a payment through the accounting information already on their system. His cover story was holding well he thought. The woman left and immediately he flew to the door, turned the catch to prevent any further visitors, and flipped the switch on the LED sign that changed from 'open' to 'closed'.

Leaving the shop floor, he headed to the stockroom where his companion had remained unnervingly quiet, although he was grateful for as much. The other man, bound to the chair and unable to move any part of him but his head, which was now slumped towards his chest, but raised only ever so slightly as he walked into the room; the prisoner's eyes now regarded him with sadness and a lack of hope was written on his face. Trying to alleviate the man's fear, he spoke to him.

'Don't worry. We're not here to harm you' and he realised how ridiculous that sounded to a man bounded and gagged. *'We'll be out of here in a minute. You will be relieved of your shift by your colleagues shortly no doubt, at which point you'll be found and can raise the alarm. Until then, I'm afraid you'll*

have to stay here. He motioned to the foreigner to come with him and leave the room.

In the corridor he found a doorway to a smaller storage cupboard, where the employee had left his coat, scarf and bag. They searched the contents in the light of the hallway but found nothing that may be of use to them. The guy's wallet was devoid of any cash that could have come in handy; the modern world had all but eradicated the stuff. The bag itself may yet prove handy. Goliath had relieved the man of a phone that had been in his pocket. They were lucky that their captive had not tried to use this when 31 had set upon him, but he doubted that there had been any opportunity, it all happened so fast. The phone would certainly be of no use to them, and as soon as the man is discovered, the police may try to track the phone and that would not be an option.

The man's coat would certainly not go near fitting the ogre, but it was passable as his own, although a little tight for his liking. The fact that the police were looking for people in a black jacket meant this red Parka type coat would be of some benefit, especially if they were to arrive at a police station in search of the woman and her belongings.

Had their cover now been blown through the revelations of the police officer? He told his companion of what he had learned, and they considered their options. After a little debate, they resolved that whoever this woman was, keeping with the police theory despite their knowledge to the contrary, if she were part of some sect or radical activist group as the police believed, she would most probably still have a day job. So, they believed they could still use this to their advantage; they would just need to make sure they did not look like they were all supposed to be in some type of uniform clothing. Whilst it was not as good as a red parker, the scarf would help to hide the details of goliath's jacket. With a satchel over his shoulder and a security tag and ID card on a lanyard around his neck, coupled with his presence with another person of similar credentials, not a loner; this would hopefully distract enough attention from what the police have been in search of.

Before leaving, they put a number of file folders, and ring binders, empty as they were, into the satchel to give the appearance of having multiple important documents. They turned off all of the monitors and machinery in the place and then finally the lights and they slipped out of the front door, pulling the door closed behind them so that it would engage the latch. Only the LED 'closed' sign was now radiating any light and the place look otherwise devoid of occupant. They moved on.

Within a few minutes they arrived back at the place they had dumped the stolen truck and were relieved to find that it did not appear to have attracted any unwanted attention. It started with ease when 31 inserted and turned the screwdriver. Moments later they were driving away. Once more the events of the last half an hour had so arrested his attention that he had failed to check on his wristband. 05:25. No new messages.

The other blue dot that had appeared to be heading in their direction had not made it closer than about a half mile from the printing place. This was a little too close for comfort considering their mission. There it is again; mission, as though he were some secret agent, with one goal in mind. He knew how ridiculous this would sound if he said it out loud. Mission indeed, how stupid was he?

The task at hand was a better phrase. Had they have been accosted by this other participant before they could continue with their task, they would have either had a problem to deal with, or another tag along with no back story or credentials. It would not be preferential to increase their numbers now, although it may assist with their ability to be inconspicuous considering the police are looking for lone persons. They were now heading away from where this other blue dot was currently located. It would not be long before they arrived at the custody suite, 31 had indicated around 15 minutes at this time of day, with no traffic.

As they moved along the open roads, he was unable to shake from his mind the fact that she had not answered her phone when he called. Whilst she may be out looking, or maybe even meeting with police about what sounds to be 'yet another' missing persons report; she must be expecting news of his discovery, and therefore would have answered immediately. She was never without her phone, always at the ready and at a time like this, it was surely a better time than ever to have the thing glued to her hand. She had answered calls whilst they had been in meetings before. He remembered how he thought it was rude to take the call from their wedding planner even though they were meeting with a prospective wedding photographer. He would never have done such a thing and would have let it go to his mailbox, where he would call back later. She on the other hand had probably never missed a call in years. Why now? Why was her mailbox full? He couldn't even leave a message.

The truck's heaters had little effect now as he was thoroughly warmed from being in the print shop and had only been exposed to the cold for a brief few minutes in between. The heat felt dry, and it irritated his eyes and throat. Another coffee would be great about now. As they continued on, he again perused the map function of his wristband in search of others. In the time it took for them to arrive at the custody suite, he had been able to spot another two blue dots, seemingly in random locations, quite some distance from the town. Neither of them seemed to be close to any other, and were such a distance away from him that he wouldn't be able to make any legible deduction of how to reach them. He wondered how they were managing on their own, how far into their 24 hours, their 'day', they were and whether they were aware of the reality that befell them?

It dawned on him that as much as he knew, it was still very little. There were so many unanswered questions that remained; so many possibilities; an endless amount of possible scenarios that could make up the situation he faced and the infinite outcomes. There had been no word from his tormentor in a few hours. Who was the author of his affliction, controlling him through an unknown, unseen terror that would likely spell his end if he did not complete their bidding? He could think of no reason why anyone would want to cause him harm. Surely this was the sick and twisted creation of someone psychologically disturbed.

Whoever this puppeteer was, they had taken him without his consent. Should he ever escape this madness, he would not give up in his search for other survivors and together they could try to figure out who their oppressor is, why they had done this, and seek to bring justice to them, even if that meant he would have to play the roles of judge, jury and executioner. Perhaps he was capable of murder after all. Perhaps that would be his ultimate calling; to locate and eliminate the creator of this contest.

With such murderous thoughts in mind, they arrived at the holding cells. As they had at the print shop earlier, they drove right by, quickly surveilling the place and went on to find a secure spot to leave their vehicle that would not attract attention. It would be a few minutes' walk back to the custody suite from where his friend considered was a good place to park up. He had a new coat, thicker and warmer than his standard issue that his colleague and all other participants would be wearing. His companion, 31, donned the scarf in a simple loop around his neck that succeeded in disguising the fleece collar of his black jacket pretty well. With the satchel over his shoulder and across his chest, and the security tags also hanging from beneath the scarf, they set off towards the place believing that their plan might just about be possible to pull off.

They discussed the fine details as they continued on foot, and in view of the larger man's foreign accent, they considered that it would be beneficial if he should open the dialogue with whomever they were able to meet, but fall back to 36 once the channel of communication was opened. They went over their phony identities, checking that the minutiae of the details were known. It was unlikely that they would be asked anything other than their professional credentials and their connections to the woman they were pursuing, so being well prepared on these matters was of paramount importance.

As they approached the doors, butterflies set in and his heart rate quickened. The fear of being fumbled in their plot was as real as anything he was experiencing this night. They needed to appear confident, but the reality was far from that. He felt he could collapse at any moment from the anticipation of it all. He stepped ahead of his colleague and pulled open the door to the reception, allowing the ogre to enter before him. Stepping inside, the place had an awkward scent, stale and damp.

There was no one at the enquiry desk and they had to press a buzzer to call for attention. The tension was growing and they were forced to wait for the desk clerk for several minutes. A short and stout woman came out, in a uniform that barely fit her. She had clearly gained weight since joining the force and was now outgrowing her attire. She seemed to be tired, weary, and not incredibly interested in two new arrivals that had clearly disturbed her from whatever she had been doing when they arrived. With near distain in her voice, she asked whether she could be of assistance.

'We believe that you have a woman in custody here, arrested earlier tonight, about 5'6' in height, slim athletic build, late 30's with blond curly hair. Does that sound familiar?' The woman just looked at the goliath with a blank expression.

He knew he had to speak next. The knots in his stomach were churning.

'*The woman is an employee of ours. We have no business with whatever she has been arrested for, and will leave you to whatever you decide in that regard; but we believe that she has taken something from us, that is critical to our production line and we must recover it at the earliest convenience.*'

'Is that so?' said the portly woman with an even greater hint of distain.

He cleared his throat before ploughing on, '*We understand that you may not release such to us at present, and you have your investigations to make. We just need to know whether she has it or whether she may have already given it to whoever her contact is. We suspect corporate espionage of our formula you see.*'

The woman seemed to be intrigued by this revelation. Their plan had clearly drawn her in, though she remained to be sceptical as evidenced through her further inquisition. He slid a neat, crisp business card through the aperture that told her he was 'Group Legal Counsel'. They offered her their fake credentials and after her brief inspection, she told them to wait right there and went back through the door from whence she had emerged, taking his business card with her. They did not know if their ID documents had been convincing enough; he was satisfied with his story, but did she buy it? If not, she could be returning any minute with more officers, who would no doubt separate them and subject them to intensive interviewing. This would bring the end of his friend, who had no more than an hour left. What would happen if the man were to drop dead in front of the police? Or if his insides suddenly erupted and caused havoc on the floor of an interrogation room?

They could hear footsteps of the woman, plodding in an unusual pattern as she was heading back towards them. A second pair of footsteps joined the otherwise solitary sound, quicker in their stride, evidently a wider gait, and sounded like they were catching up to the former. The door opened again and a man of late 50's age came through, tall but slim in his build, the grey in his hair and beard gave him a distinguished look, and the uniform spoke of his rank as a Sergeant. The rounded woman came through the door behind him.

Through the glass above the counter, the Sergeant asked them to tell him their story as he scrutinised their credentials. Repeating that which he had said earlier, this man also seemed to be intrigued. '*If you have not figured out her identity, she will have likely given you false information*' he added, hoping that they would be more taken in by the story, as much as sinking in the knowledge he had no idea at all what the woman's name actually was; Curly surely wasn't it. He explained that he was a lawyer and represented the phony company they had come up with; he had been brought in urgently to ensure the legal issues around recovery of their asset would not become problematic.

Somewhat off piste, his colleague spouted in a thicker accent than usual 'She was my partner, I can't believe she's done this, but it looks like she was only with me to expose us to this robbery. She played me from the start' and he hung his head with a look of shame and sadness.

Seeing this colossal man in such an emotional state had evidently pushed the Sergeant onto the side of the fence they hoped. It seemed to have opened him to the likelihood of their story being genuine in view of this giant being disturbed by the play of the woman. The composure of the Sergeant softened, and he suggested that he may be able to assist them, though he would have to speak with his superior. He invited them to pass through another door, which he had remotely unlocked through a button behind the counter.

Opening the door for his colleague, they were confronted by a corridor off which there were several doors only to the right. A row of thin windows lined the top of the left-hand side. This seemed to lead along the edge of the building, and at the end was a large grey metal door that looked as though it would lead to the holding cells. The Sergeant pulled open a door from a back office and asked them to take a seat there in the hallway whilst he made some enquiries.

The seats were backed to the external wall, facing four doorways along the corridor that looked to be interview rooms of some sort. One of the doors had no window and he noted that the handle was not like the others. It was round, and above it was a small section of a metal shroud around the word 'vacant'. A bathroom perhaps. At eye level on the door he noticed a faint outline of the typical 'male / female' symbols, that looked as though the paint around them had faded, perhaps a sticker of some form had previously occupied this space but was now missing. He had not realised until that time that he could do with using the facilities. His bladder felt full and this was a perfect time. He tried the handle and the door opened.

The room was small and narrow, and in darkness though there was a pull cord that would probably turn on the bulb above, the light from the hallway showed there was indeed a toilet at the other end and only a small hand basin on one side. He pulled the cord and was not surprised as the room was awash with a sterile white glow from an LED bulb. Being able to relieve himself was an opportunity he may not get again for some time.

When he was done, he found his colleague had not moved from the bench on which he was perched. There was no sign of the sergeant yet. He took a seat next to Goliath and they remained in silence, both of them hoping to hear something from the room in which the Sergeant had been. After a minute or so, the Sergeant came out of a doorway at the end of the corridor and pulled a security card on a retractable string from his waist which he pressed to a small black plate on the wall. A thick and distinct electronic buzz sounded, that seemed to echo down the corridor with force, followed by a solid thud as the door had unlocked. The Sergeant opened the door and passed through it as the door automatically closed behind him on a hydraulic arm, and a further thud burst from it as the door locked again.

There was nothing to do now but wait to hear from the Sergeant as to whether they would be allowed to inspect the woman's belongings; whether the Sergeant or another would do this for them; or whether they would be refused any assistance and told to 'piss off'. It seemed like they waited for an age, but in reality, it was no more than five minutes before there was another electronic thud and the sound of the lock releasing.

As the door opened, there she was. Shouldered by a uniformed officer on either side, and bound at the wrists by handcuffs though she had no band like those he and his companion were sporting. Her hair seemed a paler colour in this light and its tight curls were far from under control with any products. She looked almost savage, like she had been deserted in some remote place and left to fend for herself. She was not in the familiar clothing, now wearing what was undoubtedly standard prisoner issue wear. The officers urged her on with a nudge and she was moved forward into the corridor.

She looked at the pair of them, just sat there, watching her. She knew immediately that they too were part of this; the jacket of the large ogre gave them away first, but her gaze also made it to their legs and feet. To she who was familiar to the clothing, it was obvious. She was quickly ushered into one of the side rooms, and as the heavy locking door to the cells was almost closed, the Sergeant pushed his way through and went to the room also. He stood at the doorway and looked at them, and giving a wink, before disappearing from sight, closing the door behind him.

06:00

Waiting in that hallway stirred his emotions on a number of levels. There was still uncertainty as to the extent of their deception's ability to convince others. This Sergeant had to report up the chain to his superiors and no doubt, in light of the comments of the officer at the print shop only an hour ago, this woman was big news amongst the force, and would probably only be interrogated by senior Detectives.

There was less than an hour left on his companion's clock, which was counting down the seconds to his certain doom if they were unable to discover his cure from a search of the woman's belongings. It would not be possible he was sure, to speak with the woman, to learn what she knew, what had happened in that hallway where he had earlier discovered a dead man, and from which a corpse was collected.

His own time was counting down too: less than 16 hours remained. 31 had not been able to solve this riddle in the 'one day to live' they had been granted. Not yet at least. Was it likely they would figure this all out in the next fifty something minutes? And from there, what was next? Even in evading death from poison, his friend would still be pursued, at least for the next three hours. His pursuer, 32, would no doubt be desperate as their final hours crept in. And what of the continued search for 35? At least if they solved the conundrum, he would know how to save himself when he came to find them, but there was still no sign of clarity on what exactly was to spell his end, and what would save his life. It remained nothing more than Chinese whispers. The whole saga was so frustrating. He was a man who enjoyed problem solving, but this was on another level, and the constant weight on his mind was draining mentally and emotionally. He felt at an all-time low.

The corridor was bland and bleak. The floor had some kind of linoleum tiles, the walls were pale and simple; two-tone in colour but of similar plain appearance. The only thing to keep his attention from over thinking the predicament were a number of posters and flyers on a pin board attached to the wall. Reading each of these, first with a quick glance but as time passed, in every detail, it was of little interest, and sparked nothing more than a feeling of watching paint dry.

It seemed as though nothing was happening. It was unlikely that the Sergeant was extensively questioning the suspect. She was above his pay grade. What then was he doing in there, and why was he taking so long? There was no other sign of movement in this place. Aside from the uniformed men that had escorted the prisoner to the interview room, and then returned through the heavy locked door that presumably gave passage to the cells, and of course the stout woman from the front desk; it seemed deserted. No sounds, no signs of life.

He was tired now and needed rest. Closing his eyes, he knew it was likely that he would no doubt drift to the edge of consciousness. He allowed his head to rock backwards and rest on the wall behind him.

He woke with a start, and his eyes sprung open, but there was no movement around him, and he put it down to that dropping, falling feeling and jolting oneself awake. Resettling into his position, head back against the wall, his eyes closed over once more. The extent of his mental anguish was wearing him to a point that he would need to get some proper sleep, but he knew that this was not likely to happen until gone midnight at the earliest. For now, he must fight to stay awake.

The sound of a door opening woke him. He had drifted off, for how long? He checked his band, if only for the time – 06:17. The Sergeant came through a door that had seemed to be the other side of the office that lead out to the reception desk. He couldn't think how the officer had got from the interview room to the office without him noticing. Had he been in that deep a sleep or was it not an interview room further down the corridor after all, behind which there was some other passage, maybe other rooms that would lead from one place to the other.

The Sergeant was carrying a box, marked with a number, '67231'. Without needing to offer a full invitation, he simply stated 'Second door on the right please gentlemen'. They stood and proceeding to the door next to the bathroom, he opened the door ahead of them, and gestured for the officer to enter the room before them. There was a basic table in the middle of the room, metallic, cold, harsh, like the tray that had held him when he had awoken; simple chairs around it, similarly bland, two on either side. The Sergeant went around the far side of the table and set down the box on the top.

'You are allowed to look through this, but you do not remove anything' he instructed them as he presented a single pair of nitrile gloves, clearly far too small for the hands of the enormous companion. They looked at each other, both trying to hide their elation. They could not believe their rouse had worked. They were actually able to look through the personal effects of the woman in custody, through nothing more than a fabricated story of corporate espionage and some fake ID's. Maybe there was a God after all, throwing him a bone for once. '*Thank you*' he thought in a prayerful manner, knowing he could not speak the words aloud.

In the box was only her jacket, the polo-shirt, pants, black socks, black knickers, and a pair of black pumps. He was surprised they were not all in sealed evidence bags. Each item was the same as his colleagues and his own, though in female cuts and sized near perfectly for what he had perceived of the woman in the two brief moments he had inspected her. He rifled through, searching the pockets on her clothing, but it seemed they contained nothing. No signs of anything that would even remotely be connected to being the cure for some unknown poison.

'*Was there anything else?*' he asked of the Sergeant.

'Two items, but both are considered as evidence, which has been bagged and tagged accordingly. You are lucky I could get you the jacket before that got bagged. A steak knife that was covered in blood, and plastic band that had been crudely cut, presumably with the knife. The staff at the cafe she was collected from say she cut it from her wrist'.

They were thankful that their coats covered their own wrists, which despite having use of their hand out in front of them whilst rummaging through the clothing, had not been noticed by the Sergeant. After several minutes of searching, still there was nothing. Odd as it seemed, this woman was still alive, and that meant one of two things; either this was all a hoax of some perverted pig getting their kicks out of capturing people and making them think they were under some dire harm. Or she had found it, her cure, whatever it was that had released her from the timer that for her would have expired hours earlier.

If she had found the cure, she knew what it was, and that itself would be invaluable information. They were presently looking for a needle in a haystack; no, worse, they were looking for the unknown and it could be anywhere. A needle in a haystack would be easy by comparison. If the remedy to their harm was to be passed from player to player, it was missing now. She would perhaps know where it was. But getting to this woman was an impossible task. They had no leverage here and their phony ID's wouldn't hold up to interrogation if someone were to run even a basic search on the names or the company. It was time to cut their losses. They had been granted enough already.

Amazement was about the last emotional response he would have expected during this dark time, but amazement was what he felt when the officer spoke again.

'She would like a word with you' he said, looking directly at him. 'She does not wish to speak with your colleague; perhaps a little embarrassment at the... 'personal' situation, I don't know. But she has expressly forbid that we should put you two in the same room', said he, directing his attention to the ogre. 'She has only specified that she will not allow police supervision or listening. I said that I would have to discuss that with you. For your own protection, I would not recommend it...' but before he could finish the sentence, '*Yes*' came the response.

'*I will, I mean. Yes, I have no objections and will not require your protection. She will be in chains no doubt, and I am not interested in what you may have her here for. You are welcome to take whatever judiciary action is necessary. I only want what we need*'.

'Very well sir. I will make arrangements, if you would kindly wait back out in the hallway'.

And they thanked the man for allowing them to inspect the items and left the room to resume their positions at the corridor seating, he pulled off the nitrile gloves that turned inside out, a befitting premonition of what may yet become of his companion? As soon as they knew they were alone, they both just spilled out verbally. He knew that 31 had heard nothing he had said, as he had heard nothing from the other. Both seemed to stop at the same moment, realising that the other was trying to speak. They knew this was it, their chance to figure out this puzzle, to find the missing piece and complete the bigger picture. They just hoped they could do it in time, before the clock expired for Goliath. He had but 29 minutes remaining.

As they were discussing the possibilities, the Sergeant emerged from a doorway once more. 'You ready?' he asked, and with a nod, he rose to his feet and followed the officer along the corridor, to the door behind which the woman had earlier been taken. 'Before you go in, if she mentions anything about why she is here, I want to know. She may not want us listening in, but I expect to be fully briefed from you. I scratch your back, you scratch mine. Got it?' he said and he opened the door for him and indicated that he should enter.

Stepping into the room, it was not what he had expected. Blank and bleak like the hallway, but there was no magic mirror as he would have expected from things he had seen in film and TV. No place for observers to stand behind the reflective glass and evaluate the conversations of the occupants. It was just a plain square room with only a door at either side. The one behind him closed and he could hear the Sergeants footsteps moving away down the corridor. Filled with fear, anticipation and excitement, he looked at the woman who sat facing him across a table. Her hands were clasped together with her fingers interlocking, her wrists bound in handcuffs that seemed to limit her options on how she could hold her arms, prostrated out in front of her body, parallel like train tracks.

He hoped that this encounter would yield the results they needed. It was pretty desperate now for 31, who, if the these whispers were correct, would be dead at the turn of the hour. She was the key to preventing that. She was the key to preventing his own demise. She held the answers and he needed to get them. Fast. He pulled out a seat and parked himself, facing her. She looked as tired as he felt, yet she had a liveliness in her eyes that he knew he was lacking. She knew she had escaped, the madness was over for her. Except it wasn't; she was now in the hands of the law.

'Which one are you? 33? 34?' Her voice was soft, almost gentle. She had no animosity or anger in her tone, and she spoke with certainty, a clarity that he expected of someone who was well educated, a business professional, well used to having to annunciate their vocabulary in front of others, not a woman of common culture, slang speech or lazy use of words.

'*36*' he responded, a little unsure as to how to progress the conversation. His mind was so filled with questions; he did not know which to ask first.

'Whatever I say to you, I speak in confidence' whilst her clarity remained, her voice now had a slight tremor, almost nervousness. 'I made it. You can too. Unfortunately, not so good for your friend'. He could feel his cheeks and nose raise as his eyes squinted to scrutinise the woman knowing not what to make of her suggestions. 'What I tell you now does not get back to the Police. I doubt they have anything on me to convict me of murder. When I am ready to tell them the truth, the toxicology reports will confirm it. After that, it is a matter of mutilation of a corpse at best'.

Intrigue now consumed him. He was almost unable to focus on the words she spoke as his conscious thoughts raced from question to question. Every sentence she spoke seemed only to invite more questions, though she was trying to give as clear an account as she could.

In the time since her awakening, she had come to discover that she had been missing for two days. Like he, she had awoken in a morgue and believed she may have died and come back to life. The band at her wrist had told her the same as he, only she was to find her predecessor, 29. Confusion had led her to a police station, where she had wasted nearly two hours waiting for a detective to return from a crime scene, before she had witnessed a news report of a homicide, and the victim was wearing the same clothing as she.

As she had watched the TV in the lobby of the police station, 26 had arrived, looking for 25. Now there was no waiting for the detective, and with this other numbered man, they left together, and he told her what he knew. The same Chinese whispers of poison and cure. She had found only one other in all her 21 hours before her encounter with 29. It had been 26 that had told her the secret to their survival.

The cure wasn't in the possessions of your predecessor.

It was in them.

Inside them.

A wave washed over him and he threw up a little in his mouth at the sudden terror that sank in as his eyes glazed over, realising the depravity of the situation. Nausea did not begin to express the intense welling in the pit of his stomach. Mentally consumed with processing what he had heard and all that it meant, he struggled to listen to her carry on.

Whilst they slept, they had been made to ingest a tiny vial, made completely from glass, which one end would snap off. The contents were no more than a few millilitres of clear liquid that would prevent death from the poison also planted within them whilst they slept, but only if taken in time to allow it to work.

Inside her was the cure for his friend. But the ogre in the hallway could not get to it, and his time was up. She had seen his jacket and read the number on his chest, even from the end of the hall. Her eyesight must be impeccable he thought. Unless 31 were to burst through the door and rip her open whilst surrounded by armed police, he was nothing more than a dead man walking.

When she had found 29, it was too late for him. He was at deaths door and 28 had long since gone. He knew nothing of what was happening. She had shared with the now dead man what she knew, as he had no knowledge of how he could have saved himself, only that he would die when his countdown reached zero. He had prepared himself for certain doom, and on learning the truth, had instructed her to save herself once he was dead. He had given her permission to slice him open and remove what she needed, so long as she would be with him to hold his hand as he passed to lifelessness.

Once she had made mincemeat of the body, she had found the vial, which until that time she only knew that there was her cure and not exactly *what* it was she was looking for. It had taken her more than 30 minutes to find the thing in his dietary system. She had quite literally been covered in all manner of unspeakable elements that would ordinarily be contained within a human body. Having to eventually put the small bottle to her lips and consume the contents without wretching, was achieved only through the knowledge that the choice was either certain death, or probable disease.

But despite having taken the cure for her poison, she knew it was not over. As he had now suspected was likely the case, she was all too aware that she was being pursued by another, who would likely know that the only way to save themself, meant harm to her. She had calculated her options down to either run, or to hide where she could not be reached. To turn herself in was the best way to do it, to be locked up in a police cell, safe from the hands of her pursuer, and there was a blue dot following her on the map. She had to act quickly, and the cafe had seemed a reasonable option. If she spoke not a word but appeared in a traumatised state with her hands covered in blood, knife still present, they would surely call the police. Of course, the police had nothing on her except suspicion.

She had planned to tell them everything, but only once her sequel's time had expired, when she knew she would be safe from their reprise. Once 31 was gone, she had truly escaped. The game was over, and the only torment thereafter would be the memories of the deranged things she had been forced to do to survive. Of course there would also be the fallout from her butchery of a dead body, but she was certain that the toxicology report would confirm the presence of a lethal amount of whatever it was that was to kill them, and that on a larger scale, with she also being a pawn in this ridiculous game of death and sorrow, her legal team would be able to argue the case so that she likely would do no time. Her lawyer was en route and once he arrived; she wouldn't be able to speak with anyone. She wanted to help 36, and now she had given him the knowledge he needed, she felt that she had released a burden.

There was nothing he could do now to save his friend. He certainly was not about to spring across the table and murder this woman for someone he hardly knew. And when surrounded by police; it would be pure madness. All he could do now was to offer the Viking some companionship as he passed to his Valhalla. He could sit and talk to this woman for hours, but he would only be running down the clock on his own wrist, and with every passing hour that 35 remains at large from him, his demise was drawing to be an ever-stronger possibility.

He thanked her for taking the time to speak with him, and briefly explained how he had planned to search her belongings, so that she may have something to tell the police of their conversations if asked before she was ready to tell them of the true horrors of her involvement in the disappearances, death and destruction that has been ongoing. They had suspected her of industrial espionage, and that she had stolen some formula. He would tell them that he had learned nothing from her, but she had given him a lead to another.

Knocking on the door behind the woman to gain the attention of the police in the back rooms, he depressed the handle and was able to open the door. He poked his head through but could see no one, so called out for the Sergeant. There was no response and no sign or sound of any movement. He closed the door and paced across the room to the doorway back to the corridor where his friend was waiting. Taking hold of the handle, he turned to look at her '*Thanks, and good look*' he said, and slipped out into the hallway, closing the door behind him.

31 was staring at him as he emerged into the bland corridor that was yellowed by the aged strip lighting. His friend appeared nervous and seemed to know that there was no chance of saving his life now. His eyes were sad, his face gloomy. His mouth seemed to sag as though he had given up on life completely. It was only minutes until his wrist timer expired, and it was obvious he had been watching the thing as it ticked towards zero; the screen was lit and his arm was out in front of him.

'No joy?' asked the Aryan, with a vagueness of hope in his voice.

'I'm sorry' he responded *'It was never to happen; not here. We need to go, and I'll tell you what I can before the time comes'.*

With a long sigh, the giant stood and turned towards the door to the lobby. Despite his imminent death, he remained composed, calculated, callus almost; he stood firm, strong, like an oak tree being bent in the wind but refusing to break, the tower of resilience he had been for the last six hours. He strode to the door and tore it open with force; perhaps his composure was weaning, there was now anger in his demeanour. Was it likely he would go out fighting? He did not know enough to cause any problems in this place.

They were passing through the lobby when the Sergeant called to him. He turned and explained that the woman had been of little help, but claimed she was not involved in the theft of their formula, though she had given him another lead. He apologised that time was of the essence and he would be in contact by phone to update him. As he headed out of the door, the officer called back to him enquiring about the dead man. *'I'm sorry, we didn't discuss it. Please forgive me, but we must make haste if we are to save the future of our business'.*

As they headed back to the truck, he told the goliath of the location of his cure, the reason they could not find anything on themselves, in their pockets or belongings, was that *it* was within them. A small glass vial containing a potion that would prevent their death. 31 was lucky that 32 had not found him thus far, or he would likely have been killed for the thing inside him. As it happened, death was now inevitable, so it would have mattered not; perhaps, like 29 had given up hope and simply allowed his successor to butcher him when he had passed, the giant may have just accepted his fate. But surely though this monster of a man would have given a good fight to anyone that tried to subdue him.

The truck remained at the same location and again it seemed to be undisturbed or unnoticed by the authorities. They slipped into the seats they had occupied earlier. This part of the world was just waking. The sky was still dark, but the beginning of day light was breaking on the horizon. There were movements of vehicles at the end of the road they were sat on, the passing of headlights told that the road was much busier than it had been an hour or so earlier. But the silence was deafening. There was sound from the road, the buildings around them, and the breathing of his companion, which had become heavy, almost laborious. It was the lack of words that was troublesome. This man knew he was about to die and could do nothing about it.

Wondering if the deeper breathing was the psychological effect of the arrival of his companion's hour, or the physiological effect of the poison taking hold, arresting his body with some crippling manner that would result in his heart or head ceasing to function; he brought up his wrist to check his band and as he did, the time changed from 06:58 to 06:59. This was it, 60 seconds was all that was left for his colossal companion. As disturbed as it may seem, witnessing what would happen seemed like a good idea. It would prepare him for something more and he would perhaps gain some idea of what it was that was killing them.

The giant put his hands on the steering wheel at the 10-2 position, exposing his wrists and his band that was now displaying his countdown timer, reducing by the second.

'Goodbye my friend. I hope you make it' the ogre said with compassion.

'When I get out of this, I will find them. Whoever it is that has done this to us. I will make them pay!' he returned with both contempt and comfort in his tone.

In silence they watched as the timer counted down. 31 seemed to be like a statue, so focused on the dropping seconds that nothing else in the world existed but the tiny screen of the wristband. As the clock hit 10, he held his breath with anticipation, not knowing what was about to happen.

04....

03...

02..

01.

07:00

———

Fear had choked him as the hour turned and the timer had hit zero. The anticipation had culminated in such tension that his heart felt like it had squeezed so hard, there was nothing left within it to pump. Being unable to move and so captivated by the dropping clock, he realised that he had not taken a breath in longer than his heart and head would have liked. His composure suddenly dropped, and his body sagged as he observed his friend who sat motionless in physique though his eyes darted around as though he was trying to make sense of it all.

The screen of the bearded giant's wristband had turned off and reverted to the white plastic paper appearance that was now a common sight. It was as though it was a deliberate shutdown. As the timer ran out, so did the functionality of this futuristic technology.

'Nothing' the giant exclaimed in a flat and monotonous style. 'I don't feel a thing'. Nothing looked different. No shock or jerking motions, no choking or gasping for breath. 31 just sat there, still alive, as though nothing had changed. Maybe nothing had.

A roar of laughter erupted from the ogre, deep and disturbing, the kind of belly laugh from so far within a man that it seemed simultaneously filled with hilarity and horror.

The deep roar slowly melted to a muddled chuckle of a laugh, which was itself a funny thing that brought the first smile to his face since his awakening. His companion was now creased with laughter, giggling in an infectious way and before he knew it, the pair of them were sat there, chuckling with tears streaming down their faces.

Maybe this was all a hoax after all?

But she with the curly hair had confirmed this was real. She had a first-hand account of witnessing death for one whose time ran out. A sobering thought that caused the laughter to subside and he wiped the tears from his cheeks.

Questions continued to consume his every thought, too many to process. What on earth was happening, and why was his friend still alive? He realised that he was grateful for that fact. 31 should be dead, but there he sat, as alive as he was minutes ago, as alive as he was hours earlier. More so even, animated as he was in laughter.

No poison had taken hold of him, and he sure as hell had not taken any cure. Perhaps his physical size had been too much for the poison to master? The dilution of the thing in comparison to Goliath's stature may have been enough to have prevented it from a lethal conclusion?

Whatever had happened, or not happened for that matter; he was pleased that his friend was still alive.

Until now, they had not given any thought to what came beyond the expiration of 31's hours. Their plan had been only to find the means to preventing the certain death that awaited him. And now he was still very much alive, despite being unable to get hold of the potion that was with the woman. They had to think ahead. What was next? Was it worth continuing with the pursuit of 35 in search of a cure now that there were no effects from the poison to the goliath?

In view of the woman's account of the demise of 29, and the others before them, it was probable that whatever the situation with the leviathan beside him, was some form of malfunction to the system, something had gone wrong with his poison. There remained a very real probability that in 15 hours' time, he would not have the same joy.

The search must continue, and it began with the map. 31 could no longer use any functions of his band. It was now superfluous to him, and it was understandable why the woman had removed hers in the cafe. His own band continued to work just fine, or as fine as he was used to; this thing should not even be on him, it was not what was expected, and was not a welcome edition. This whole predicament was less than desirable, and he would not wish this upon so much as an enemy; not that he had any, and again his thoughts drifted to searching his mind of anyone that would have any grudge with him, as he scoured the map on his wrist in search of the nearest other blue dot.

He could not be sure, as he was so close to his companion, but he was almost certain that he was still able to see the presence of two blue dots at their location. Moving the screen about, it was some time before he located another. He had felt the pickup rock on its aged suspension and heard the creak of the leather as the ogre shifted in his seat, now leaning over his shoulder to see, and he could feel and smell his breath on which the scent of stale coffee lingered. Working back through the streets, they gained an idea of the direction they needed to be heading in so they could interact with this other. 31 inserted the screwdriver and fired up the engine.

Trying to get a sense of bearing, he jumped to the 'compass' function and tried to make use of it. The numbers were reducing as they progressed along the road. The arrow around the edge of the dotted ring was far from stationary. At every curve in the road, every turn, it moved in tandem with their orientation. Surveilling the area, it seemed as though they were passing through some commercialised zone. The buildings that rose around them were industrial looking, warehouses, and factories. Steam emanated from exhaust ports of heating systems that were poking out of the sides and roofs of them. The roads were now well travelled by people beginning their day, heading to work on the morning commute. Traffic had not become a constant stream, not here at least, but it was likely that the city was thickening with people and vehicles.

The industrial estate gave way to an undeveloped area of greenery that was likely arable farmlands on the outskirts of the town. Hedgerows turned to open fields, with infrequent lay-by's that were mostly vacant. The roads here were icy and had been out of the reach of the gritting vehicles that kept the city's streets free from such perils. The conditions weren't dangerous if one was careful, and 31 had slowed his progress a little that was befitting of the lacking grip levels.

07:19. Getting back to the map on his wrist, he could see that they were indeed getting closer to the dot with whom they were hoping to meet. What's more, it appeared as though the dot was heading towards them. Maybe this dot was trying to interact with them, with him at least, as to anyone else still caught in this madness, 31 was either dead, or had found the cure to his condition. Depending on what this new dot already knew, it was likely that there would be some sharing of knowledge, one way or the other, perhaps even both.

He was studying the map with intent, trying to decipher the most convenient route and instructing his friend to take a left or a right turn at different junctions. As if out of nowhere, the truck bumped harshly as it ricocheted off a parked van, which jolted him with force enough to know in an instant that he would suffer from whiplash to the neck. He stole a glance at the driver and found that 31 was slumped back against his seat and the driver's door. He looked pale, lifeless, dead.

There was no way he could prevent what would happen next. There was no time to react other than to throw his arms in front of his face in a cross like position. The pickup collided with an oncoming car that sent him crashing into the dashboard with force.

He felt dazed and knew that he was coming too; he had been knocked unconscious in the crash and the truck was now on its side with him in a crumpled heap on top of his companion, who was certainly dead, if not from before, he had been killed in the wreck. His shoulder ached and his arm felt limp as he tried to move it to lift himself. It must be dislocated. His head was ringing although with the adrenaline pumping through his system, there was little pain at this moment.

His left arm had been pinned between he and the giant. He wriggled it out from beneath him and took hold of the steering wheel, pulling himself to a near foetal position, from which he could stand, but that meant on top of the corpse of his dead friend. Reaching up, he was able to release the passenger door, but he struggled to push it open and knew he needed to resolve the issue with his shoulder before being able to climb out of the mangled heap.

He had dislocated a shoulder once as a child and recalled the agony of the reseating back into the socket.

Opening the red jacket he still wore, he was surprised to see that his white t-shirt was stained crimson, dark and almost black, just below his ribs on the right-hand side. He had not felt the pain of this at all, but the small round hole in the shirt spoke of some form of puncture wound, though he could not fathom what had happened. Raising the shirt from his waist and inspecting the wound, that too was small and round. It did not seem very deep, and he was satisfied that unless it became infected, it would not cause him any major problems. There was a biro poking out of an inside breast pocket of the coat and knew this had been the cause.

Dropping the coat from his left shoulder first, he was able to lower it from his right, where he found that the top of his arm was perpendicular to his torso. He slammed the front of his shoulder against the seat back which sent a sharp and shooting pain right through him but had not re-seated the ball in the socket. He tried again, screaming out from the pain that felt like a carving knife had been sunk right into the joint, but disappeared as quickly as it had arrived. He had succeeded in setting the shoulder back into place, but his arm was incredibly weak. Satisfied it was no going concern, he allowed his emotions to creep in once more, and began to sob.

Was it emotional overload? Was it the passing of the giant? Was it the pain of the injuries? Likely a mixture of all, and more. Though he wished to continue, to get to the end, one thing after another made the whole situation just seem hopeless. The crying continued for several minutes.

He was surprised that no one had come to offer assistance. The road on which they were travelling had been fairly quiet and was boarded by fields and a spattering of trees. There was likely no one else around. He thought of the person, or people, in the other car they had collided with. Were they stuck too? Or perhaps significantly injured and could not get free. He must escape this vehicle, and that made him think of the tomb in which he had first awoken. A shudder shot up his spine and the terror of that first hour was not a welcome thought.

The windscreen was cracked and battered, so perhaps he could kick this through.

He sat on the deceased shell of his friend to steady himself and braced his legs across the dash with his feet on the screen and his back on the seat. With his right heel still suffering from earlier in the night, he brought up his left leg to a right angle at the knee, and whilst pressing against the screen with a firm and constant pressure with his bad leg, he slammed his left heel into the glass, which dislodged it from one corner at the lower A pillar.

Hitting it several more times, the seal had split most of the way around, and he could certainly climb out. Scrambling across the dash and forcing his way through the gap between the glass and the truck's frame, his feet reached the tarmac, and he wriggled his way out until he was lying on the floor outside. There was a smell of oil on the air, and the sounds of hot metal clicking and creaking as it cooled. He drew himself to his feet and could see over the edge of the truck's bumper that the car with which they had collided, was on the other side.

He was still unaware of the extent of his injuries as he felt almost euphoric, riding a high from his system being flooded with natural chemicals to combat his condition, all he knew was that taking steps was rather difficult, sluggish, laborious. As he rounded the front of the truck, there was a small hatchback type car, still upright, but had been twisted on the road and was at 90 degrees to its original direction of movement; the front corner of it severely caved in. Its driver was slumped against the steering wheel, but the airbag had clearly deployed and hopefully she was without significant injury, though she showed no signs of movement.

As he drew closer to her vehicle, intent on opening the door and seeing if she was in fact still alive, there came the sound of an approaching engine rising above the noises of the broken vehicles. Turning around, a pair of headlights approached, and the vehicle slowed as it arrived. With the motor still running, the driver's door opened, and the silhouette of a nondescript man stepped out. The headlights of his vehicle made it impossible to make out any details of this newcomer, but somewhat out of context to the situation of finding a car wreck needing his help; verbal expletives erupted from this man's throat with violence and anger as he slammed his door shut.

The silhouette of the man approached, and he spoke again, this time controlling his choice of language, 'What the hell happened? Are you okay?' asked the man, but he was unable to respond with anything meaningful. He hadn't quite realised, but he was in shock, and unable to string together a coherent sentence. The man approached the driver of the hatch, and opening the door, reached in and checked for her pulse, whilst continuing to ask questions about what had happened.

Still unable to muster the words to offer any form of answer, he mumbled something he didn't even understand himself.

The man stood up and turned around, at which, for the first time, he was able to take a good look at the newcomer, who was now being lit by the headlights of their own vehicle.

This was the dot they had been heading towards. The same clothes, the same jacket, black with a fleece lined collar, a '3-' on the chest, but the shadow being cast by the angle didn't allow him to see which of the other numbers this was. The man grabbed hold of him by both shoulders, and shook him a little trying to get him to sober up and answer; pain shot through his right as the man's thumb pressed right into the hollow of his shoulder.

'You're bleeding.... pretty badly.... want me to take a look?' but he could still offer no words, the shock of the crash and this new arrival had caused only a blank expression, with his eyes being glazed over, staring as though off to the distance. The man lifted his shirt and saw the wound, and he grimaced with disgust written on his mouth and lower nose. 'Perhaps it's not that bad' he said, but there was no hope in his voice.

The man moved off around the truck to look into the cab. There he found another body inside. Coming around the truck himself, he watched as the man grabbed hold of the edge of the windscreen and pulled at it, moving his hands along a little at a time, breaking off what was left of the seal, until the entire screen came away and fell to the floor. 'Shit' came from the man, as he got onto his hands and knees looking at 31, crumpled in the corner. He reached inside and checked for a pulse before rising to his feet and wrapping his hand across his mouth as he stood there deep in thought.

The new numbered man bent down again and grabbed hold of 31 by the lapels of his jacket, and heaved at the corpse trying to free him from the wreck. '*He's dead*' managed 36, as he watched the man struggle.

There on his hands and knees, the man turned to look at him with inquisition, and he watched the man's face change. It had dawned on the newcomer that this injured mute was wearing shirt, pants and pumps all befitting of his own.

'Were you with him?' asked the man with urgency in his tone. He nodded.

'33?' came a befuddled question with a quiver of fear.

He shook his head.

The man turned back around to the truck's cab. He reached inside and pulled out the red Parka and threw it towards him. 'Put it on, it's cold' he said, before turning back into the truck.

He struggled to get the coat over his arm and shoulder that was now starting to ache with a pain that was reminiscent of the ligament reconstruction surgery he had had to his ankle some years earlier. It took him at least 60 seconds to get the thing on, and it provided instant relief from the cold, still warm from his body, having only been taken off only minutes before.

As he looked over to the truck again, the newcomer was backing himself out of the hole where the windscreen should be and stood upright, turning something over and over in his hands, until he found what he needed. The man turned around and was holding his standard issue jacket, '36 eh?' he spoke as he looked at him. 'Welcome to the party, I'm 32'.

He knew instantly that this was a man in his desperate final hours. Beyond all the odds, he had found his predecessor. Despite the fact that the predecessor was dead, he could obtain his cure, as the curly haired woman had with 29 back in that hallway of horrors. How much did he know? 'You'd better get in my car' said 32, 'We need to get away from here before anyone else arrives', and he proceeded to continue to drag at the body of the dead man, attempting to free it from the vehicle. He watched as 32 tried in vain to pull the mountain of a man from the wreckage and knew that he needed to help.

The biggest problem they faced was the steering wheel and larger portion of the dash around the control panel. Being the weaker of the pair following the incident he had been involved in only a short while ago, he supported the body whilst the other dragged it towards them and out of the truck. The legs of 31 got stuck and now rather than supporting the body, he was desperately trying to free the legs whilst 32 continued to pull. Eventually, the carcass came loose and moved enough that he could hook an arm around the ankles and lift the feet over the steering wheel and they were finally able to remove the giant from the truck completely. As the feet were dragged out of his view, there were the toolbox and satchel. These may still come in handy. He reached inside and grabbed them, placing them one at a time on the floor behind him, before backing out of the windscreen cavity on all fours.

Rising to his feet, he was still dazed. His orientation was off and his balance not what it ought to be. He had to place his hands on the overturned bonnet of the truck to stabilize himself from falling. He took a deep breath and held it for several seconds. There was a flavour of fuel and oil to it that tasted foul in his mouth. He wanted to vomit again for the second time in the last few hours, but this time was likely from the dizziness and the concoction of taste and smell of the air about him, polluted from the broken vehicles, leaking, bleeding out from their organs, cracked and bruised from the impact.

32 had his arms wrapped around the chest of goliath, under the arms of the dead man, and was dragging the corpse backwards, heels scraping at the floor. As the dawn was starting to arrive, there was now a wash of dim twilight creeping ever brighter, that allowed details previously hidden in darkness to slowly and steadily awaken like the blooming of petals from the first flowers of the spring. As quickly as he could, which he found was not very fast at all, he headed towards the vehicle to which the leviathan was being manoeuvred.

32 was a man of average height, average build, average appearance. There was nothing remarkable about him at all. He had a look about him that was filled with weariness and

tiredness. This man was at the end of his journey and the finish was in sight. There had clearly been trials and tribulations that were etched onto his appearance. He had suffered, but endured and now would be rewarded, if that's what you could call getting to live the rest of your life carrying the horrors of your 24 hours of torment.

Shifting the dead weight was cumbersome for him, unsurprisingly so, the lifeless man was massive. The body being dragged looked battered. The remains of the giant looked as though he had been 12 rounds with a heavyweight champion without offering any defence, face caved in from impact against the steering wheel and dash. Trails of blood streaked down from open wounds across his nose, cheek and forehead.

'You'd better just get in' 32 said as he struggled to open the rear door, not really watching him attempt to walk, but clearly aware that it was not an easy task for him. As he rounded the car, he was transfixed on the non-descript newcomer who was trying to bundle the mangled monster on to the rear seats. Putting the satchel and toolbox into the opposing side of the rear seats from the dead man, he took out the roll of insulation tape that had been used to mask the registration number of the stolen truck and found a craft knife with a retractable blade. He dropped on to the front passenger seat with a lack of grace, placing his new items on his lap, he fought with his legs to get them up and into the foot well, using his hands to aid them.

Whilst 32 struggled with the giant's legs and finally shut the door, he lifted his shirt to inspect the wound again, before cutting several lengths of tape and crudely covering the hole. As the car started to reverse, he realised that 32 had got into the driver's seat, which he had clearly failed to notice, being still in shock and focused on his wound. They left the scene, and his new companion was grateful that no one had arrived before they were able to get away. The police would find a driverless stolen vehicle, and assume that the thieves had fled from the place once they had totalled the truck.

'*Was she still alive?*' he asked with concern for the driver who had been an innocent victim of his friend's misfortune and was pleased to know that she had a pulse, even if it was weak. She would likely have some significant injuries, but 32 was satisfied that she would not suffer from any lasting damage. She had seemingly remained unconscious throughout the ordeal in removing the body of the giant from the truck.

He checked his band for the time, as he had no idea how long this episode had taken of his remaining hours. He could have been unconscious himself for any length of time. 07:55. The end of another hour was approaching, but he hadn't lost too much time in the wreck. What had happened to 31? He played it over in his mind. One minute everything was fine, they were merrily plodding on their way towards another player, in the hopes of finding something more to further advance their goals of solving this madness. 31 had seemed to be free from poison, but at the next moment, he had slumped and seemed to have been dead. Whatever had happened, it was as though the man had just died, sitting there, driving. Like a switch had been flipped and out went the lights.

Was it the poison after all? Perhaps this venom, whatever it was, had taken its time to work into the system from when the countdown had expired. Slowly being absorbed and working its way to the brain where it would cause catastrophic chaos and in the absence of the cure, death would arrive.

The interaction with the woman in police holding had given him enough to help the man who was now his chauffer. Perhaps he knew enough already, he was certainly wise enough to have taken the body of the man-mountain; surely he knew that the potion he needed was hidden inside the cadaver of his predecessor. This man had but two hours to live but would need only a place to operate to gain access to the vial that would release him from captivity and certain cessation of life.

He thought of how odd it would be in any other scenario. The grotesque and gruesome task at hand was to help this newcomer dissect the man-tank that had been his companion in recent hours. It was a strange thing to consider how this didn't repulse him. Not only was this the desecration of a corpse, but the mountain had been his friend. They had laughed together less than an hour ago, and now he was to aid and abet the butchering of the body. Had he grown emotionally cold in less than half a day? Who could blame him he thought?

His whole being ached as his thoughts drifted back to himself. His shoulder was in agony, and the hole in his chest was growing to be an ever more intense pain. He leaned his head back against the headrest and closed his eyes.

08:00

He was unsure of what exactly had woken him, but he sensed that more time had passed than he would have preferred. The car was at standstill, and he saw that the new companion was missing from the driver's seat, though the engine continued to hum. The clock on the dash said it was nearly quarter past the hour. Outside the day was almost at full light; within a few minutes the sun would be cresting the horizon.

There was woodland around him with old stone buildings off to one side. This place was dead to the world, somewhere quiet and away from the watchful eyes of onlookers. He knew their purpose at this place was to interrogate the dead man's innards for the vial that would save 32. The realisation that the newcomer was gone, caused a horrible sinking feeling within the pit of his stomach, a well of despair. Had he missed it? Was the ogre gone too? Had the gruesome act of butchery already taken place? Would he still learn anything from this?

He turned in his chair to see if the corpse was still on the back seat, but the aches and pains shot through him as he tried. He was somewhat relieved to see the body remained slumped on the rear seats.

A door opened on the building and there was darkness within; at least, it was lighter outside than in, as though there was no artificial lighting. 32 stepped out into the daylight and strode towards the car, his coat was undone and waved in the breeze as the unexceptional man approached. Bending at the waist, he took hold of the handle and pulled open the driver's door; and leaning in, he spoke 'Welcome back to the land of the living. I feared you wouldn't wake in time. If you're feeling up to it, I could do with your help'.

The well of despair instantly returned. He thought for a moment before responding. Not an hour earlier, his companion had been balling with laughter, and now he was considering rummaging through the man's intestines to aide this new arrival.

'*I may need a minute to find myself, but I need to see this for myself, if nothing else*'.

Pulling open the passenger door, there was pain through every fibre of his being that had moved in that motion; arm, shoulder, chest, neck. He felt as though rigor mortis was setting in, although he was far from dead; yet. He almost wished it upon himself, as his body had been all but destroyed in the impact.

How ridiculous he thought, and he was thankful to still be alive, for now.

Every part of his entity felt worse as he tried to get his legs out of the vehicle; it was a chore to move a fraction, yet he was required to stand, to walk, maybe to lift and assist with the movement of the monster in the back seat. If there were to be anyone watching them, they would undoubtedly expect some foul play between they and the corpse in their care.

Standing was arduous, painstaking, a lengthy process. He would be of little help with any manual labour. Hopefully, 32 was up to the task of moving his predecessor without aide. The man must surely be feeling a euphoric rush of excitement and adrenaline at the thought of obtaining the thing that would save him from the grip of the reaper, whose sickle was being drawn, ready to swipe and take his life.

The newfound friend was propping open the darkened doorway with a rock and moved with purpose back towards him, where he stopped and regarded him with a befuddled look. 'Are you going to be okay?' he asked. Was this a trick question? It seemed to be loaded at least. How could he be okay after what he had been through in the last hour? He had been smashed about with the force of a head on collision that had tipped the truck onto its side. He had come to, crumpled upon the dead body of his companion, and been forced to escape from a second entombing in the space of a few hours. He was battered and broken. It was still possible he had actually broken bones. The pain in his chest was now stinging and sharp where there was a hole, punctured by a pen. How could he possibly be okay?

More than the physical ailments, in view of the events of this night, how would he ever be 'okay' for the rest of his life? The mental anguish and scars would plague his existence until his mind was lost to old age; if he were to ever get out of this nightmare. But the question 32 had given seemed to infer at something else. Are you going to be okay? Going to be? It was as if his question lacked a certain ending; ....on your own?

He knew in an instant that 32 did not plan on sticking around. Once they had obtained what they needed, they would need to go on the run, to escape and evade 33, who would be hunting him down like a wild cat chasing its prey; when once more, he would be alone and left to pursue his own predecessor, 35, struggling with the notion of possibly having to take a life in order to save his own.

It seemed an answer wasn't needed, as 32 had continued in his task of retrieving the body from the rear passenger seat, with his arms under those of the dead man, grasped around the chest, and was heaving the weight trying to free it from the car. He watched as the ogre fell, limp and lifeless, his feet flopping to the ground. The massive man looked awful, as though he had been beaten to death with a two-by-four. His face was ruined by heavy impacts with gashes and grazes in multiple locations, the beard seemed to be heavily stained from the blood being leaked out into it, now starting to coagulate and thicken in clumps. His legs and arms all appeared to be broken, the left forearm in several places, as it waved about too freely than the natural form would otherwise dictate.

The sight was almost comical, observing the one of modest stature attempting to manoeuvre the mountain sized mammoth. But persistent was 32, if slow and backbreaking it was to drag the monster towards the doorway, they managed a few feet at a time, before readjusting grip and composure, and continuing on again. Eventually he had to move with them, to head inside, but his body was so stiff and wrought with pain that he wanted to just collapse. Any normal stride was simply not a possibility; his feet could merely shuffle, one at a time, moving slowly on.

The journey towards that door seemed longer than the walk to the city following his awakening. He remembered the look on the woman's face that had nearly ran a red light and could have ploughed right through him. He felt as though she had. The last ten hours had been lengthy yet seemed to fly. The toils and trials he had already faced, were more than a lifetime's worth; yet he was not even at the halfway point. In his current condition, he would surely look like a half decaying zombie to anyone else, shuffling slowly towards the door, contorted in pain at the chest and abdomen.

The other had managed to take the body through the doorway, and it seemed like darkness washed over them as they passed inside. The murky daylight that was still slowly gaining in luminescence through the thick cloud overhead, had no reach within. He watched as the flailing legs and feet of the ogre were pulled into the blackness, like descending to the depths of the ocean, dragged slowly out of sight. Following behind, he was unable to keep anywhere near the pace of his new companion even with being weighed down by the load of the dead that they bore.

His eyes were fixed in the abyss of the blackness through the doorway. Beyond the very distant noises of traffic, and the sound of the birds and woodland creatures, singing and scurrying about in the thicket; there emanated a sound from within the darkness, clicking, scraping, scratching. Light flooded through from another doorway within, and he was able to observe the two figures again, one pulling the other. Readjusting their grip on the lifeless weight they towed, 32 pulling it through yet another aperture, until once more, blackness descended as the inner door had closed.

It took more than a couple of minutes to reach the doorway. If he could only progress at this pace, he knew that it would not be worth his efforts to continue his pursuit of 35 and the others involved in this deranged game. His progress was too slow for him to make any meaningful advance towards the prospects of completing his task and obtaining his potion. He needed to rest. It may be that resting would waste some of his time, but it may be better to lose half an hour, an hour, or even two; than to continue at a snail's pace and never make it to the finish line.

Stepping into the doorway, he could see that this was some kind of cloak room, a place for muddy boots, wellies and waterproofs. The room was not much more than ten feet wide by twenty feet long. Along one side were racks for shoes, and hangers for coats. A dog's bed lay in the far corner, but the animal was absent. Aside from the door through which he had entered, there was only the other door through which he had watched the two forms fade. No windows, nothing to give any natural light.

Taking hold of the handle of the inner door, it turned with ease, but it required more strength than he felt he could muster, to be able to make the thing budge. It was heavy, solid, and the hinges were mechanical self-closing types that fought against him as he pushed hard. Light sprung forth through the gap around the seams as the door began to move. As it opened enough for him to pass through, he was confronted by a large expanse, it was a picture of beauty.

A huge open plan living space, at least 700 square feet, and glass walled along two edges that gave a picturesque view over a lake to more woodland. A dining table, leather sofas, a kitchen area with a huge island; but here the view was spoiled as the giant had been pulled up and onto the surface, and was lain there, prostrate, exposed up the middle as his clothes had been torn and peeled back.

'Pull up a pew' called out the other, with a half-smile pursed at the lips. 'It's time for me to get my hands dirty. Do you know what it is I'm looking for?'

His information had come second hand. It was only Chinese whispers, although he placed a degree of reliability to what the curly haired woman had told him, and he explained the glass vial, with one end that would snap off, the contents no more than a couple of millilitres.

Armed with a Stanley knife, a selection of kitchen knives and several polythene bags, 32 dropped his jacket to the floor, and extending the blade of the craft knife from the handle, he placed it to the chest of the corpse, and sank it into the skin.

Shock and horror slapped them both as the body let out a groan and a long breath of air and he watched, wide eyed, as 32 recoiled in terror. Was his friend not dead after all? Surely he would have made some protest before now at his being manhandled as so he had been? But there he lay, cold, unmoving, and absent of any further outburst. After expressing their 'freaked out' disconcert to each other, they chalked it up to post-mortem noises of the lifeless corpse, nothing more than trapped air escaping, passing over tightened vocal cords.

32 resumed his position, knife in hand, and with a shiver passing through his shoulders, neck and arms, proceeded to make a large incision from the bottom of the sternum to the pubic bone.

Observing the man go about his makeshift surgery, he was surprised that there was not much blood and figured that his friend had been dead now for more than an hour and was likely beginning to solidify.

The man cut open the belly of their predecessor from one side to the other, and peeled back the flaps of skin, fat and muscle like the leaves of a lily, and reaching inside, began to pull apart the innards of the ogre, squeezing, and feeling for anything solid, but trying to be careful as to not cause it to break, and spill out its contents before he could consume it. It was fascinating, yet disturbing to watch, and he knew that he may have to go through this same procedure in only ten hours or so time, if he were to locate 35 and obtain what he needed.

If the cycles were indeed in three-hour increments, his predecessor would be dead by 7pm. That gave him three hours to locate his antidote, if he had by that time located 35. He would need somewhere to work, somewhere like this place. He looked around him again, taking stock of the finer details.

This was a place of wealth and affluence; the home of someone not short of money. A cabinet along one wall contained a multitude of fine whiskey and cognac; there were two paintings, which although he knew not their provenance or artist by sight alone, it was evident that they were of significant value; the furniture here looked pristine, and of significant cost.

'What is this place?' He asked of the surgeon.

'It's my place' he responded. 'I like to escape from the city, so I commute to work from here. It's pretty quiet and secluded. One of those places that no one seems to know about but is only half an hour from civilisation'.

The man told him whilst he worked on the wounded warrior, of his life as a stockbroker, and how he had come to great wealth from one investment portfolio that had grown at an exponential rate and given him the life of luxury since his early 20's. From the return he had achieved, he had gained traction with layering his money in different markets, and was now predominantly involved in overseas developments, putting his wealth to good use, building block housing in areas that had been shanty-towns in third world and war torn countries, teaching labouring skills to and employing the local peo'ple in the construction.

It was nice to meet someone whose key priority was not themselves. Though this man had wealth, he did not have greed, and greed was the social disease that was rotting the heart out of society in the modern world. It seemed that those with money only wanted to make more, and at the expense of those who had none. Avarice was the cancer of the common man. But this man was not common. A model citizen, a rare breed of giver, not taker. His plans were to build communities, towns and civilisation; to help the deprived areas out of their poverty. The people of these under-developed places knew nothing of greed, for they had nothing to begin with. When he was a child, he had seen advertisements for charities and something had stuck in his mind – give a man a fish, feed him for a day; teach him how to fish.... how to build.... how to teach.

Teaching people life skills in design, construction, electrics, water systems and the like, had seen such change to these areas. He wondered why he had never heard of this man and his charitable efforts; the guy was not just a genius, he was a saint. His investments continued to grow in capitol but though he lived a more than moderate lifestyle, he knew he would never be able to spend as much as was already in his bank unless he had put it to good use. Why sit on a gold mine if you can't build a legacy?

The intrigue of this man's character seemed interrupted by the thoughts of their oppressor. Who was it that would take such a man as this, a pillar of society; and subject them to the toil and torment of this wicked game? The players seemed to come from all walks of life, no holds barred on who had been selected. They were more than picked at random, of that he was sure, for the clothing they wore, the jackets at least, with embroidered numbers on the breast depicting their position in this twisted fate, were the perfect fit for the shape and size of each one of them.

His mind clouded over with a depression that he seemed unable to shake, dark, gloomy, squashing his soul like a vice. Whatever was happening to them all, seemed to be nothing more than a perverted obsession of a sick weirdo, who simply wished to enjoy putting others in this state of shock, horror, confusion and chaos. What was the end game? Was there an end game? Whoever their oppressor was, they could vanish like the flame of a candle, destroying, consuming, then gone, leaving only the tell-tale signs of having burned. The remaining trail of smoke that would soon dissipate as civilisation continued, paying little regard to 'that event', as had been the case with so many horrors gone by, would be a final remnant to anyone not directly involved.

The man continued to fumble with the innards of the deceased, drained of life and lying as though on a butcher's block, being separated into pieces, stripped of his giblets like a turkey being prepared for a feast. He thought it odd that there was no smell. It was a gruesome sight, but he felt no emotion towards what he was witnessing; only an inquisitive mind, that he would be prepared for when it was his time to do the necessary and retrieve his vial from 35. He wondered who his predecessor might be, what kind of life they had before this nightmare, and whether they were likely to find their end to this madness and escape the clutches of the poison. Would he result to violence; could he bring himself to take charge of 35, to maybe even take their life; or would he have nothing more than desecration of a corpse to tend to, if they slipped from life by some other means.

Goliath had lived passed the end of his 24 hours, but it then seemed as though they were taken in an instant, driving along, then gone. Nothing more than an empty shell still sat behind the wheel of a moving vehicle. That crash had ruined any possibility to know for sure, but it looked as though the giant was dead before the impact. There was no scream in pain, nothing that would indicate that there was anything wrong with the man. They had considered it all a hoax, mind play simply to get them to cause the chaos and carnage of killing others. But then the life was sucked from the behemoth. He wondered again whether the poison had taken hold, perhaps having slowly worked its way into the system and capturing the ogre's mind, stopping all functions as the chemicals seeped into the grey matter.

Would the same fate capture him too? There was no knowing as to whether he would catch up with 35. The odds were weighted against him.

Would he ever see her again? Once more he was engulfed by the love that he felt for her, and the fear of missing out on the rest of his life, growing old together. They had talked of their future beyond the wedding, they had even made a five-year-plan; but everything would change now. What would life be like if he were even able to escape the venom within him, but living with all he had witnessed, all he had experienced, all that he may yet be forced to do? Could he ever tell her of the depravity of the depths to which he had stooped?

His body would heal, his mind was more fragile. If he were forced to kill 35 to save himself, would that even be a life worth living? Was their existence any less important than his own? Why should he rob another of the chances of escape, if he were only to be imprisoned by the mental scars of taking a life?

Playing it over and over in his mind, exploring every avenue and possible outcome as he watched the other set about his work; he resolved to an outcome that he considered to be decent of him.

If he can find 35 before their time is up; and if they have found their cure; he would leave them to live out their life, and he would surrender to the serum within him, and pass as peacefully as his friend had before the impact. But if by the time he found 35 they had no chance of escape, he would try to do as 32, and cut up a cadaver to get what he needed.

As a final thought on the matter, if necessary, if on the off chance there was any need for him to, he would kill; but only if 35 had lost all hope of securing their antidote.

32 seemed to suddenly become animated, and he realised that he had sat in silence, consumed by his own thoughts, like a statue for the last 15 minutes. The other had found something that excited him as he was feeling around the contents of a sack covered in blood. He'd found something solid, cylindrical, and reached for a blade to free it from the organ. As he sliced through the tissue there was an eruption of faecal matter discharging itself through the opening, oozing out, having been forced around like toothpaste in a tube whilst the man had fondled the intestines in his search.

And there it was. About two inches in length, and the circumference of a pencil; the exterior covered in the elements from the contents of a digestive system which now had indeed raised a pungent smell. With joy on his face, 32 spun around and strode across to the sink, where he washed off the vial. Sat there observing, he couldn't help but feel excitement and elation for the man, who with his persistence over the last twenty two and some hours, had been able to get his hands on the thing that would save his life. He hoped that he would find the same end.

The man turned and held the thing up to the light spilling in from the glass walls, inspecting the content; a clear and colourless liquid. Of course, neither of them had any idea as to what the contents were, it could have been anything, water even. There was a remote possibility that whatever this was, in view of the twisted mind of their tormentor, could have even been a poison that would bring about their end. But the story given by the curly haired woman had supported the other accounts of this being the cure they each needed.

The man snapped off the top and smelled the opening, before pursing his lips and placing the opening to them. He tipped back his head, raising the vial and spilling the liquid into his mouth, where he let it run a pathway down his throat until he needed to swallow only by natural reaction. Having consumed the contents, he placed the thing down on the worktop and exclaimed 'It's not over yet'

'You have a little over four hours left you mean?'

'Four hours to evade death. Four hours to escape from capture. Four hours to prevent being butchered like him' as he pointed with a head motion to the body cut open on the kitchen island. I'm going to get showered and changed, then I'm leaving and will be going far from here. Forgive me for not telling you, but I cannot take any chances now that I have actually drank that vial. There is a very real possibility that I may yet get to live'.

The man headed towards the far window wall, beyond which the lake, woodlands and scenery, looked more beautiful than it previously had. There was something about the man's way out from this madness, that had rubbed off subconsciously and had given him hope. He was observing this picture with renewed eyes; eyes that were now focusing on a positive outcome, rather than the negatives that were berating him. The other had disappeared, having slipped out through what had looked to be part of the internal wall, clearly a concealed door.

He stood from his stool, an arduous task. Pain continued to wreath through his body, and he felt stiff all over. He felt as though he had been shot in the chest and would need to take care of this wound quickly or it was likely that infection would set in.

Staring out of the glass wall, he was lost in thought, churning over the next steps and how he would manage to move about with any freedom in view of the state of his body since the wreck. He hoped that the escapee would at least give him passage back towards the city before they made their flee to safety. But walking around as he had in the first few hours, would be a far greater task now than it had been with only a limp. He should wait for the man to comeback from changing and ask for his help in at least getting to the city. Waiting, he slowly lowered himself on to an ergonomic chaise that was positioned by the window, and laid himself out, trying to relax.

09:00

_____

A great disturbance of noise came like a cacophony, waking him. Confused in the half sleep he couldn't figure out what it was; a constant thud, thud, thud, that was hollow and fast moving. The low tone and pitch seemed to rise as the speed of the sound grew. He bolted upright, and immediately regretted having moved so fast with the pain shooting through him. The sound changed in pitch again and he noticed along the top of the window line, there was a disturbance of air, almost like a heat haze from the engine of a car in the peak of the summer, distorting the image beyond it. The nose of a helicopter, followed by its body, came into view and moved forwards from the roof line and headed off across the lake; like a dragonfly over the water, it disappeared to the distance.

He was sure that the thing had taken off from the roof and knew in an instant that 32 was making his break for safety. He was now alone again, miles from any others and still prisoner to the poison that would kill him in half a day. He checked his band and was amazed to see that he had lost at least half an hour to sleep. There were no signs of others anywhere near him on the map of his wristband. All of the other players, except from 32, were around the city and suburbs. He had no idea which of them was 35, the one who holds the key to his own escape.

He realised for the first time that in searching for 35, there was a very real possibility that any of the dots towards which he would be heading, could possibly be his pursuer, 37, who by now could no doubt have learnt what they needed to do to free themselves of the chains of this oppression. He felt sick to the pit of his stomach. It was no longer about simply finding a cure, but also avoiding capture. 37, whoever they were, could set on him in an instant if they realised who he was. The red Parka would still come in handy, not only for allowing him a degree of anonymity as he would approach any other blue dot in the cold light of day, but also from the authorities, who knew the black outfit of the perpetrators of the odd happenings of the last weeks.

That thought echoed around for a moment, and the maths were playing through like mechanical cogs turning, processing, all slotted into place to produce a final result. The cop at the shop had said weeks. 24 hours divided by three hour windows, meant 8 new players per day. Two weeks multiplied by eight players would mean that if it really had been so long, there were likely at least 100 players that had already taken part in this. He wondered then why he was 36, and why those with whom he was interacting, were those numbers around his own, that would seem to sequentially fit with the timing of their escape from the morgue; or was it their release?

Surely there could not have been 100+ people involved in this already? The tormentor, the puppeteer, whomever they were, was evidently a clever and well planned, meticulously operated individual that whatever their reason for subjecting hundreds of people to this perverse reality; was able to organise the capture, release and communication to each of the victims of this torture. The mere fact that there were eight people per day to kidnap was no mean feat. The organising of transport, and storage of the players, the administering of drugs, both to keep them unconscious until their given time for release, and to instil the poison within them; along with the vial that would be the cure for the one they preceded; would be time consuming and a logistical nightmare. Was it really possible that this was all the doing of just one person? Had it really been weeks? Surely this could not have been ongoing for 14 days straight. He would have seen or heard something about it by now, especially with the speed at which news breaks in the modern world.

The woman from the cafe, now in police care, would surely be giving her story to their interrogators now that 31's time had come and gone. She knew that there was no hope for him, as she was 'safe' within their custody, and it would be impossible for the ogre to rip her apart and secure his cure from within her. If she would be giving the true account, then the police would at least have some understanding of the reasons for the strange happenings of the last number of weeks. It was quite odd, he thought, that they had not been able to capture one of these numbered men and women before now, but each of them must, like he, be cunning in their going about in search of the others. The woman had only been apprehended as it was her plan; she had intended to in order that she would be safe from the hands of 31.

The police had caught none of them despite how long this seemed to have been going on. Surely this was not right? The officer from the print shop had said as much, but for 'weeks', and with the amount of people involved in that time, it would be a little unrealistic to think it had been so long.

He needed to move; his time was wasting away. It took him much longer than he would have liked to get up and get sturdy on his feet, but as he did, he could see the body was still there, laid on the countertop. He walked over towards the giant and a feeling of sorrow washed over him for the dead man. His friend of but a few hours had been incapable of escaping, yet being unaware of what he was required to do, he had remained hopeful in the face of adversity. It was literally only in his final minutes that the goliath knew it was certain that they could not escape death.

As he approached the kitchen area, he saw that on the corner of the island, by the head of the body, was a note and several items. A bottle of pills, two loose tablets, a key for the car, some fabric strip plaster and a roll of duct tape. He read the note;

"You will excuse my having to leave. I didn't want to disturb you though I hope that you do not sleep for too long. I had to take my leave before I was being hunted by another. I am sorry for the mess of your friend, but I will have to deal with this tomorrow once I know that I am safe. Help yourself to whatever may be of use to you. There is food in the fridge. Get yourself something to eat, you will need the energy."

He looked around for a refrigerator but couldn't see one. He assumed it must be concealed within the kitchen units. The note went on;

"The white pills will help with this. Take one now and one in six hours time. The bottle is prescription meds. They will help relax your muscles of the tension since the crash and act as a pain blocker. They are very powerful, and if you plan to take them for a few days, I recommend you take one every four hours, rather than two every six hours as the bottle says."

He picked up the bottle and read the label. He had never heard of this medication before, and it was certainly not something you could obtain with ease. He continued with the note;

"I'm afraid that my medical supplies do not extend to wound dressing anything more than basic strip plaster and there is very little of that. I would suggest you cover that wound on your chest and then cover over that with duct tape. The car is yours, use it as you see fit. It is my gift to you and there is no need to give thought to returning it, or anything else that may happen to it. Do whatever you can and have to. Good luck"

As he thought about food, he realised how hungry he was. He moved around the kitchen checking all of the units in search of the refrigerator. Inside, he found that it was about half stocked with various food stuffs, cold meats, cheese, raw chicken and the like. It was too time consuming to cook. Perhaps a sandwich would be well suited. There were several bottles of water, and he pulled one out, took one of the white pills and washed it down, then popped open the bottle of painkillers and took one of them too.

Searching around the kitchen further, he was able to find bread rolls, and working on the side countertops away from the body, he set about making a selection of ham and cheese sandwiches that he could keep some in his bag for later, then began to eat. Observing the ogre, cut open on the island, he considered the grotesqueness of the situation, the man's innards spilled out, drying blood pooling in the cavity of his abdomen, as he stood emotionless, eating a cheese and ham roll as if it were an everyday occurrence, numb to the obscenity of the gore.

Beginning already to feel a little revitalised, he searched the kitchen for other portable foods and found a number of snack bars and biscuits, putting some into the satchel and eating two of them. He could see nowhere to put the rubbish, so left it all on the top next to the body which needed disposing of at some point. The note gave little indication of future intentions, but he trusted that the man, with all his wealth and seemingly moral code, would do the right thing by the giant, search out his family and give the man a proper burial.

He needed to tend to his wound, so stripped off his coat and t-shirt that was now soaked in blood around the area of the puncture hole and had leaked out onto the jacket also. Slipping off the jacket came with little difficulty, but the shirt was a problematic task between the decrease in his flexibility since the impact, and the pain he suffered at the ribs, particularly around the puncture. He wondered if his ribs had also been cracked, though he had no difficulty in breathing.

He padded slowly across the room to the place where 32 had slipped through part of the wall that was a concealed doorway. On closer inspection, he could see the lines in the woodwork that spoke of the perimeter of the door and pressing against this, found nothing more than a little mechanical resistance keeping the thing in the closed position. There was a hallway on the other side, which had a grand and fantastic appearance. The ceiling was part of the roof, constructed of opaque glass that flooded the hallway with natural daylight. The flooring seemed to be slabs of quartz stone, glistening with a mirror fleck amongst the white finish, perfectly bespoke so that the joints of each slab followed the curvature of the hallway that meandered softly from one end to the other, boarded by curved walls with strip wood finish, and evidently a number of other concealed type doors leading from this to other rooms.

As he pushed against the first, he saw a large bedroom inside, almost as grand as the hallway, but a room with a view. The outer wall was also curved, this room was almost round; but the wall was glass, like the large living space, and looked out across the lake from a different angle. Then, only a bed, huge though it was, but nothing else to fill what was otherwise a void of a large size. The disused administered clothing of 32 lay on the floor, cast off as he had gone to shower and change. He had given no care to clearing up, wanting to leave as quickly as he could. On the bed was a sight that caused a smile to split at the corners of his mouth. The now defunct wristband of 32, like discarded handcuffs from an escaped prisoner, released from the chains that had bound them. He would still need it had it not been for the helicopter escape.

There was another outline of a door, this time being made with light, glowing around the edges of another would-be entrance. Behind this was a bathroom, again it was huge, bigger than the bedroom of his own home, yet this room had much lesser of a purpose. There was a glow being emitted by the entire ceiling that looked like one huge light, bright, white, clinical; which was amplified by the white tiled floor and walls. The shower was enormous, a walk-in type unit, that required no glass screen as the floor was a wet-room kind, off to one corner where the wall tiles were segments of interlocking grey slate with a copper tinge.

This room also had a view through a large glass wall, looking peacefully over the lake. To take a bath in this setting must be blissful. There was a basin in the middle of an internal wall, white porcelain, round in shape, that looked like a giant egg cup, stood on a glass table that was one curved piece from floor to tabletop and back to the floor. He made way towards it, and was stunned to see himself in the mirror. His face was swollen and bruised along the right cheek, and his left eye looked as though he had taken a blow from a boxing champion. His jaw line was cultivating a few days worth of growth that had not been there the last morning he could remember, when he had shaved before going out for breakfast.

He thought of her again as he washed himself off in the sink, first cleaning the dirt and grime from his hands, then face, before gently dabbing a wet towel at the area around the wound on his chest. He could think of nothing but her as he stood there, a shadow of his former self, physically beaten, mentally near broken, knowing not what he may yet still have to face. After a few minutes, he was satisfied that the wound was clean, not from debris and germ, but that it was neat and would hopefully cause no problems in its healing. He needed to find something else to wear.

Heading back to the bedroom, he looked around for any signs of other doorways, as surely the man of money would have an extensive wardrobe. A faint outline of a darker tone told of another concealed door, but this time when he pressed against it, the door moved only a few millimetres, before being totally stuck. As he released the pressure from it, the door popped open in an outwards motion, springing out towards him, the first few inches with some pace, before slowing.

As he pulled open the door, he was not surprised to view the contents, meticulously aligned in banks according to type of clothing. A section for suits; a section for jackets and blazers; one for dress shirts and another for casual shirts; space for jeans and casual pants, a whole bank of polo-shirts and t-shirts. The man had more shoes than he had seen in any woman's collection.

There was a dressing section with a mirror behind, above which a light was casting and was toned in such a way as it made him look a million dollars, despite the beating his face showed. The top of the dresser was boarded by an array of colognes and aftershave, and through the glass top he could a see a drawer specially made, and filled with all kinds of ridiculously priced wristwatches that would be more than a year's salary for him to afford.

All he needed was something simple, and he chose a plain polo, dark blue in colour, that would hopefully hide the seeping of his wound if he was unable to prevent the bleeding from continuing. He took if from the hanger, which he replaced in the row, and carrying the shirt in one hand, whilst holding the damp towel against his chest with the other, he headed back towards the kitchen area where the carcass of his friend remained open on the worktop.

As he moved slowly through the house, he could feel that he had a little more inertia about him, he was able to move more freely and with less pain. The pills were starting to take effect, and he remembered how the ogre had obtained some ibuprofen for him in the fast-food place only a few short hours ago. Back then he had wondered who this man was, and whether he intended him any harm. Back then he knew nothing of what was happening to him. He had learned what he knew from the goliath and it seemed odd that he thought of this man as his friend, a man he had known for so little time, yet had shared so much with.

As he approached the body, he had a renewed mindset, knowing that this corpse was a real possibility for him to be in 12 hours time, if he were unable to find his predecessor and obtain what he needed to survive the poison. He must continue on with his search, to find 35 and bring an end to his woes, if that is, they were not already in possession of their cure and making way to safety before he could reach them.

He was not a murderer and would never bring himself to harm whoever his predecessor may be if they had any real possibility of escape from all this. There may yet come a time where he would have to 'man up' and face death to allow another, or potentially others, to live.

It dawned on him that if he allowed 35 the freedom from his grip, that his ultimate end would also benefit 37 who would be in search of him, hoping to collect what then needed from within the belly of the beast.

The pursuit of others would be difficult for him, but at least he had a mode of transport as the helicopter pilot had gifted him the means to get back to the city, and to move about with ease. At least this time he would not be cruising around in a stolen vehicle, fearing that any sight of authorities would be problematic. He should have no problems in finding a place to park, as they had with the truck they had taken from the old man's driveway. This would not only save valuable time; but would limit the amount he had to bear weight on his legs and allow his body more of an opportunity to recover.

He packed his satchel with his stash of bottles, biscuits and sandwiches, and rinsed off the Stanley knife and set it down on the side whilst he searched for something to dry it with. He longed for a stiff drink and the whiskey cabinet looked like an attractive offering, though if he were to be driving around, it would not be wise. Given his physical state and the concoction of drugs in his system, he should not mix that with a healthy dose of 40% Scotch.

He had not noticed earlier, but one of the machines on the bank of appliances was quality gourmet coffee maker, from bean to cup in a variety of different styles to suit the taste of the individual. Coffee would be perfect for him now, and he found a mug in one of the cupboards, set it into the machine, and pressed for a deep black coffee. The aroma of the brew was intoxicating and he waited with anxiousness as the machine slowly filled the cup. The contents were hot but drinkable and he chugged it down with disregard for the taste as he was too excited to just drink it. He knew it tasted good, but he was never a connoisseur of coffee and could not give an account of the flavours beyond it being of significant quality.

He replaced the mug in the machine and pressed for another, then set about looking for a thermal flask to 'take one for the road' and was pleased to find one in a corner unit among small kitchen appliances. He poured the fresh mug into the flask and filled it again from the machine. Waiting for the brew to complete, he was lost in his thoughts and starred with blank expression, losing focus on what he was doing. The machine had finished its cycle a good minute or so before he had realised. His mind was so lost. He found it difficult to remain focused on such a mundane task, so over consumed with the planning of the events ahead.

It was the cold at his bare top half that brought him back around. The shocking sensation of being semi-naked, had reminded him of the morgue, where he had felt vulnerable before dressing. He collected the mug and held it over the flask, tipping the contents from one to the other. This would be a welcome treat later in the day of madness he was yet to face. He placed the thing into his satchel.

Rinsing the towel, he cleaned up the wound again, but was glad that it was weeping only a little. The blood was congealing and was mixed with a clear liquid as the body was trying to clot and form a scab. Drying the area with a hand towel, he used the Stanley knife to cut a strip of plaster from the box, and peeling back the cover, placed the mesh padding over the hole and pressed the sticky parts to his skin. As he collected the roll of duct tape from the counter, he thought of the employee from the print shop, who by now must have been found by his colleagues, strapped unassumingly to a chair in the stockroom, having been accosted by a powerhouse of a man with a foreign accent and thick beard.

The sound the tape made as he ripped back the top was another reminder of the crimes he had committed in the last 12 hours. Breaking and entering, burglary, theft of a vehicle, false imprisonment, kidnapping even, identity fraud, failing to report, fleeing the scene of an accident, the list went on. The next 12 hours were likely to be as bad, though he doubted this could get any worse, despite knowing that he may need to mutilate a dead body, the same as he had witnessed here at this countertop.

He pulled off a strip about six inches long, having bitten one edge and torn the tape from the role. Gently, delicately, having regard for the wound beneath, he covered over the plaster, and pressed the tape down, securing the hole with some pressure to help stop the bleeding. Satisfied that he had made a reasonable job of it, he put both the tape and the plaster strip into his bag, and collected the shirt from the side. Pulling this over was painful, and his movement whilst limited from his ailments, was also hindered somewhat by the strip of tape, as he was cautious to not stretch it so that it started to peel away.

The shirt was an okay fit, a little on the large side, but nothing outside of how most off the peg clothing would be around the waistline of a man with broad shoulders. The red jacket needed wiping down on the inner edge of the chest by the wind flap. The blood had set in and stained it, but it was nothing serious and would be much less visible when the coat was being worn. His 'standard issue' jacket, sporting his numbered pawn piece in this game of doom and gloom, had been left in the vehicle parked outside. He had no idea if this would be of use to him yet, but at least he still had it.

Putting the coat on, he collected the bag and keys, bid goodbye to his friend on the counter, and left through the doorway to the cloakroom and out to the fresh air of the forest. The car remained as it had been when he left it not much more than an hour earlier, with the doors open, lights on. He wondered if the battery would be drained, in which case he was screwed. He headed to the car with still more vigour as his body absorbed the chemicals of the medicines, digested the foods and soaked in the caffeine.

Arriving at the car, he approached the passenger door and threw his bag down on to the passenger seat, closing the door through which he had earlier got in and out of this vehicle. Pushing the rear door closed, a passing thought for the ogre came and went, and he walked around to the driver's door and slowly lowered himself to the seat, gripping hold of the steering wheel and the A pillar for stability. With hope, he closed his eyes as he pressed the 'start / stop' button, willing for the thing to start but nothing happened.

Shit!

The dash told him that he needed to put a foot on the brake pedal to start the engine, and he tried again with the correct procedure. It fired into life and set him at ease. He could now begin his travels with speed and comfort as he searched for his cure. Raising his arm to check his band, he gave a flick of the wrist.

09:59.

He was halfway through.

10:00

―――

He slid up the screen in the familiar way and immediately went to the map and began searching for any signs of the others. It took him a good few minutes to locate the first, but then trying to find a means by which he could head towards them, he lost their position again and spent a further few minutes looking. Coming across another dot, in another location, he at least could see the direction he needed to travel. Manoeuvring about would be a problem as he had no sense of bearing, and if the roads were to twist and turn, he would soon get disorientated.

He had always been generally good with such things, his sense of direction impeccable. He always seemed to be able to navigate without issue, unlike her, who could get lost on a high street, not knowing whether to turn left or right as she walked out of a shop. He had called it one of her more 'endearing' traits, when he teased her about it. But now he was in the middle of nowhere, and though he had a general idea of bearing, he was a long way from where he needed to be and figured that it would take at least half an hour to get there.

Putting the car into reverse, he carefully manoeuvred backwards using the mirrors and reversing camera, it was still too painful to twist his body. Turning the car, he set off along the driveway which seemed to go on for a half mile before reaching any distinguishable public road. Pulling out, it was a narrow country lane, single carriageway in either direction, with no signs of other road users in the vicinity.

It was a several minutes before he passed another car, a random by-passer, going about their daily business, knowing nothing of what was happening to a select group of people, perhaps picked with haphazard selectiveness from their daily happenings, to be thrust into the torment and torture of poison and potion. Being alone with his thoughts on that journey was one of the most mentally difficult tasks he had ever faced. Turning things over and over, from one thing to the next, but all interconnected, intertwining; gave no clear thought path or direction to focus his mind.

It was troublesome and tiring, the infinite quantity of avenues and possibilities were draining his mental capacity. The scenery slowly changed from rural to suburban; from suburban to commercial and from commercial to city. The roads became awash with traffic, that grew thicker and thicker as he grew nearer to the town. There were more and more people on the streets, and he wondered how it would be possible to find these other captives of the wristbands among the thick of bodies walking the pavements, if it were not for the help of their positioning on the map, and their standardised clothing.

He hoped that he would blend in with the other people, pedestrians and others going about their day. His red coat would help to hide his involvement in this fateful event and give him a degree of anonymity if one of the others were looking for him. The dash of the car told him that it was now 10:28 as the traffic came to a standstill from a collision ahead. This gave him a chance to have a good look at his map and to narrow a route towards the closest blue dot.

Poking at the screen, moving the map around, he was engrossed in the roads depicted on the tiny screen as he searched, when he felt a buzz that filled him with horror. The thing had vibrated again which he knew told of another message from his tormentor.

As he tried to navigate to the message function, there was a beep from behind as the vehicles ahead had moved on but he had failed to notice. He had to abandon looking so that he could move forwards on the road from being an obstruction to the other users.

Anxiety built. He had no chance to look at the new message. A sinking felling dragged him down, descending to the depths of an internal abyss. Peripheral vision became blurry. His stomach knotted and he felt nauseous. He needed to know what it said.

Willing for the traffic to come to a halt again, it just kept rolling, slowly but surely. Whatever this message said, it was not likely to cause him any more distress than he had already experienced in the 12 hours of horror; there was little more that could stir him further than what he had already been exposed to since his awakening. Surely there was nothing worse to come? But what if there were? What if this new message gave more horror to an already horrendous unravelling.

The knot in his stomach tightened.

The traffic still crept forwards. He was approaching the scene of a collision, nothing major, just a commuter bump, but the drivers involved were out on the carriageway engaged in a heated debate, no doubt concerning who was to blame. It was clearly the fault of the driver of the second car, which had shunted into the rear of the first. The queuing line of traffic was forced to cross into the opposing lane to pass the damaged vehicles which blocked their path, and this was causing the holdup whilst they waited for a gap in the oncoming traffic. He was now at the front of the queue waiting to go around the obstruction.

The wanting desire to read that message was burning within him. Could this be another cryptic clue to aide him on his challenge to find 35? Was there something more that the puppeteer was throwing at him, trying to steer the course of his future for some unknown purpose? In a moment, he would pass the vehicles and drivers blocking his way with their shenanigans of fault and blame, and then he could find somewhere to pull over and review the latest communiqué that had arrived at the wristband that controlled his life.

The head-on string of traffic was relentless. Too many people with their head up their own backside to realise that there was a tailback on the other side, and allow a gap for the cars to pass; everyone just busied on with their own journey, having no regard for those caught behind the incident at which they all gawped as they passed slowly wanting to inspect what had happened. Face after face, in vehicle after vehicle, all slowing to look, with no courtesy for those waiting behind the stricken cars. It must have been three minutes before someone eventually stopped and flashed him through.

By this point, he was building a red mist at those who had passed with no regard, and though he was grateful to the soul who had relented their position to allow him to pass, he was so infuriated that he simply floored it, carelessly waving his hand in thanks as he shot passed the man who had stopped for him. The road ahead was clear as all other traffic had moved on whilst he was stuck there. He had reached 50 before realising what he was doing. This was a built-up area, with busy streets and footpaths; and he rolled off the throttle.

There were kids about, from pre-school to teens, which at this time of day meant that there was no school. It seemed too busy for a Sunday. Surely it must be a Saturday, but that would mean he had been missing for at least a week! Surely not, he thought as he slowed the car, and pulled into a side road where he parked up at the curb side.

He took a moment. With his hands grasped at the 10 and 2 positions, he closed his eyes, took a deep breath and expelled it over a long few seconds before checking the wrist band once more, the knot in the stomach turned even tighter.

Navigating to the message function was simple, but the anticipation of reading the message made it seem to take forever. The expectancy was deflated quickly as he read the words. It was nothing important, but rather pointless, all things considered. The eagerness he had felt to read the message made it turn out to be somewhat disappointing. "12 down, 12 to go – half a day to live" was all it read. It seemed silly now that he had been so frustrated by the traffic, and then rushed as he had, shooting up the road in a rage at the other motorists that had blocked his way, preventing him from reading the message sooner. It could have waited; heck, he wished the tormentor hadn't even bothered.

At least now he was closer to the others, and parked up at a relatively safe and unobtrusive spot from which he could be a voyeur from above, looking down at the map on the blue dots about him. They were all moving, none together; not even close to one another. He wondered if there were any that would be in a pair, as he had been earlier, but maybe appearing as only one dot on the map, being so close to another.

He thought then of the newest member of this helpless situation. If they were each awakening three hours apart, and if they were all trapped in a body bin having need to escape; it would be sometime around now that the next player would break free of the cadaver cooler to discover their fate, number 40 as he calculated.

How much longer could this go on?

He had vowed to his enormous friend that if he is eventually able to escape from this torment, that he would do all in his power to find the fiend that had enslaved them, and bring justice for the lost ones, whether it be lawful, or a cold hard serving. That was a murder that he could truly contemplate, the killing of the one who had captured so many and subject them to death by poison or person. Who knew how many had made it out? Who knew how many more would be party to this? If anyone had a chance to stop it, even if that meant murder, it was a price worth paying to avenge the fallen and prevent it from continuing.

But before that, the next task; the task at hand since his escape; was to find 35. These bands gave no indication of which numbered person these other dots were. Only the map and a faulty compass. Surely there was something more to the compass? He brought it up and studied the thing for a while. The number read '2112m'. The arrow was pointing to his right, and as he moved his wrist around, the arrow floated around the ring, always pointing in the same direction. It wasn't north; he could tell that by the navigation system of the car which showed the direction was more like south-east. The number was decreasing, slowly, steadily, with rhythmic timing, but not in seconds. What did it mean?

Getting back to the map, the closest of the blue dots was perhaps a little over a mile away. He would need to turn around and get back onto the road from which he had pulled off, heading in the same direction as before he had turned to read the stupid message. He checked the mirrors and satisfied he could pull across the road and turn the car in one smooth motion, he indicated, put the car into gear, and moved off. As he arrived at the crossroads from which he had detoured, he realised that the blue dot towards which he was intending to go, was in the same direction that the compass was pointing.

As he waited for the light to change, he quickly swiped up and brought up the compass. Sure enough, the arrow was pointing off to his left, towards the place that the dot was. He switched to the map, and indeed he was right. Back to the compass, still the same, but the counter was now down to '1829m'. What is the 'm'? Why was it counting down? The number was higher than earlier in the night, he was sure. So why the rise; why now the fall? It made no sense to him. But if this compass was pointing to another player rather than north, perhaps this numerical element also pointed to another player? Metres!

As he moved off from the junction, rounding the intersection to make a left turn, he watched as the arrow spun to face ahead of him. The number was reducing quickly now that he was on the move; surely it must be meters. It was now down to 1730's and falling. At this rate, it would only be a couple of minutes before he could come upon the other.

A well of hope filled him as he considered that this compass may be directing him towards his predecessor, towards 35. He may soon be upon them and close to his goal, the cure that would save him from the poison within. But if this is 35, he would have more than eight hours with them before their time was up. That meant eight hours of having to try and help them find their cure, find 34, but that would mean with every passing minute they were closer to their escape, and the escape of 35 meant doom for him.

He had resolved to allow 35 their freedom if they had located and secured their cure before their time was up; which meant only death for him, an outcome he was prepared to face. If he were to help 35 to live, he would be helping himself to die. Maybe he could follow them around for the next few hours from a distance? But he was sure that if they were to keep checking their map, they would realise they had a tail, and his game would be up pretty quickly if they then searched for him.

As the road meandered along, it was clear that whoever this was, this dot he was seeking out, they were deep within a suburban housing estate that would require some negotiation. He flicked back to the map as he moved along, less than half a mile from the dot was showing on the 'metre-meter' as he left the compass. He took a left turn and pulled over again to search out a route to find them. They had stopped, wherever they were, it would be a number of turns now to reach them, but as they were not moving, it should be fairly easy going.

Within a few minutes he was almost upon them. Pulling onto the street the dot was resting at, he slowed the car and pulled over, shutting off the ignition. Silently, he sat there, surveying the road ahead, his eyes searching, pouring over every detail. Quaint houses, manicured lawns and gardens; late model cars of modest value outside many. But no signs of life, no one walking about; nothing but a cat that moseyed across the road before darting with speed to tackle a six-foot fence with grace and elegance.

There were telltale signs of the houses being occupied beyond merely the cars on their driveways. Windows were open in places, a mist of steam emanating from the exhaust ports of heating systems warming the houses from the cold that remained. The thermometer of the car said it was just above freezing.

It seemed from the map that the dot was likely in a house off to his right about four properties along. There was nothing obvious happening there that he could see, though it was evident that people were inside. He slipped out of the car and placed the keys in his jacket pocket, where he found an object that had thus far escaped his attention. How he had not realised this was here before now mystified him, but sure enough, there was a phone.

His immediate thought was to call her again. Earlier he had been unable to get through, unable to leave a message. She would not even know that he had tried, never mind that he was still alive, albeit far from safe for the present time. He found that the phone was locked and he would have no access to make any calls other than to the emergency services. Calling the Police right now was not a sensible option, especially after all he had done.

He thought then of the man at the print shop, the owner of this jacket, the owner of this phone. By now he would have been discovered, the alarm would have been raised, and that meant there was a very real possibility that this phone could be being tracked by the police in search of the attackers who bound, gagged and robbed a man in the middle of the night. He must get rid of this thing quickly. He held the power button to turn it off and then slipped it through the opening of a rain grid, and into the sewage system beneath the streets.

He hoped that his current location was not already a target for the authorities. Was it worth fleeing now, waiting at a distance perhaps to see if anyone swoops in to capture the assailants from the print shop? But this may mean losing the possibility of engaging with the blue dot, that was now less than 200 metres from his grasp. He needed to press on and the chances of the police giving such priority to tracking that phone now seemed more and more remote than in his haste to have disposed of the thing. Regardless, he was not tech savvy enough, nor did he have the equipment to have by-passed the phone's security and use it to his advantage. Getting rid of it was a smart move.

Ahead of him, there was an eruption of noise on the otherwise quiet street. It had seemed almost picturesque until a front door had evidently opened and a family spilled out, one at a time, clearly in a rush, late for something; parents yelling at kids to get in the car, kids yelling back causing a scene of embarrassment should any of the neighbours be witness to this event. The front door slammed as the mum stormed down the driveway yelling aloud, but mostly to herself about how the kids were disrespectful and ungrateful; before she tore open the car door, jumped inside and slammed the door shut again. The car fired into life, reversed with some ferocity, and shot up the road towards him with pace, before passing and heading out of the street the way he had come in.

No one had given him the slightest regard. He walked on towards the place that the dot was resting. A modest size house, similar in construction to the others, but this one had undergone some extensions that perfectly blended with the original characteristics and were only obviously additions due to the manner in which this house was different from those around it. The white finish of the exterior seemed to be well kept, unweathered, fresh looking. A break in the clouds had temporarily allowed the sunlight to flood the place, and in that moment, this house, gloriously adorned with planted boarders, hanging baskets and window pots; it looked like a summer's day in a place of beauty.

He couldn't decide how to approach this property, to seek to engage with the dot. Should he sit and wait it out, or go head strong and knock at the door. Why this house out of all of the others? There must have been something that had drawn them to this specific place, as they had left the city, moving further away from the other captives who were surely all looking for one another. What connection did the dot have to this house and the occupiers? Was it worth him finding out? Perhaps they had come here to seek help and refuge from the occupants, perhaps friends or family, and if he called knocking, looking for an unidentified person, it may cause him problems.

But on the other hand, if this dot was one of the newer participants, a number that had been released after himself, perhaps they knew little of their situation. He could be of great benefit to them, giving the details of what he had come to learn of being poisoned, having to find your cure, what it is, how to get it..... This may all be invaluable to any successor of this numbered sequence.

There was a small possibility that this dot was 35, the one he has been looking for, the one who holds the key to release him from this captivity. If it was, he would need to work out how was best to go about the eight hours they had left to find their cure. What if they knew nothing of what was happening? Could he honestly live with the guilt of not coming clean, allowing their time to pass, then seizing the opportunity to take hold of his cure?

He was a better man than that and he knew it. If he were to come across 35 at any point, his conscience would not allow him to do anything other than offer his help to them, even in the face of that bringing death to himself. It was the decent thing to do, and he considered himself a decent man. He knew that his life had no greater value than anyone else's, and therefore, he could not take the life of another, or allow them to die solely for his own benefit if there was a chance of their escape. There would be no victory in that, only remorse; remorse he would have to live with forever.

The mental scars of this event would be much more permanent than the physical damage his body had sustained.

He knew that he must approach the house, and resolved to knock and seek out the participant. He looked at his band a final time, 10:58, then looked back at the car sat peacefully on the quiet roadside where still there remained no other signs of life; and then began to walk up the driveway towards the door. As he approached, he could hear noises within, people talking, and he hesitated before knocking at the door. The murmured voices didn't seem to stop, but one was drawing closer to the door as they spoke. He forced a smile to his face as he heard the latch release.

The door opened.

11:00

A man was stood the other side of the door, late twenties perhaps; early thirties at a push. His hair was styled from the day before and had clearly been slept on, his face awash with a few days growth since when he had last shaved. Clothed in a tour t-shirt from a band that he recognized from yesteryear, a pair of slack jogging pants, and bare footed; this man had been nowhere this day, and clearly was not the 'dot' he was in search of. 'Hello' the man spoke.

'Hello and good morning. I am sorry to bother you, but I wonder by any chance is 35 here' he said, hoping that the man may know something if indeed a numbered person had arrived at this house seeking help.

'Sorry pal, we're number 16. 35 will be across the road and further along'.

'Excuse me, perhaps you have mistaken my intentions. I am looking for a someone, not a somewhere' he responded with as much pleasantry in his tone that he could manage.

Something registered with the man in his makeshift pyjamas, and the look on his face changed. Clearly, he knew that whoever this random caller at the door was, they had some knowledge or involvement in the matter he too was aware of. It was as though his face spelled out the words 'who are you and what do you know'.

'35? I am looking for 35, but you may have another number here? 37, 38 maybe?'

He heard the footsteps of someone else approaching as the man in pyjamas just stared at him not knowing how to respond. Another body appeared from around the door, a young man, 20, 21 years old maybe, but at first, nothing registered about the characteristics of this other, as 36's attention was grabbed by the same standard issue clothing that was now ingrained in his mind, being worn by the youngster. '39' spoke the man with a quiver of apprehension.

Wanting to seem as approachable as possible, he could think of no other way of showing that he too was a part of this, than to show 39 his wristband. He put out his arm and pulled back the cuff of his coat exposing it. '*36*' he spoke, and he watched the eyes of the other dart from his wristband, to their own, and then fix their gaze intently on him.

'I think you'd better come inside' said the man in pyjamas.

He was ushered through to the kitchen, where evidently these two had been sat conversing when he had interrupted them with his arrival. Mugs were out on the table in front of chairs that were haphazardly arranged compared to the otherwise pristine look. The oven was humming and the room was filled with a mixture of the scents of fresh bread, coffee, sausage and bacon. Immediately he was hungry.

He was invited to sit down at the table and offered a coffee which he gladly accepted. A pot that had been freshly brewed not long earlier with a good quality gourmet bean.

All things considered, he was sure this was the best coffee he had drank in a while. 39 had seated too whilst the other man went about turning the meats in the oven, and took the fresh loaf out of a bread baking machine.

39 looked at him with interest and expectancy, though in return he only needed to know what 39 knew already of this sordid tale, so asked them to tell him their story in order that he would know where they were up to. That way he could explain what he had come to discover, picking up from wherever the youngster left off.

This young man, barely out of his teens, seemed to have been missing for 10 days, and the last he remembered before that, was getting in a taxi on the way home from a night out with friends. He too had woken in a morgue and had to escape from a cadaver chiller. He knew nothing else from this, and had simply got dressed and started walking. At first he did not recognise anything, but then realised this was not his home town. He remembered various landmarks from visiting his cousin; the man in the pyjamas, and from that had tried to find his way to the cousin's house; this house, but he had only been once before, for a random weekend, and his memory had not been great. He had no means of contacting anyone, so simply walked around hoping to recognise various things that would guide him to this place. Eventually he saw his cousin's car on the drive, it was an import and there weren't that many of them around, particularly not in that striking orange colour, so it must have been his cousin's.

The boy had not interacted with any other number; he knew nothing of what was happening. He had only considered the possibility of '38' being another person when his cousin had pointed out that he was bearing the number '39'. Until then, he had no idea as to what 38 may be. He had wondered if it were an amount of things, a monetary value, something tangible. The idea that it was a person had not entered his mind.

He was clearly confused about what was happening to him, and his cousin had got in touch with his family back home. They had feared the worst when it had been more than a week since anyone had heard from him, and were relieved to hear that he was safe and had been found.

The reality of course was that he was not safe, far from it. Thinking how unfortunate this young man was, right now just beginning his journey of discovery; he began to tell his own account. He told of how he had escaped from the mortuary, found the other dots on the map.

Retelling it seemed surreal; how he had watched as the curly haired woman was arrested and goliath had told him what he had learnt. From there to the copy shop, the holding cells, the kitchen counter and the rich man's helicopter escape.

The man in pyjamas was now sat at the table with them, intrigue and interest written all over his being. Both he and 39 were dumbfounded at the story of this random man who came calling at the door. They could hardly believe it true but for the fact that they shared experiences, had identical wristbands except for their own sequential numbering. Their pants and shoes were identical, though his story told how he had come into possession of the dark blue shirt and red Parka that seemed an obscurity.

He had all but brought them up to date when the pyjama man stood again to tend to the food. As he finished his coffee the man produced a plate adorned with a bacon, sausage and egg sandwich that was slid across the table towards him; 'It sounds like you need this more than I do' said the cousin of 39.

Having thanked him, he asked for another coffee as he picked up the sandwich. The yoke of the egg popped causing the content to ooze out and drip from the bottom of the butty. The smell was incredible, and as he sunk his teeth and tore off a large bite, the taste was better than he could have imagined. Perhaps there was something in the impending doom that made the food seem more enjoyable than ever before, but he relished every morsel of that sandwich, taking his time to slowly devour it.

Pyjamas had floated in and out of the room several times and presently was absent as they heard his call from another room to come quickly. He and 39 shared a look that they knew something serious was happening as they stood from the table and their sandwiches to head towards their host. He grabbed his coffee as they left the kitchen and headed to the hallway, from which they could hear the television in another room. 39 went ahead of him as they entered the lounge and he saw Pyjamas stood watching the news;

'....fortunes building an empire on the stock market, but in recent time has focused his efforts on humanitarian projects in deprived nations; has been missing for more than two weeks. Today, police tracking fugitives from an assault and robbery at a down town shop, were led to the home of the billionaire via cellular triangulation, but instead found the mutilated body of an as yet unidentified man. We'll bring you more details as the story unfolds' told the reporter.

It sounded like he was a murderer. It came across as though he and the leviathan were nothing more than bandits and had tortured and killed for their gain. Would these newcomers think of him this way? Could they trust what he had said? He was now a suspect in a horrendous crime.

For the others, this report was validation of the stranger's story, but for him, it was worse than he could imagine. He wasn't safe here! That bloody phone, the police must have been tracking it after all. What about the car? Was this a risk he could take? Could he use it now that the police may expect it had been stolen given that the owner had been missing for a fortnight? Automatic Number Plate Recognition was so advanced, he was lucky he had not been stopped already, and arrested for being in charge of the stolen vehicle. At least he had the letter from the owner that would exonerate him of theft; but by the time he was processed and dealt with, it would have wasted too many of his hours, he would be near death with no hope of finding 35, if he was not dead already.

The car was of no use now. He must retrieve his bag from it, and leave the car there. He explained to Pyjamas and 39 that he had to leave, it was time for him to set back to his task of finding 35, and he implored 39 to set about his task too. This man was young, had no life experience, and no wits about them; and asked if they could accompany him on his travels in case the would find 38 together by chance. Having a companion had been somewhat relieving earlier in the night, but it would not be wise to start gathering together if the police were looking for people in certain clothing.

They returned to the kitchen table where he showed the newbie how to use the wristband in full effect to search for others, and the compass which pointed to another user. It was for this reason that he could not partner with the youngster, as his compass would always be pointing two feet to his side if he walked with any other numbered man. They would have to go about their own ways he apologised, but suggested that the cousin may be able to help him.

Before long, the police would soon have an idea of what was really happening, as the curly haired woman would by now have spilled the beans as to her capture, the poison, her mutilation of the man who had died before her very eyes, and the ogre that had arrived at the police station in pursuit of her. Armed with this fresh information, once they had made some enquiries, completed toxicology on the dead man from the hallway of horrors and learned the truth of his death to poison; they would doubtless be putting out an appeal to help those who found themselves caught in this tormented tale of terror.

It would likely be another half day or so at least before they had collated their evidence and corroborated the account of the curly locked lady, which would mean his time would be up before the police could reliably intervene; but 39 had a real chance of their help if he could survive the next 12 hours or so. Pyjamas came up with a plan to sit in the house and ride it out until the police do appeal. The problem with that however; was that there was no guarantee that they would. Moreover, he pointed out how he had found 39 with ease, simply by using the map. Others may come looking, and though the successor of 39 was just at the point of waking and joining the group of unfortunate puppets of the wristbands; who knew how quickly they would learn of their situation and what may be needed to save themselves.

That third cup of coffee in as many hours had not only given him a buzz from the caffeine rush, but seemed to have over filled his bladder quite quickly, and he asked to use the facilities. Pyjamas showed him through to a bathroom, and explained that he would gladly give him a lift into the city before going on to help his cousin to find their predecessor, and he turned around and disappeared towards the stairs. Having used the toilet, he emerged and made way back to the kitchen where 39 remained in the same position, staring blankly at the wall. It was almost as if you could see inside his mind, turning like the wheels of a clockwork motion, trying to make sense of the predicament. His eyes had enlargened and his face had lost all muscular tone and had started to sag, the boy clearly weary of what was to come, but frozen by the thought of it.

He left the youngster alone in his thoughts, not wanting to interrupt. He observed the man for the first time, properly taking in the detail of him. Slim and slender, a little less than average height. Despite his face having not seen a razor for as long as he had been missing, it was clean and showed only the slightest '12 o'clock shadow' around the four corners where a goatee would grow. This man was barely more than a child. He wondered what the two of them may have in common, what the rich Samaritan would have in common with either of them? What was it that connected them; Goliath: the woman? There was nothing that he could think of, yet whoever had taken them, seemed to be hand picking from the crowds of others that swarmed the streets both night and day. Why?

Pyjamas returned to the room, evidently having changed, dressed for the adventurous day ahead of him. He wasn't Pyjamas anymore, just an Average Joe. Getting changed may even be a good idea for 39 as it would allow him to blend into the crowd, and less likely to be set upon by any other trapped contestant searching for their cure. He remembered how Goliath had told him of having been near run over by someone in their desperate final hour. New attire would help prevent such madness.

He suggested to 39 that he change, and the cousin agreed and went to find a suitable outfit. Wanting to appear grateful for the hospitality displayed by Average Joe, he set about washing the dishes whilst the man was gone. 39 remained planted, almost rooted, as though he was overwhelmed by all that he had learned of his situation. The man was like a statue, fixed, inanimate; it was unnerving. He had barely moved in nearly 10 minutes by the time that his cousin returned with an outfit for him to change into.

Needing to collect his bag from the car outside, he informed his host of the same before slipping out and into the daylight once more. The sunlight streamed through the otherwise clouded sky, and it was as though this was a sign from God himself, that there was a ray of hope for his future. He stopped for a second, closed his eyes, and drank in the air through his nostrils. If he ever makes it out of this mess, he would grab life by the horns and learn to let go of the trivial things that possess people's everyday lives.

The street was busier now. A small gathering of 10-12 year olds were a short distance away, playing ball games on the road, another family of people were leaving their home, in a much more civilised manner than he had witnessed an hour earlier. The car was undisturbed, with no sign of the police around. As he walked towards it, he wondered whether they were even aware of the car and if they were actually looking for it? It was not the type of car one would expect a billionaire to drive around in. Heck the man's home was the most impressive he had ever stepped foot inside, and the guy flew away in his own helicopter! A low grade hatchback seemed out of sorts with the man's character. Perhaps it was registered to a corporation he owned?

It would be too great a risk factor to think he could continue to drive around in the thing without being quickly apprehended. Regardless of whether the police had been able to track the whereabouts of the handset, the car may be low-jacked. Abandoning it would be a wise move. He retrieved his bag from the passenger seat and closed and locked the door. Heading back towards the house, it dawned on him what a chore it must have been for 39 to have spent hours searching for his cousin's home. More so, it was remarkable that he had not come across others in this twist of fate, as although he had no idea what he was doing, there were others out there looking for more blue dots.

Pyjama Joe and 39 came out of the front door and opened the car on the driveway, putting some items in. As he approached, Joe was heading back to close and lock the house. He suggested that they could be in for a long day, and it may be worth them getting some supplies, but the man just waved his wallet, as though they would buy whatever they needed whilst they were out. It was the first time in a while that he had realised that he had no money, and so far hadn't needed it, but now that the day was in full swing, having some funds may be useful. In this day-in-age, cash was almost all but extinct. Getting hold of any tangible payment method would be problematic, but the owner of this brightly coloured import was of course no part in this melancholy and still had access to his regular items. He slipped into the rear of the car behind the driver's seat, putting the bag down beside him, and 39 sat across from him in the front.

'You better hope you know what you're doing buddy, you've got only ten hours left' said the youngster, with a hint of compassion in his voice.

'*The odds are now in my favour of finding 35, so long as I can move about with ease*' and in speaking those words, he realised that the pain he had earlier been experiencing, had become so subdued, it was hardly noticeable. Those tablets 32 had left him were a modern marvel he thought.

The driver got in, and the car fired up. Soon enough, they drove away, passing the borrowed car of the billionaire, and turning out towards the main arterial roads. Traffic was modest, people were about. The sun was now obscured by the cloud that had earlier opened like a window to the blue above, and through which the sunlight had poured in. Now it just seemed grey, muggy, bleak. He thought how his day was reflecting the weather, momentary and specific elements of sunlight joy were surrounded by the grey clouds of doubt, fear, anticipation and sorrow.

How much more of this did he have to endure?

Could he?

12:00

———

Noon came as they approached the border that unwittingly separated the city from its residential suburbs. Not having any strong inclination of which direction to head, the driver was seemingly just on autopilot heading towards the downtown area. Both of his passengers were preoccupied with their thoughts, being somewhat overwhelmed by the situation they faced. Average Joe just kept rolling, not wanting to distract either from their train of thought.

After a while, knowing that they needed to be somewhat specific in their destination, the driver asked for some kind of directions. The sound of the gruff voice broke through the silence and disrupted his tiresome thoughts of all that lay ahead. He knew he needed to refocus rather than allow the wandering of his mind to continue, his time escaping in vain without any advancement to his goal.

It would be simple to read the map and direct the driver to the nearest other dot, but the youngster needed a chance to get to grips with the makeshift cuff that served to be its own brand of imprisonment. He instructed the boy once more on how to use the band and search the map for others. Thereafter, the kid was able to give clear direction to his cousin that would take them ever closer to a mysterious blue blip that was yet one more unknown number of this sadistic state of affairs.

Buildings grew ever taller as road after road became thicker with traffic, both vehicular and pedestrian. The general attire of people was a good mix of business and casual, but in today's society, casual was the norm in many places where once only the smartest of dress code was acceptable. Briefcases had all but been replaced with knapsacks and backpacks. Any one of the people lining the streets could be either a professional on their lunch break, or a weekend shopper out to peruse the high street's delights. He still had no idea what day it was, and enquired of the momentary companion that was currently at the helm of his destiny for the next few minutes.

Saturday? Was this the same Saturday that he remembered? He could have been missing for only a matter of hours...... Surely this couldn't be so. How stupid of him to think it. He had been awake for 14 hours already since the morgue and had already been through the night. He must have woken on a Friday night if today was Saturday. And that meant he had been missing for at least six days.

For six whole days at least, she would have been going crazy with the thought of what may have happened to him. Exploring every avenue of his conscious memory, he could remember nothing of his disappearance. Was she there? Was he snatched from right in front of her? Did she see it? He had no idea what had happened since their walk that morning, or how that day had ended in their separation. For the first time, he considered the possibility that she may not be fearing for his safety. Had they had a falling out?

He could never imagine a time in which she wouldn't love him enough to care, but if from her perspective he had simply been dodging her calls... What if from her point of view, he had given her the slip whenever she came calling; she may have been hurt at his snubbing. She could think he was simply being awkward, not knowing that he had been abducted; taken against his will; imprisoned; poisoned and forced to partake in this perverted pastime of the obscure puppeteer.

It dawned on him that there may be no one looking for him, no one truly concerned that he was gone. Surely this was madness, as even if she felt betrayed by his eluding her, she loved him enough to still care for his safety, especially if it had been a week since anyone last saw or heard from him. Surely, she would have answered her phone when he had tried to call? Perhaps she simply hadn't recognised the number, though he expected that she would take any and every call she received if she were concerned for his well-being. He thought about trying to call anyone else, but he realised how reliant on technology the little things had become, that he didn't know anyone else's phone number from memory.

He was now free from the elements of attire that the Police had been chasing. He was lucky that the handset from the Parka's pocket had not led them right to him before realising how much of a danger he was in. The man from the print shop would by now long be free from the makeshift bondage that the giant had put him under; though the trauma of the event would likely result in lengthy counselling for all but the most resilient of people. That poor man was simply a victim of their circumstances.

The cops had been chasing after people for weeks already, and he wondered how many other unfortunate victims of circumstance had resulted from the capture of the cuff adorning their wrists? How many people had been traumatised by the crazed persons in strange uniform that had done all manner of unspeakable tasks to advance their position in seeking their cure? This death sport had a much greater toll than simply the numbered participants. Their spouses, families, friends; and all those that had in some manner become involved or interacted with the kidnapped, now criminals seeking to murder another for their own gain. The count must be immeasurable by now, especially if the cycle had, as he now suspected, played through numbers before, if he wasn't the first 36.

It was just gone quarter past the hour as the front seat passengers became elated at having turned on to the same road as another dot. In less than 200 metres they'd be upon them. There were few vehicles moving, but a number parked up in laybys at the roadside. A cluster of people walked in unison on one side of the road, whilst on the other, there were just three individuals, separated by a good 10 meters; the one farthest from them was moving at a much slower pace than the others who were gaining ground on them. The progression of the first was as though they had almost given up on life, more of a slow slump forwards than a walking pace. Whoever that was, it was likely that they were the one that the map was leading them to.

As they approached this other, the walk was awkward, odd looking, as though they walked with a limp, but on both legs. Slowly this zombie like rapt mess of a human wilted onwards with an apparent lack of hope; it was as if they had been bled dry of anything that resembled life.

They drove past and observed the character better, a man of early 50's, weathered, tired in the face. He was remarkably average, though he had clearly been a good-looking man in his everyday life, but the troubles he was facing at present gave his appearance to be more haggard than normal. His hair was short, un-styled, with a salt and pepper edges around the temples. The coat was evidently that of a hostage to the futuristic plastic paper wrist strap; his pants and shoes also had the same unexceptional appearance of the other participants. None of them could make out the number on the man's chest.

They pulled up ahead of him, allowing them enough time to disembark the less than conspicuous vehicle they travelled in, without seeming like they were deliberately intent on accosting the man. Without a word to each other, they alighted the brash looking import and congregated at the rear wing, Pyjama Joe leaning against the body work, but directly in the path of the zombie. It seemed to take an age for him to get within the distance that they could read his number; 33.

This man was about to die. Heck, it looked as though he already had died inside. He wondered what the man may know of his circumstances, and how much he knew of the impending end? It looked like he knew it all. This man has less than an hour to live and had obviously given up trying.

They caught his attention, but none of them knew how to open without sounding like crazed madmen. He knew it was up to him, the others were new to this; one of them was nought more than a bystander, an onlooker, simply offering his assistance to his youthful cousin whose future he may be able to massively alter by helping in this time of desperation.

'Excuse me - 33?'

The man paused, without a look of bewilderment or befuddledness as one may expect, just a soulless corpse stood still and looking back.

'I am 36, and this here is 39' he explained hoping to immediately catch his interest. *'We found you through our maps, and.....'*

What was he expecting...... this man is on the edge, about to fall, there was nothing to prevent his demise. His pause was followed by a long exhale and

'Is there anything we can do for you?'

The man looked at him with hollow expression that was a continuation of his walking dead like appearance. Truly he had expended the entirety of his emotions and was at the end of his tether. He cared not who they were or what they wanted.

'Who can do anything for me now?' came from him in a muttered mumble with a rhetorical tone that needed no answer.

'*I knew 32*' he said in response, '*Briefly anyways. I spent an hour or so with him. I know it won't make it any easier for you, but he got out. He was able to secure his antidote and once he had taken it, he got away. There was no chance of you catching up with him.*'

'Well he's the first I've heard of that has actually made it out of this madness' spoke the stranger. 'I have seen several others die, and not one has ever found release. I began to believe it was all a hoax, accept from the deaths I have witnessed, and that gave me false hope of a cure'.

This man was a mix of puzzle and intrigue. He had survived for nigh on 24 hours since his awakening and was now knocking at death's door; but he spoke as though he knew little of the potion that would free him, only that he was looking for it.

It was by pure chance that he and the ogre had happened upon the solution. Curly Locks had clearly picked up on elements of it, but how many actually knew what was needed? Was it really possible that this wandering near corpse had no understanding of what it is that would save him?

'*Do you know?*' he asked; '*What it is? The Antidote?*'

'Antidote? Oh, to stop the poison! Don't tell me it's something ridiculous like a code from the band of another; as I've interacted with so many that had tried anything and everything. No one seems to know what, or how'.

It was evident that he knew nothing. How could one break the news to another with any subtlety? He would need to say it like it is. '*It's a potion*' he said, '*A vial of colourless liquid that....*'

But the man interrupted him, 'What vial?'...... and the whole place seemed to fall into silence as they peered at one another 'Where's yours?' he asked and then paused, almost for dramatic effect, as his question seemed empty; 'Aren't you supposed to hold the cure for the one who follows?' now he was animated, as if the thought had provoked something in him, made him sit up and pay attention.

He continued..... 'I don't have one. I had nothing, never have. From what I gather, no one has. I woke up bare ass naked: as naked as the day I was born, and all I've ever been given were these clothes. You've got to have seen the same..... emptied your pockets too? Ripped the lining out of the jacket, insoles out of the shoes'.

This poor man really was clueless. It was sad.

'*We all have it*' he responded and left his own slight pause for that to take hold. '*Yes, I've been there; wondered if its real; whether I had some magic cure for 37. At one point, we questioned whether it was even a poison, or possibly a small electrical or otherwise explosive device, perhaps deactivated in*' *some way by interaction with your predecessor. But the reality is far worse.'*

'It's inside', spoke the youngster for the first time in this interaction, looking down at his abdomen with a hand placed on his belly.

A look of fear and grotesque voyeurism washed over the man's face as he came to realise that he had been carrying it the whole time, and what it would take for him to have got his hands on what he needed; or what his successor would do to him if they found him. In that very instant, he seemed to almost welcome the death that was staring him in the face; utterly discombobulated.

This man needed time to think, to process, but in reality, it made no odds to him now, with what the situation was. He was nothing more than a dead man walking. If 34 should come around the next corner and murder him for their antidote, he was no worse off than he would be in 35 minutes. His time was too close to the end, there was nothing he could do about any of it.

Feeling compassion for the man, he wanted to do something, some act of kindness, anything to show that he cared for the welfare of even a total stranger such as he. But there was nothing that could be done. It was no more compassionate to take his life now and prevent his mental anguish over the next half hour or so, than to simply let him succumb to the venom that would rage within him. Fallen from his animated display of conversation moments ago, he was evidently regressing to his zombie like state, starring off into the middle distance, as though he were an extra in a movie scene. Only, with this man, it was truly a case of being lost in his thoughts.

'Your 35 then, I take it you've not found her?' said the zombie with no animation or expression whatsoever, just a dry and almost shrill tone.

Her, he'd said 'her'; and he said it with such a simplistic expression that it was as though he knew it for sure. 35 whomever they are, is a 'her'; a 'she'; a woman. This was some news, as in that very moment, it excluded 50% of the population from being the one he was looking for. In an instant, half of the swarms of humans that inhabited this Godforsaken city were ruled out as being the holder of his fate. With any luck, this man may know more of her.

'No, I haven't. In fact, I didn't even know it was a woman until you said. This woman, what is she like?'

'If you mean is she kind, compassionate and caring, the sort of woman any man would be lucky to have, she would tick all your boxes; but I'm pretty sure that you're only interested in wanting to know of her appearance, that you could filter her out of a crowd of strangers,' his tone now held some disgust and animosity.

He shrugged, with a half-hearted smile, his head tilted to one side. The man had clearly caught him out.

'Well she's pretty easy on the eye, not strikingly beautiful, but a real looker, 'bout five-five I guess, slim, athletic. Dark hair, shoulder length. Probably half my age or she'd of been the type of girl I'd go for.'

She sounded like the type of girl he would go for. *'Was she local, did she know her way around, carry a foreign accent?'* he asked, wanting to gather as much data as possible about his target, but then immediately feeling bad for thinking of her as his victim, when the reality was, they were all victims.

'I dunno kid. She seemed to have some wits about her that's for sure. She knew what she was doing and was on a mission to see this through. I mean, we all are, but she had gumption, drive, determination'.....she really did sound like his type of woman.

'When did you last see her?' he enquired

'Must have been around 6am, she went off on her own to carry on looking'

'And where was she headed?'

'East is all I could say' he mustered, not really too sure of himself, 'off through the park on the other side of town. I don't know what was beyond the park though'.

'Thank you friend' he responded, and excused himself from the group of would-be stage folk under the instructions of the theatre director, influencing their course of action to continue with their play. A tragedy more brilliant than the historical greats or Greek mythology.

He wished the man peace in his death, the youngster luck in his progress, and instructed Pyjama Joe to look after his cousin and to keep an eye on the breaking news that was surely imminent. If he was right, it would be any time about now that the Police would start to place an appeal for them all to 'come in'.

The day was bright now, but still overcast with cloud. If it hadn't been for the height of the buildings that surrounded him, he knew that he'd be squinting to see in the absence of his glasses. The day was much warmer than the night had been, but having been stood motionless in one spot for more than ten minutes, the cold had started to creep in. His borrowed Parka was zipped up to the top and he pulled the hood up over his head, and tucking his hands into the cuffs of each sleeve, he set off intent on heading east, where he would find the park and then search his map for other dots.

Movement was now far easier than it had been only a few hours earlier when he had all but given up since the wreck of the stolen pick-up. He wondered how long those miracle pills of 32 would last before the aches would start to consume him again? And in thinking of 32, he knew that it was finally over for him. His successor was at the end of his time, and at the turn of the next hour, there was no danger left for the helicopter pilot billionaire. The world would be a better place for it; this man of vision, of positive influence and social action; could continue his crusade to change the lives of others in desperate need.

How sickening a thought though, that this was only achievable through the death of another. 33 must die for the champion of justice to continue to do good. And as good of a man as the Samaritan was; why was it that he should be any more deserving than his successor who was now slowly walking to his grave less than half an hour away?

Life had always moved in cycles, he thought. Be it hunters and prey; survival of the fittest; or general evolution of the species; life was always fluid, always moving, always fleeting. Death is a daily occurrence, the only natural part of life that is left. From the moment of birth, every breath, every step, every action, was one closer to the end. Death was the only constant in life. The one thing that without fail, everyone who has lived and ever will live, has only death to look forward to.

He realised how his life until the shock introduction to his world in turmoil, he hadn't truly been living, merely existing. Days came and went, and he planned out his life to 'live', normal, mundane, boring. Mortgages, life insurance, dental plans, car maintenance savings; what the hell was his life for?

A singular moment of clarity seemed to break his consciousness, like an epiphany, a lightbulb moment, from darkness to instant glorious light.

Life was for living.

Until death came not just knocking, but bursting through the door; his life would be to live, and live to the fullest imaginable. That started right now. His entire life had been until this time a calculated sum of decisions, risk assessment and analysis, a playing of the most favourable odds; but now that seemed to pale to obscurity. Risks would be taken, chance would be a fine thing. It was time that he stepped out of himself and into a life that was actually worth living. A life worth enjoying. And should it be that his new found purpose resulted in him being released of the enslavement to the wristband, cut free from the strings of the puppet master; he truly would go on to 'live' his life.

The sounds that surrounded him were a mix of dull tones of engines, air conditioning units, heaters; the rippling of rubber on tarmac as vehicles passed, the hum of a hundred conversations all within his earshot as he walked along the ever busier pavements. People spoke on phones as they walked, vehicles were making drop offs and deliveries. The whole world continued in the day-to-day activities.

No one gave regard to him more than any other. He seemed to fit right in to the society of people moving about the streets. He passed two uniformed cops stood on one corner, who were obviously on the lookout for something, but then were inattentive to his passing, and clearly his present attire attracted no attention, despite his lower half remaining of the same appearance as the other numbered participants. He realised how little regard he would ever give to someone's legs and feet in everyday life. The detail was usually 'face, hair, shoulders' type area where the eyes would focus, and in that you would gain a reasonable idea of what a person was wearing on their upper half, but unless it was something out of the ordinary, with loud colours or extravagant patterns, people don't seem to pay much attention to below the chest. His plain pumps seemed to go unnoticed.

Though he had not long earlier consumed his first proper meal since his awakening, and was satisfied with his fill; there were wonderful smells emanating from the cafes, restaurants and sandwich shops, all of which were getting busy with the lunch time rush. At one place, there was a scent that arrested him, and brought memories of his childhood. He couldn't work out what it was, but the smell made him stop and drink it in through his nostrils.

As his gaze flitted around the establishment through the streetside windows, he saw a corridor that lead out towards the back. The horror of his early interactions with a dead body in the doorway suddenly took hold of him and caused terror to fill his very being once more. He allowed the thing to play on his mind as he began to walk on, remembering how he had learnt of what had been the fate of the dead man, and how the hallway of horror had actually been a saving grace to the woman who had later gifted him the knowledge to save his own life.

He remained uncertain as to whether this information was in fact a gift or a curse. Though she had given him the knowledge to obtain what he needed, and he had witnessed 32 butcher Goliath and retrieve what was required; she had also given him a moral choice, a great debate causing him internal conflict and turmoil. To save himself, it was likely that he must kill another. If 35 were able to get hold of their cure, her cure, the only way to redeem himself would be to take her life.

13:00

———

As the hour passed he had reached the edge of a park that seemed to be east of from where he had not 30 minutes earlier interacted with the hollowed soul who would now be dead. The time on 33's countdown would by now have expired and the zombie of a man would be nothing more than a corpse. His ogrelike friend had suddenly dropped, from being alive and kicking one moment, to being a shell. Nothing more than a vessel in vacant possession, perversely itself symbolic of the truck that moments later had its own sudden stop. Having thought about the situation over and over, he knew that his companion's consciousness had instantaneously removed itself from the body that slumped as the vehicle began to lose control.

He wondered whether 33 would, in similar fashion, just stop and drop at the roadside in the middle of the pavement? Surely this would gather a crowd of onlookers and calls for the emergency services. It was best to be well away from such a scene at this time, lest he may be waylaid by the commotion and lose valuable minutes of his remaining life.

With the death of 33, their successor would now be in a desperate state, and he pondered how the misfortune of another may have a positive impact on his own predicament. If 34 could not retrieve their potion, they too would ebb from life and that meant 35 would also be in a sticky situation. She, as he now knew them to undoubtedly be a woman; would have only three hours from now to locate her predecessor and engage in an act of unspeakable revulsion, of gore and carnage, to ultimately consume the vial that contained the medicine to her punishment.

What he had thus far learnt from his interactions with others, was that hardly anyone knew the truth of what they would need to do; of the bloodbath and butchery that necessitated their freedom. And if she didn't know, the three hours she presently had available were but nought to the greater picture. Even if she finds 34, she may very well lack the knowledge to avert her own succumbing to the venom that would in less than six hours time, also take hold on her.

If she was not able to preclude her own demise, then he was almost home free. All he needed to do now was locate her. He had resolved that he would not take the life of another if they had indeed been able to save themselves; but if she, whoever she may be, was not able to procure her potion, then all he would need to do is await her end, and then as the wealthy humanitarian had done in the cabin in the woods, perform an impromptu surgery on the body, before fleeing as fast and as far as he could possibly go, to get away from the one who would be hunting him.

Though the clock was ticking his life away, he began to feel a sense of confidence that he may actually be able to dodge death. Unwittingly, this thought had brought a smile to his face that he only came to realise when one after another, strangers passing by in the other direction gave a returning smile. He pondered how society, for all of its misgivings, still maintained a number of its very human characteristics. People seemed to always return a smile that was sent in their direction. It was certainly one of the more endearing traits of the human condition.

Compassion, however, seemed to be somewhat of a lost art in the everyday life. When a significant event happened that rocks a community, a district, an area, or even a country on a mass scale; people would always rally together in droves to offer their support, to uplift and encourage one another, create donations and collections and offer gifts of finances, materials, aid, and personally invested time. But in the footsteps of any lone individual, compassion was lacking on a large scale. The lowly were neglected, the orphans were mistreated, homelessness was rife, yet blind eyes were turned at every corner.

In this world, the individual was only concerned with one; themselves. It had become a tragic state in not much more than 100 years. With advancements in transportation methods, the far side of the world was easily in arms reach. No longer was one confined to their own community without a significant walk or travel by animal means. Where business, trade and commerce made individual communities thrive and depend on each other, creating links, ties and bonds to those who lived nearby, these unions were all but erased in less than a century. Mankind had grown to reaching not just the local and regional villages nearby, but foreign nations, continents, hemispheres. Thereafter stretching out even beyond the ball of rock it inhabited, searching the depths of the void outside of the atmosphere.

Not only had the transport advancements resulted in such expansion that people lost connection with their neighbours; everyone was now interconnected, on a global scale, being instantly able to send and receive immeasurable amounts of data, pictures, video and information; all instantaneously from the palm of a hand. The individual had all but shut off from social interaction, being so concerned and obsessed with the piece of picture glass they could hold on to, that revealed the world to them like a crystal ball, showing all manner of news, media, and 'social meeting places'. Personal interaction had all but been replaced through mobile communication technologies. Droves of people would endlessly stare at the device in the hand rather than talk with those in the room.

These thoughts seemed to have killed his mood, and the smile he had been wearing had now faded from his face, replaced with a furrowing of the brow and a drooping of the eyes as he felt saddened by the state of the world and his thoughts drifted to the one who was in control of his destiny for the next seven hours. Why would someone want to take him? What harm had he caused anyone that they would inject him into this?

As he wracked his mind trying to think through why he was the one that had been selected, he remembered that he was not alone. He was one of many. How many, he did not know, but as the time continued to pass, it was now the turn of 41 to break out of the tomb within which they had not long awakened. There were more than just he that had been plucked from life and injected into the game of torture, he was just one more participant, one more pawn on the board.

Maybe whoever was taking them had no ulterior motive in their choosing. Perhaps it was all random selection. But eight people a day was no mean feat. The sheer logistics of the matter were remarkable. Not only did it involve the taking of the players from their otherwise menial lives, but the preparation of chemicals, the clothing, the body cooler, the vials of whatever they contained that would break the cycle of the poison; this had to be the work of a number of people, or have taken years of planning and preparation.

If it were one person, acting alone, they would need to have been so well prepared, that with each passing day, the only thing to do was to take eight more innocents by whatever means they used, and administer both poison and potion from sequential hoards, before placing them into the cooler, which no doubt had some form of gas pumped in to keep them unconscious until their chosen time. This would still be a logistical nightmare.

And what about the messages sent to each player? It is likely that they could have been automated, set up by a computer program to send out the cryptic clues at specified times, synchronised to each numbered band? Maybe this would not need a manual input at specified times. Whoever this puppet master was, they were meticulous and fastidious in their planning and preparation. The skill was almost admirable had it not been for the reality of what the situation meant to him.

As he approached a gateway on what he determined to be the far side of the park from which he had entered, there were a greater number of people seeming to be heading into the greenery amongst the harsh grey tones of the city's buildings. Taking the opportunity to rest his legs a moment, he parked on a bench for a while and checked his band; 13:25. There were no other dots near to his current location. Moving the map to view ahead his position, he still saw nothing. Using an ever-increasing arch motion, he swept slowly, thoroughly, with exactness, with painstaking precision, in the hope of finding another blue blip on the tiny screen that adorned his wrist.

It was some time before he was able to locate one and the sudden sight of that little dot caused his heart to flutter with excitement. He watched for a minute or two, gawping at their movement, which was nothing exuberant, just a methodical progression. Perhaps they were heading towards another. He searched briefly, but gave up, and focused instead on the means by which he could approach and intercept the dot on their path.

Having worked out an efficient route, he rose to his feet, again thinking of the ease in which he could conduct his movement in light of all he had experienced and the injuries he was carrying, now masked by the miracle pain blockers left for him at the house on the lake. He was grateful for the drugs, and knew that without such, he would be little use in making any progress without some mechanically assisted aid. Even the ease at which he could breathe was greatly improved from the laborious process that he had earlier suffered.

Setting off in the direction of the new dot, he moved with vigour and a renewed energy. He felt sure of himself, of his ability to abscond the death that ogled him now with envious eyes.

A new thought came upon him. What of those who had already escaped? Was that really the end? Would this tormentor, whoever they were, simply allow them to just walk away? Did they give no regard for the continuation of the others still enslaved to the torment that raged and ravaged the souls of the damned? Did their persecutor give no further thought to those who had escaped his grasp? Were they so disposable to the wide picture that whoever this oppressor is, this game of life and death was their entire focus?

As his mind wandered, it seemed to him that there was some possibility of being not just free from the grips of demise that presently stalked him, but also he could be free to pursue this tormentor, to seek them out and bring retribution for the countless numbers that had already been caught up in the human hunt horror that had been going for countless days.

Thoughts of killing, of murder and massacre, had now plagued his mind through the night and long into a new day, but now the thought of taking the life of another living person, felt almost justified. As wrong as he knew that it was, that the law should be the one to bring this tyrant to justice. But he was by virtue of his immersion in the current state of affairs, personally invested in ensuring that the orchestrator of this madness should be terminated with as brutal a force as necessary; and with as much torture and depravity as they had inflicted on those who had been injected into the drama. Revenge could be sweet.

He scolded himself for his thoughts. He knew that as much as he would like to, he lacked the ability to deplore from decency and bring the demise of someone in cold blood in such a way, even if in his mind they deserved it.

Though the streets at this part of town remained filled with people, he felt completely alone and isolated from humanity. Those around him were oblivious to the conflict occurring amongst them, of the countless acts of horror, violence, robbery, kidnap and any other unspeakable acts that the numbered contestants had stooped so low as to engage in. He knew that he would forever be mentally tormented by the things he had witnessed in this day, of the horrendous sins he had committed against his fellow men to advance his position to where he is now. Such horrors would be embedded in his psyche for the rest of his days. Was it something that could be forgiven?

All through his life he had tried to be a good person. Though he was of no particular religious persuasion, he had tried to lead a life that was good, and morally upright, not wanting to upset the apple cart, but try to be a good neighbour, and a blessing to others. He pondered how it may be possible for him to personally interact with the people he had wronged, to offer a heartfelt apology and an explanation of his acts in the hope of forgiveness.

These people were not to know why they had been kidnapped, bound, robbed; but within a matter of hours at best, the story would likely break in the media from the exposé of the curly haired woman who had deliberately been captured to avoid the imminent death at the hands of the bearded giant. Perhaps then these people would come to understand why such unthinkable acts had been committed against them, what had driven the criminals to lie, cheat and steal from them. The news would likely traumatise the entire city and its suburbs, in a way that only the most heinous of crimes does, like the scenes of high school massacres, of bombings at public events and gatherings; this situation was really an act of terror; an attempt to break the spirit of a few, but have lasting impact on a much wider network.

The inhabitants of this metropolis had endured weeks' worth of carnage going from what he had gleaned through his deceptive acts at the copy shop and police holding cells not half a day ago. It surprised him still that their ruse had worked to such a degree that they were granted access. He knew that it was in fact not entirely of his doing, nor that of the ogre; but the woman had been marched through the corridor as the pair of them were sat watching, and it was she that had spotted the elements of their attire which spoke of their involvement in the entertainment of some twisted tormentor.

Still, it was a dazzling deception that had passed with sufficient credence to have them sat where they were at the time. It had been quick thinking that had led to such possibility, and the suggestion of there having been a relationship between his gigantic companion and the red-head. It seemed as though this was the element that had pushed the superior officer to believing their tale. The fake ID's had been worth it in gaining some attention, and as much as he regretted the manner in which they had left that store employee bound and gagged in the stock room; he was grateful for all they had accomplished in the short time they had been there.

His heart went out to that young man who had been so helpful in assisting their ploy of phony identification documents, going out of his way to contribute whatever he could. It was as though their illegal act had given him something to entertain himself from the otherwise sheer boredom of the graveyard shift. And in an instant, his joy at being of service to them was stripped from him as he was instantly turned from patronage to prisoner.

As time moved on, the streets beneath his feet did also. Cafés and bistros were much fewer and far between than earlier, but there appeared to be one at almost every corner. It occurred to him that as he knew nothing of his geographical location, and his bearing had been skewed from all of the commotion he had already endured, it was possible that any one of these establishments had been the place he had viewed earlier, when the cops arrived in force to tackle the woman with blood soaked hands wielding a knife.

It had always amazed him how the 'Chinese whispers' effect had a way of exaggerating reality, and he thought of how the ogre had explained it to him, that there were only 'Chinese whispers' that gave them any information at all about what was happening. How odd it was to him now, having gained the knowledge that he had, that those 'whispers' had such an understated expression of the dismay that actually befell them.

He had now gained much ground and though the end of the hour was vastly approaching, he knew that he was not far from where the blue blip had been on his map. He searched again, and was surprised to see that the dot now appeared to be heading in his direction. They must have spotted his dot on their map and began making a beeline towards him. He watched with fascination as with every step he took, the distance between the two seemed to close by twice as much as his own movement. He was certain they, whoever they transpired to be, were on course for interaction, the both of them intent on engaging with the other.

At this point, he was glad of his replacement coat, not only providing additional warmth over his standard issue item, but the lack of the 'uniform' bearing his number meant not being an obvious tell of his part in the unfolding events that would connect him to the other. He knew not who this other would be, and it was entirely plausible to him that they were not a predecessor of his, but he may be a predecessor of theirs. Depending on where this other would fit into the numbering system which they had so methodically been assigned, with such attention to the details of what followed;

he could prove to be a blessing to they, or they may prove to be a curse to him. From the camouflage of his Parka, he hoped to be able to observe the mysterious other for a while before the ultimate encounter.

In every passing moment that drew closer to their meeting, something stirred within him, a welling up, growing larger with every step, with every breath. It felt as though this happenstance of coming together was intended, was fate, was the all the forces of the universe conspiring to direct the pair of them to interact. Somehow, he just knew that he was supposed to come to connect with this new dot. The emotion provoked within spoke of only two possibilities; either they were his predecessor, the one from whom he could secure his potion; or he was theirs, bearing the gift of life to the mysterious dot that approached. It was more than chance, more than opportunity; he knew that he was *supposed* to interact with this one; of all the dots that would be somewhere located on the map at his wrist, this one was connected to him.

With his gazed fixed on the tiny screen that adorned his arm, he moved with vigour through the streets, turned a corner, and stepped across the road, so buried in the image of this meeting of destiny, that he had given no regard to the vehicle approaching.

14:00

There was a new pain, strong, deep. An ache that seemed to fill his whole being. His head swirled and he relived the moments within the tomb of his first awakening; dazed; baffled; confused about who he was, where he was, and what was going on. But this time it was not dark, it was daylight.

He became aware of the commotion that was gathering. People, voices, noises; the sound of an engine rolling over and over, idling away just inches from his ears. As his hearing became less dulled, less filled with a tinnitus ringing; the noise was immense, with every sound being near indistinguishable from others, just a melancholy of audio overload, throbbing in his head. As his eyes began to regain focus and his vision slowly returned to him, though not to any legible extent. The wavy and obscure figures of people standing over him caused him to know that his initial belief was correct. He had been so intently looking at his band that he had stepped out in front of moving traffic. 'What an idiot' he thought.

He'd been hit, knocked down.

The ground felt cold, again it somewhat reminiscent of his first awakening, but this time he knew he was clothed; no feeling of the shame of nakedness where the onlookers around would see. He knew he was outside; he knew there were other people present. He felt wet. Had he fallen into a puddle? It hadn't rained that he could remember.

The voices around him were muffled, mumbled almost, and he couldn't make out the words of any one individual. He couldn't make out their faces either, and as hard as he tried, his eyes were straining to tell whether individuals in the crowd of folk around him were male or female, with the only discernible tell being the shape of their silhouette determining longer or shorter hair. How could his eyes fail him so monumentally?

The pulsating of the engine droned with a resonating chug that all but drowned out anything else from his earshot. He longed for the owner to shut it off, but he was trapped, a prisoner within his own body once more as he had been the evening past, and which now despite his every effort to move, was unresponsive to the electrical impulses firing from brain, to cause muscular contraction. He willed for his brain to send to each of his body parts some usable signal. Each would usually respond without complaint, silently, swiftly, unconsciously causing the movement of person that one takes for granted in any ordinary circumstances. It was as though he were having an 'out of body' experience, only he knew for sure he was not 'out of body'. He was captive within, contained within an unmoving case that were it not for the respiration and the open eyes darting about, all bystanders would assume he was dead.

There he lay, frozen, bound, restricted from pursuing his cause and his goal. How long had it been he wondered. He had certainly lost consciousness, but for what length of time was now a mystery. He figured it could not have been long, as emergency services would likely have attended the scene, assessed his condition, and transferred him to a hospital. The reality that this may yet occur, struck him hard as he thought of the one he had been in search of at the time he was knocked down.

He knew not what had hit him, nor the severity of his injuries, but if he were unable to become lucid and mobile before the arrival of medical aide, he would then be bound in a further prison of the hospital bed and would lose valuable time in his quest. He was close enough to the finish that a deviation such as to be in need of any attentive medical assistance, he would surely reach the end of his hours, ebbing away with every passing second, and thus he would cease to live on.

He willed even just for his fingers to twitch, to show him some sign that he was still in control of his own body. He wished he could drum them on ground and thigh as he had in the cadaver cooler, but there was no such luck, it was as though he had taken such a shock to the system, that it had completely shut down. His mind remained active, but his functions were far less than. It had taken several minutes for his eyes to begin to gain proper vision, and now several minutes later the silhouettes were looking more like distinguishable figures. Shapes and contours were beginning to show and the appearance of colours broke forth, slowly seeping in as though a fade switch was blending the spectrum gently rather than the surprise shock of colour as used by the film makers in the tales of Dorothy's arrival in the mystical land with the Emerald City.

He took some comfort in the fact that he was able to feel. The sensations of cold and wet remained, but the sheer notion that he 'felt' them, caused him to know that his central nervous system had not been obliterated, and it was unlikely that there had been any significant spinal trauma. He determined that it was his right hand and around his lower torso that had the wet sensation. Was it likely this was blood, seeping out of him, soaking his clothes, his skin?

The noise level suddenly dropped as the chug of the engine ceased, the driver having evidently shut it off. A thankful release. He could hear the voices more clearly now, and one particular seemed to be talking to him, or more appropriately, at him. The voice was male, soft, yet assertive, reassuring; evidently they were attempting to let him know he would be alright and that paramedics were *en route*. His vision recovered enough to make out the owner of this voice; dark skinned, tanned from a winter holiday with very short hair. He was unlikely the driver, as he was adorned in a suit, shirt and tie, wearing a woollen trench coat and scarf, which suggested they had been outside, exposed to the chill of the air, not behind the wheel of a heated vehicle. It was probable that they were simply a witness, or passer-by as the incident had occurred.

In the periphery of his vision there were many people walking about, some of whom may also have been witnesses or other passers-by; and yet others may have been they who had hit him. Perhaps this had caused other vehicles to be involved also. He felt sorry for the driver that had been unable to avoid him, like a train track jumper from the platform of a railway station just as the carriage approaches. The driver would have had no control or ability to make any evasive manoeuvre. At very best, they may have been able to scrub off a few digits from their forward speed before colliding with him, but it was likely they were going at regular pace at the point of the impact. He knew that he was the cause and that he had stepped into the road without giving due care and attention to the other road users travelling at right angles to him, and whom had priority on the carriageway.

The man kneeling beside him rose and began waving as though to gain attention, gesturing for others to come to his whereabouts, and then started pointing down at him. This had suggested the arrival of the emergency services, and within no time at all, two uniformed police officers stepped around him to inspect the vehicle that had evidently been involved and speak to the other peripheral persons. They were followed momentarily by two paramedics who began asking him questions that he would expect as he had seen in TV shows and movies. The smartly dressed caretaker explained that he had been unresponsive and it was likely he had concussion and cranial swelling, and suggested administering certain medications that he had never heard of before. This man must have some medical background.

Within only a few minutes, the paramedics responded appropriately and having used two hypodermic needles to inject some unknown substances, he felt a sudden jolt that seemed to raise him ever so slightly from the ground and changed the feeling of pressure against the way he laid. Evidently, they had got him onto a snap board, and then proceeded to lift the lot, and place it on to a trolley bed. They hadn't restrained him he realised, no neck brace, no straps to prevent his body from significant movement. He took this as a good sign, as it was likely that he had no lasting damage.

As they began to wheel the trolley, he lay there, looking upwards, only having sight of the sky above him, cold grey clouds floated like a layer of rolling canvas with patches of light and dark. The edges of the building roofs around him encased the view like a porthole looking out to the ocean, slowly moving as he felt the wobble of the trolley wheels passing over the tarmac.

Having arrived at the ambulance, he was transferred to the vehicle and one of the paramedics got in with him and began to connect him to two intravenous feeds, as the other stood at the rear doors talking with the attending police officers. The one tending to him was wearing a large digital watch and he managed to catch a glimpse of the time.

14:41.

He had no concept of how long he had been laid there on the tarmac since he regained consciousness as every minute had felt like an age. He had only lost just over two thirds of an hour so far, but in his condition, this was likely to continue. The paramedic gave him another shot from a needle, and within a few seconds, he began to feel unfrozen. It was as though he was thawing out, slowly from his extremities, sensation of movement began to return, creeping closer to his inner core. Whatever the newest drug to be administered was, it was something miraculous to his condition.

He could articulate his fingers and was soon able to form a fist with his left hand, and he felt the tug of the IV needle in the back of the hand as he did. His right hand was being treated by the medicine man, bound with fabric bandages. It seemed far less than optimal, and as he tried to move his fingers and show that he was regaining function, the paramedic told him not to. Another few minutes passed, and the man had finished a basic swaddling wrapping of the hand that now felt heavy with the extent of materials used to encase it.

He heard a new voice at the rear of the ambulance, a female voice that sounded familiar to him. He was unable to distinguish the words, but he knew the voice well. It was difficult, nigh on impossible for him to ever forget that voice. He was certain of its owner. His heart began to race, signalling an increased speed of repetition to the beeping sounds from a machine to his left, and this caused the paramedic to take note. 'Calm down' he said, 'we have you under control now, don't worry'.

Being unable to offer a verbal response, and still not having enough function in his arm to gesticulate to the direction of the new vocal owner, he tried as he may to point with his eyes, engaging the medicine man, then darting to the door;

back to the man then back to the door, repeatedly, before finally fixing his gaze at the door. The medicine man seemed to understand and got up, placing his hands above his head resting on the top of the opening of the rear doors, he leaned out in a nonchalant way, and engaged the discussion of those gathering outside, and gave them an account of what actions he had taken in fulfilment of his roll with the patient.

The Police were happy for the ambulance to leave, stating that they would catch up with the injured man later to take a statement. They asked which hospital he would be taken to, and a name was given. Despite being several feet away, the noise of the machines around him, and the hum of the ambulance engine, he was sure he heard accurately, though it was not a hospital familiar to him, clearly not being from this area himself.

'You can ride with us' a voice said, evidently the other paramedic. He assumed at first that he was speaking to one of the police officers, but then he continued 'She's his fiancé,' he told the medicine man.

Now his heart pounded in his chest, he knew that the voice he heard was indeed hers. It was unmistakable, unforgettable. All the attributes of her personality were strangely encompassed in her voice. The tone, manner and speed of her speech had displayed her kindness, gentleness and caring heart and was one of the qualities he had first remarked upon when they had initially started dating.

How was she here? How did she find him? What would she think of all that was happening to him? She'll know of course of the incident of him being knocked down, but he had so much to tell her of his last 16 hours, how would he even begin? Could he even begin? Presently he was still voiceless, unable to engage his mouth to create speech and vocalise all that he wished to say.

Her face appeared at the rear door as the medicine man turned to take a seat. She regarded him for a moment before climbing inside. The look on her face spoke of desperation and despair, despite which, she somehow seemed to him to be more beautiful than ever before. Her make-up wasn't done, and her hair a little wild; she looked as though she had been frantically searching for him since his disappearance.

She had evidently observed him in such a state that there was a look of hopelessness sinking across her being as she began to climb into the ambulance. It was then that the situation went from bad to worse. It seemed as if time had slowed down as she slowly rose into the rear of the vehicle, and he wondered if his eyes were deceiving him, or his mind playing tricks. As she came into view, there it was, fur collar, black jacket, plain white polo, pants, all spoke of her connection to the same sordid affair as he was engaged in.

35 was written on the breast of her jacket.

There was no comprehensible thought that followed, as everything concerning this began to swell in his mind at once. This is why he couldn't contact her. This is why her voicemail box was full. She had been taken as he had, possibly at the same time. She too was infected with the deadly toxin that was likely to kill unless the potion was taken. She too was approaching the end of her time, in fact, she had only four hours and change.

The reality suddenly smacked him with such force that it was worse than the vehicular impact he had suffered not an hour ago. She was his predecessor!

She was the one from whom, out of whom, he needed to retrieve his potion, she was the one that would give him life, but this meant death for her. And if she were to die, what good would there be for him to live onwards, and what reason would he have to continue?

As she took a seat within the cabin, the medicine man was explaining his condition, being unresponsive et cetera, but that they had given him something which showed early signs of good results and he hoped that within a few hours they would know more of the long-term effects. His condition in general was quite alarming, and they could not be sure there was nothing broken without further tests, however; they were concerned with the head trauma and wanted to run some scans before saying any more.

A few hours? He did not have the luxury of sparing a few hours in dealing with this. He cursed himself for his naivety and stupidity in not having paid proper attention to his surroundings. How ridiculous of anyone in normal circumstances, but when time is such a significant factor, what he had already lost to this was more valuable than any wealth he had accumulated in his years since birth.

One of the officers also stepped into the vehicle, and the dialogue that followed suggested that the curly haired former player may not have got her message out at all, or if she had, it had either not been believed, or had not filtered down through the masses of law enforcement, and certainly not to the general public through bulletins and broadcasts. He was reading her her rights, a formal police caution, though he had agreed to not engage any restraints. It was very clear that she, his fiancé, 35, was under arrest.

As the vehicle slowly began to move on, she attempted to explain her position to the uniformed warrior and what she knew of what was going on, but the man shot her down and advised her that it would be for her own good not to say anything at all until she were being formally interviewed by the assigned task force, one of whom would be meeting them at the hospital, where she would then be taken to a station for questioning.

She asked the paramedic for permission before taking hold of his hand, her right interlocking with his left, and her left cupping them both. He felt the warmth of her touch and it was an intense sensation of pleasure to have her so close, after the longing, yearning, wondering for the last 17 hours and the thoughts of never seeing her again; to be able to feel the embrace of his hand in hers was near climactic.

He could feel the pulse of her heart rushing through her hands, it was fast, but not overly so, just elevated from what he thought was natural. He did a quick count and figured on about 95 beats per minute before wondering why this mattered. He was simply doing all he could with the sensations available to him. He was otherwise a vegetable, lay there with no ability to move or to speak. An inanimate object wasting away, wasting time. The longer he lay there, the more likely it was he would get them both killed.

Time was running out, and though he lay there, still feeling like every passing minute was an hour, it seemed like the countdown to doom was moving more rapidly than before.

15:00

The ambulance would stop every so often, which he assumed was due to traffic or signals, and it occurred to him that the driver felt no sense of urgency as they were not proceeding with emergency lights and sirens blazing, just steadily gliding along with the rest of the road users. Amid the noise of the vehicle's engine, the machinery surrounding him, the chirping of the two radios, one at the dashboard and one on the officer's collar each emitting muffled voices telling of other incidents needing emergency responder assistance; there was a faint sound of her humming.

He had always enjoyed her humming and had found it soothing; a melodic tune of her own making, never something he had heard before. She was gifted. The humming was a technique she had been taught as a child to help her deal with a specifically traumatic event that had occurred when her father was killed in front of she and her mother during a home invasion robbery. Since therapy, she had always hummed during times where her mind was overly active, especially when dealing with stress and anxiety. Regarding her as he lay there, otherwise unable to move, he could see that her eyes were fixed, her stare engaged at a point over his shoulder; not that she was looking, but that she was lost in her mind, her eyes had glossed over, and she was deep in cognitive processing.

The ambulance had stopped once more, yet the noise outside spoke of moving vehicles. Horns sounded and there were various indistinguishable shouts from frustrated road users, all of which were unlikely to elicit any reaction that they intended. From complete standstill, the ambulance lurched forward with vicious force. It was evident that this was not the doing of the driver. All of the seated occupants were shifted uncomfortably from their positions with expressions of horror and surprise across their faces. They each tried to steady themselves as a second jolt caused the vehicle to spin with the rear coming around towards the front. It must have shifted 90 degrees so he thought. They had been hit by something else. The fact that there was second impact, was either careless driving of multiple people, or it was deliberate intent.

The commotion that erupted within the ambulance was a ruckus of expletives and profanity. There was as much happening outside, with lots of shouting. The officer jumped to his feet and went to reach for the door handle but the air cracked with the sound of gunshots from outside. 1, 2, 3.

The officer, alarmed by this took a half step backwards and drew his side arm, and whilst he held this pointed downwards by his waist, he took hold of the door handle in his free hand, but as he did, he found it was ripped open from outside. Startled, the man let off a shot, discharging his firearm as more of an autonomic response to the forceful opening of the door, than any calculated decision to open fire. It was careless, and without aim. The noise of the discharge within the ambulance was deafening, with little room for the sound waves to dissipate, instead bouncing off every internal surface, causing an intense sound of thunder. It had been the officer's counterpart and colleague that he had just displaced with a 9mm slug, whose sure footing had given way with delayed reaction and he slumped to his backside clutching at his shoulder.

The one who fired, jumped out to aide his wounded colleague. Heaven only knows what must have filled that man's mind at that time, having just given friendly fire to his companion. But as soon as his feet hit the floor, another crack burst forth and in simultaneous action, the sound was accompanied by one side of the man's head exploding outwards, and his body was felled like a tree, keeling over to the ground lifeless. The seated wounded man drew his hand from his shoulder and appeared to shout out, though he heard no sound, his head filled with tinnitus ringing from the shot that went off inside. And the wounded man was now lifeless too, spread out in a star shape on the tarmac.

She began screaming, and the driver pressed the ambulance into action, but it was clearly blocked in by other vehicles and there were several impacts as the one at the helm tried to ensure their escape from the scene. With more cracks of thunder from outside, they suddenly stopped, and the engine revs increased to the red line for a few seconds and then dropped, returning to an idol hum barely audible over the continued inner ear ringing. Though he could not see him, the driver was doubtlessly dead.

The attempted manoeuvres had caused the rear door of the ambulance to swing back around and it was almost closed, letting light spill in through a crack only a fingertip wide. The door moved. It was opened a few inches, then closed completely. As it did, there was a thud and a hiss inside. The cabin began to fill with smoke and she and the medicine man gasped for breath. He felt like he wanted to also, but his body was still not responding to anything more than making a fist. He tried to sit up, and realised that he had some motor functions, he could feel the twitch of muscle fibres through his stomach and chest; but did not have the strength or ability to raise himself. The others were now on hands and knees, choking. It was perilous, and despite his desire to do something, he was confined to the mercy of whatever was happening now. He had never felt so hopeless, so useless.

The vehicle was thick with a white gas until the door flew open once more. The other two were evidently incapacitated to a degree near to his own, as they lay there, wrestling their own chests struggling to breathe. The silhouette of a man appeared at the door, and he began to methodically disconnect the two IV lines and the monitor from him without any sense of urgency or speed, before dragging the trolley outside. This was some scene. Whoever this newcomer was, he had wreaked havoc, causing a major road traffic incident, and seemingly had gunned down two police officers and the ambulance driver.

Now in the daylight, no longer surrounded by the gaseous substance, he observed that this assailant was another of the participants of this wretched debacle. The clothing gave him away. He was late thirty's, maybe early fourties', and had a look of having not shaved for a week. There was a large scar on his left cheek that did not have the appearance of a clean cut but was jagged and of differing thicknesses. It was not fresh, but still remained a slightly purple colour showing that although it was likely a few months or possibly a year old, it had not fully healed. The man's frame was thin but broad, yet he had somewhat of a muscular form hidden beneath that jacket. He could not see his number.

As the man moved around the trolley bed, the fur collar of his coat was stained with blood on the right-hand side, and he noticed that on the opposite side of his head to the scar, the man had a stripe of flesh coloured bandage tape from the temple to behind the ear just above the blood stains. The trolley span around with a few bumps from the uneven surface of the tarmac below, and he was shoved into another vehicle, a much smaller van with a dark interior, with bare exposed metal work and no interior fixings. All he could see were the back of the seats in front of him. The doors behind remained open yet he was aware he was alone.

After a few score of seconds, the assailant returned, and behind him, seemed to struggle to climb into the back of the van. It became clear why. She was with him, unconscious and carried over his shoulder. There was no care or consideration given to how that bastard dropped her onto the floor in a heap beside him, like a discarded piece of furniture. Despite the willingness to display graphic violence this newcomer had just bestowed to the emergency responders; if he were in control of his currently defunct body, he would put up whatever effort he could to give this guy a good hiding.

But presently he remained a prisoner confined within his own carcass. There was still little movement he could muster, but he knew that it was not completely elusive. Only a half hour ago, he couldn't move at all, then a finger, then a fist, and now there were twitching fibres all over his being, muscles straining to work hard enough to result in real movement. He prayed again, the second time this day. He asked God for strength and returned function that he could escape from this new menace, and to save her also. She, his prize and his pride, would be like putty in this man's hands. She was not more than a metre and a half tall, and maxed out at 60 kilograms when carrying 'holiday weight'. She was petite to say the least.

Why had this scar faced man taken him; taken them? Evidently, he was one more lost soul, dancing to the tune of the tormentor, unseen and unknown, directing the debauchery of their demise. What did he want with him? What did he want with her? They had obviously been visible dots on Scarface's wristband. Whilst the red Parka of the copy shop clerk would throw some fleeting glance from immediately connecting him to the sordid story, his pants and pumps would confirm him as a contender. She was in full garb, the uniform of the damned, mirrored in the pawn of the puppet master that now commanded control of their direction.

Perhaps this scar faced arrival had come to their rescue?

But the bastard had been bullish and beastly. He had killed without cause and taken them both. What did he want of them? Was this a dying man, approaching his final hours, and like he had heard of earlier players, was relentlessly rampaging to do all they could to see an end to this madness?

Perhaps he had deliberately targeted one of them?

Unconscious and slumped there, looking more dishevelled than she had a half hour ago, he remarked at her features in a way that he never had before. Perhaps it was because he was unable to do anything else, so there he lay, gawping, taking in every detail, as for all he knew, these may be their final moments. Her cheekbones were strong and solid, riding high in her features, her jaw line a little wider than average form for her size, something that she was not fond of. That one element all women have that they hate about themselves; this was hers. Her nose was round and dainty and the remnant of a once rebellious phase remained in a pretty little metallic dot to the top of the right nostril. Her eyelashes were thick and full and even since she was a babe-in-arms it had been something that everyone had commented upon, how she would never need mascara. She looked a little older than she was, again something she wasn't best pleased with, and at times had tried to dress herself younger. But she was six years his junior and she felt it was immature to continue to dress like a teenager when they had become serious.

How her life had been taken from her in so few years she had lived. She had been dealt a rough hand in her past and now she was possibly living her last. Even if they could get out of this, it was a further trauma to deal with trying to move on with life. And then he realised......

She had less than an hour left to find her predecessor before their clock ran out.

He wondered what she knew of what was going on, how much she was aware of in the twisted Chinese whispers that had worked its way through the 'players' of this insane game of misfortune. Would she have discovered anything of the truth? Did she know the reality of the poison and the presence of the antidote? Was she as naive as he and the ogre had been in thinking that it was something their predecessor had on their person? The horror of the truth was all but unspeakable, the kind of thing a man would want to protect his family from, but she had been exposed to this in such a way that he could not hide it from her, he could not protect her from this horror.

And what of 34?

Now, at this very time, whoever they were, however close they were, was right now so far away. They may have been within easy striking distance of him when he had been stupid enough to have been hit by the car. Had he been able to reach them, could he have overpowered them, and taken from them not only their life, but the ability to give life to her, his future wife, who now seemed to have little hope?

But could he have? Really? He had spent so much time already pondering his ability, physically and morally, to take the life of another person to save his own; but had not until now considered the possibility of taking the life of another innocent to save his beloved. Would he? Could he go the extra mile to ensure her survival? What kind of future would that mean for either of them? To live with having taken the life of someone else in order that they could live?

HOLY SHIT

For the first time, it dawned on him.

There was no way out of this for him now.

If by some miracle, they were able to locate 34 again, and retrieve from them the vial that they held within, then his fiancé would surpass the affliction of the toxic substance that would otherwise take her life - and that meant he would be unable to retrieve his vial from her.

She had lived with loss before, her father had been her world until she was eight years old, a true daddy's girl; and then he was snatched by the clutches of evil. With difficulty she had coped, she had managed, and he was sure that given time, she could do it again with the loss of him. His sole focus now was to ensure her survival, though the chances of this were slim!

And then what would have become of his own fate? If he was able to secure her survival, then he faced only certain doom. There seemed no way of retrieving what he needed to save himself without harming her. But presently, there remained a very strong probability that there was no hope for her now. Where was 34?

He lay there, motionless, still confined by his inability to force any significant movement from his shell. And as he did, he wandered through the memories formed not so long ago, pacing the streets of his mind, back tracking to those fleeting interactions he had had with others, who may now give him clues enough to secure the thing vital to his predecessor, his fiancé, the body now heaped beside him.

Time seemed to pass, and in his concentration on trying to recall any information that may help them find 34, he gave no regard to the thoughts of fear one may ordinarily expect if they were kidnapped in such an aggressive way by the now driver of this desolate vehicle in which they were captive. Once more, he remarked that the van seemed to stop and roll intermittently, again as if filing in with other traffic. It seemed that this newcomer was not in any rush to get anywhere, despite having killed people to attain the captives.

And all the while, he could see the back of this man's head from where he laid. Nothing about him gave any clue to who this scar-face was. He recounted the works of Doyle once more, and the ability of a certain Mr Holmes to read the subtleties of a person and make deductions about their background, life, vocation, social status. In this day and age, such was a much more difficult task, but with these numbered people running about in the uniform attire, having witnessed, encountered, contributed to such atrocities as they had, it was not likely he could make any logical inference. This whole business was illogical to him.

His functions were presently returning. He now had limited movement of both arms and legs, and very soon he may be able to move about, though he considered that the pain was likely to prevent much of his mobility. He would surely be once more remanded by the inability to use his body normally, as he had from the car wreck when Goliath had collapsed at the wheel.

This day was going from frying pan to fire. The sequence of events that had unfolded over the last 18 hours had undoubtedly been the singular worst day in the life of anyone he knew. Was it possible that it could get any worse, he thought? There indeed was still so much possibility of that. The likelihood of saving her was ebbing away with every moment that passed as the pair of them lay immovable in this rolling prison. He needed to take control. Was it possible that he could overpower the captor? Even if he regained full control of his bodily functions, would he have the strength and ability to get the drop on the newcomer?

He would likely need some form of weapon, something at least that he could use as a club to smack the man in the head with enough force to at least render him unconscious, if not causing some lasting damage. He needed to create sufficient time to be able to get away. But she was still unconscious, and how soon after she woke would she have control of her functions? Perhaps this vehicle provided their greatest opportunity of escape. If he could somehow get the other out, and be able to drive away himself, this would be most beneficial. He looked about resolutely for something to wield as a mace upon his captor.

Yet as it was, he could still not even sit up. Slowly but surely, his body was regaining the ability to utilise itself, but it was not fast enough. He knew not how long the newcomer would keep them in this vehicle, nor to where they were being transported, though he could hazard a guess as to the why. Time had been in short supply since he woke up in that cooler the previous night, and time was now much shorter.

Then he noticed that she was awake. Her head had raised ever so slightly, and she was looking directly at him, with baffled confusion etched into her features. Evidently, she could move with ease. She placed her palms down on the floor, and straightening her arms, she shifted her body position to be more upright. And with which, she silently took stock of the situation, seemingly aware that there was need to be as inconspicuous as ever.

They exchanged a dialogue of silent conversation with intense and expressive looks and eye movements. He hoped that he had been able to convey that they needed to escape. She seemed to understand. There was a small powder fire extinguisher above the seats in the cabin of the vehicle, which she was now pointing at. As quietly as possible, she manoeuvred herself to her knees and on all fours, positioned herself to take hold of the thing. As she tried to remove it from its housing, she realised it was strapped down. A simple fabric strap with a Velcro fastener.

Without further thought, she pulled at the strap and released the extinguisher, but the tearing of the Velcro went with an instant audible ripping noise, that alerted Scarface to something happening. As his head spun around, he looked at her with anger and disgust. 'Bitch' he shouted, as she pulled the pin and let off the thing in his face. Powder erupted from the nozzle filling Scarface's eyes and mouth and causing him to slam on the brakes. The vehicle came abruptly to a stop and just as it did, she raised the canister and drove it downwards, heel first, into the top of the man's skull.

She repeated the action and then swung the thing from the side, striking his head a third time, and driving it into the door pillar, rendering him incapacitated. With a fear that he may yet take hold of her, she reached over the man and pulled on the door handle causing it to open a little, and she shoved at his shoulders trying to push him out. And out he went, slumping down to the road outside.

Quickly, she clambered over into the driver's seat in a flash and tried to pull the door closed. But Scarface was not as subdued as she thought, and he put up some resistance to her efforts, pushing back against the door. She tried several times to viciously yank the door closed, but the man resisted, though clearly able to do little else, as there was no sign of him getting back to his feet, or putting up more of a fight to take back control of the situation. She slammed the vehicle into gear and gassed it hard to get away, leaving the man behind.

She had been the hero to him that he was contemplating of himself being for her.

She drove for several minutes, seeming to calm with the passing of time; as the adrenalin rush was fading, so too was the speed, urgency and erraticness of the vehicle. After a brief few moments, believing that she had put enough distance between them and Scarface, she pulled into a disused automated car wash, and drove into the old machine, in an effort to camouflage the van.

As the vehicle stopped, she looked about for what must have been only 30 seconds, but seemed like a half hour. Satisfied that they were safe, for the next few minutes at least, she climbed back into the load space, knelt beside him and took hold of his hand.

16:00

As she knelt there beside him, she sobbed and sobbed, pressing his hand into the side of her face. Her skin felt cool and he took this to mean a sign of her fright and alarm, that her systems were still working hard in that fight-or-flight mode, pumping oxygen to fuel the muscles not the flesh, thus draining her skin of additional heat. She lifted her head, and sweeping her hand across her reddened face, gathered her hair from one side and pulled it backwards across her scalp, exposing her beauty as she gazed at him, her eyes full of tears.

It seemed like a long while before she spoke. 'What the hell is happening to us?' she asked.

He tried to respond, but he was only able to make muted sounds more akin to an interrupted signal with phone calls on the old cellular networks that had dried up when he was only mid-teens. His ability to control his functions had clearly not extended itself, thus far, to his speech.

Realising that she was only able to convey her messages, and unable to receive any legible verbal response, she decided to bring him up to speed. Consistent to his calculations, she had been awakened at around 7pm the night before and found herself naked in a morgue. She too had wondered whether she had been mistaken for dead and left there. She had found a pile of clothes neatly folded, dressed herself and went in search of help, only to find the place desolate, with all doors locked, save for those which led outside.

Her first instinct was to stop a passer-by, but they had been dismissive of her and carried on their way. Moments later, her wrist band buzzed and lit up, giving her the instruction to find 34. She had been confused and could make no sense of it. What was 34 she had wondered?

She had tried to get hold of him, as he had her; she stopped another passer-by and asked to use their phone, but he had not picked up; each time she tried, he was not there, no answer; and she had been unable to leave a message. At some point, she realised that they had been together that she last remembered, and she had considered the possibility that he too was party to what was happening. Was he involved in some sinister way even? She had considered every eventuality, even things she never thought possible, she had questioned his integrity among the myriad of possibilities.

Being led by the map on her band, she had engaged in several interactions with others, and determined that 34 was, in fact, a person. She hadn't even noticed her own number, until someone else had pointed it out. She had come to hear tales of death, peculiar stories of clock watching, and time running out. With more messages through her band, and further investigation of its functions, she had seen the 'one day to live' message that she had somehow previously missed. With what she had learnt from others, it then came as no surprise to her that this countdown was 24 hours from the awakening.

She had understood that this had been happening for some time. If she was 35, there were at least 34 predecessors. One per three hours, that meant eight per day, so she was almost four days into this madness. Had all of them died she had wondered? She had postulated the rhyme and reason for the torment in this bizarre turn of fortune, and why these people, herself included, were now sheep to the control of a hidden shepherd, herding the numbered folk through the instructions on their bands.

She had been told of a poison and an antidote, but believed it untrue as neither she, nor anyone else she had interacted with, had found anything of the sort on their person. Yet that gave no explanation for the mysterious deaths that were reported to her of the previous numbers. She had believed that something had been twisted somewhere, and the most likely explanation was in some way connected to the strange hospital like tags at the wrist of each of the unfortunate souls caught up in this nonsense.

Perhaps in some way, the interaction with their predecessor would deactivate some timing device that would otherwise bring an end to life. As she spoke of these things, her gaze drifted subconsciously to his wrist, and she saw that he too had such a tag. He too was a player in this sickening sideshow.

She suddenly became animated, energetic, and flung herself to her feet, grabbing hold of his other hand and twisting his arm to expose his band to hers. Excitement was in her being, but in futility, she touched the two together, over and over, with ever increasing pressure, until she was virtually banging their wrists on one another with some force. He remarked the pain becoming more and more intense, and he knew this was a good sign that as feeling was returning, it was likely that his motion would also.

But presently, she was deflated that there had been no magical display of the two bands getting so close. She examined the two with great intent, hoping to find something new she had not seen before, something that could connect the two together. After a time, she gave up. He knew of course that her efforts had been in vain, for he knew that the reality of what was happening was far more monstrous than she would care to envisage.

As she had conducted her inspection in the hope of being able, as his predecessor, to save him from his ill-gotten fate; he was all too aware that his only hope was her doom. He remarked to himself that he had never seen a movie, watched a TV show, or read a novel, that was quite as deranged and twisted as the situation in which he found himself entailed. He wondered how much of the truth he would tell her, as it now seemed impossible to save her life. 34 would have passed from existence, to be more of a shell than even he was presently; lifeless, innate, hollow.

The reality of her imminent death, in less than a trio of hours, began to weigh heavy on his mind. Need he subject her to the mental anguish and trauma of the worry for the next three hours, knowing that she will at some point likely cease to be mentally with him; or was it more humane to pursue a search for 34, even in their hours of death, to give her a false hope? He knew the latter would serve him better, as she may otherwise simply give up now.

At any event, he resolved that he would be with her in her dying moments, and that although there was no hope of him saving her, he would be able to prevent his own demise. But the truth of this was too horrifying for her to know. He would have to butcher and mutilate her corpse to retrieve from it that vial that would end his affliction, and if she knew what was required, she would never forgive him, even in death; even if that meant he could live. She would haunt him, and he knew it.

As she came to realise there was nothing of value in her search, she regarded her own apparatus with conviction, and poked and prodded at the thing clearly deep in intense engagement, staring at the miniature screen. He presumed that she was taking stock of their whereabouts in relation to any other numbered player, and then for the first time since they had come to rest within this desolate machine, he thought of Scarface and his probable pursuit of them, subject of course to any lasting damage she may have inflicted with the fire extinguisher.

Wherever he was now, if he was of able movement, there was no doubt that he would be chasing them down. His purpose was sure, his goal was known, and he had already extended to significant violence to achieve it. Murder and mayhem. This man would be relentless, unless she had given him sufficient injury to prevent his pursuit.

She became alarmed, 'He's close' she said, 'We'd better move', and she leant over and pressed her lips softly against his forehead, her hair falling back down and tickling his ear and neck as it did, before swiftly brushing across his face as she turned, rising to an upright position and resolutely set for the driver's seat. She jumped over and pressed the start button, but there was no life in the engine. She tried again. And again. She became frantic, 'Just bloody start' she shouted, but still there was no chug from the engine, just a low electrical 'ding' from the dash. 'Shit' she cried, 'the automated services have run the remote shut off, probably because of the impacts.... We're stranded in here, shit'.

The technology had initially been aimed at preventing drivers from fleeing the scene of an accident. Fat lot of good it had served here, he thought to himself. The shut off had been way too late, he figured it had been at least 10 minutes to get from the ambulance to the car wash. But now they were trapped, unless they were on foot, and his feet were just not working. They needed another solution. They had to run, but how?

She had opened the driver's door and slipped out, seconds later pulling open the rear of the van and heaving with every inch of her miniscule frame, she forced his trolley prison to move and spill out on to the mishmash of concrete and metal that formed the innards of this auto-wash. She dragged the thing as best as she could until they got to the mouth of the machine, where the ground, now solid and devoid of any grooves, rails or other deformities, allowed her to spin the trolley about and push him along. 'Shit' once more erupted from her. He came to a swift stop and was aware she had walked away but as she was behind him, he was unable to see what she was doing.

Within a few short seconds she returned, and with one hand on the back of his bed, she swung around to his side, and placed his satchel and a moderately sized pistol in his lap. 'I'm Solo, you're Skywalker' she said, 'I'll be the pilot, you're the guns, okay flyboy!'. He realised she wasn't joking, and it suddenly occurred to him that he had grabbed a hold of the sides of the mobile bed on which he was now partially laid, partially seated, and had in fact pressed with sufficient force to slightly change his position. *I can move* he thought, '*I can actually move my arms!*' and he realised that it being something one ordinarily takes for granted, he had failed to note the significance of his doing so whence he had.

He tried to speak once more but failed. Again, simply a grumbled muttering of half spoken words spilled out of his mouth, only this time, he felt the drool that accompanied it and ran down his chin; so instead, he raised his arm and gave her a 'thumbs up', before taking hold of the weapon and drawing it down off his lap and next to his side. Though he knew he had the ability to move his arm, move the gun even; he doubted that he had the strength to raise the thing, take aim, and squeeze that trigger with enough might to let loose a miniature missile towards Scarface or any other would-be assailant.

They were moving along now and though it wasn't necessarily uncomfortable, this rolling quasi-bed-chair did anything but glide along the uneven surface of the roadways and footpaths beneath him. The oddity of their appearance drew strange stares from onlookers and by-standers, pretty much every soul that passed by would glare at the strange site of a man being wheeled down the street on an ambulance trolley, jostling him about, near rattling the teeth out of his head.

The streets continued to move, unchanging, unaltered by their presence, and it occurred to him that the news had not yet broken, the curly haired woman from the police station had been thus far unsuccessful in getting the story known to the masses. He wondered whether the police would accept her account, whether they would give any credibility to the bizarre exposé of a seemingly mad woman who had likely murdered a man, disembowelled him, and gave herself up to the authorities. Yes, her actions had been more akin to the psychotically deranged psychopaths.

Her intentions could well have fallen at the first hurdle. All her talk of opening Pandora's Box to the authorities would most likely have been swept away, dismissed and debunked, as a feeble attempt to distract their investigations into the crime for which she was responsible. But... he thought, what if they had believed? What if they accepted her account? Lord knows there was evidence enough with the stories of strange happenings for weeks, the 'cult' of people, unknowns, nobodies, being involved in such atrocities. What of the wrist band she had worn, the information she had that could be verified, corroborated?

And if she still had the vial in which her antidote had been, there was a possibility of analysis, experimentation to determine the chemical make-up for the purpose of reproduction. She would of course also have a complete, unopened, unused vial insider herself. Perhaps the police were at this very minute working frantically to replicate the contents for the purpose of saving the remaining players. Perhaps this was why the news had not already broken, maybe they would put out an all-ports broadcast to call forward anyone involved once they were sure that they could save them?

It was all speculation, and quite fanciful at that, so he thought.

Daylight was fading fast; street lighting had already come on, providing an orange tone to the pallet of colour that laid before them, as the grey of the sky held a purple hue to what he perceived to be the west, where the last remnants of the day's sunlight remained low in the sky. The cold was creeping back in. It had never fully left, but with the tumult that had occurred over the last few hours, he simply hadn't noticed. Now he was exposed on this rickety platform, but unmoving in himself, generating no heat from movement. The chill was biting.

With the motion of cars and other traffic sweeping past them, the air rush created had caused him to grimace and again, he knew that his motor functions were returning. Releasing his grip on the pistol, he tried to raise his arm, hand gun-less, but pointing with a finger and thumb in a 'gun-like' action, testing his abilities. His hand still was a little limp at the wrist, but in another few minutes, he would be able to hold the weapon out if needed. He realised he was facing the wrong way. She was pushing him from behind. If Scarface was pursuing them, surely, he would come up from behind. He wondered how she was monitoring this.

He could hear sirens in the distance behind him, and another approaching from ahead. An ambulance appeared into view and raced through the traffic, dodging, weaving through the cars as it screamed past them. He wondered if it was heading to the wake of destruction left by their pursuer. It dawned on him that he was now able to see his own wrist band, he raised his arm, and gave the familiar flick. As he poked at the screen with his free hand, the trolley hit a bump and a sound followed that was a thick thud, as he grasped to support himself from toppling off.

'Sorry' she called out from behind. 'We need to get off the roads. Any changes going on with you? We need you off this bed'. He again raised his arm and gave a further 'thumbs up'. Glancing around, they were approaching a side road on his right. She had begun to manoeuvre the trolley as though to swing its weight around the bend and ready herself behind it for the change in forces as it did. As they started to turn the corner, he could feel her struggle to stabilise the thing, fighting hard for it to not get the better of her.

It was no use, there was no way she could prevent the altering weight distribution and the rolling motion of the thing to want to keep going in a straight line. The momentum continued, causing it to career to the edge of the footway and the front left wheel went over, and nose-dived towards the road. The buckaroo effect shifted him, and gravity was far too great a foe for him to battle in his weakened, debilitated state. He was going down and he knew it. There was little he could do to even break his fall.

Though it was nothing compared to other impacts he had experienced so very recently, hitting the ground sent a shock through him that he felt in every muscle, every joint. But, he could feel it! He could feel the movement of his limbs as his torso was shifted, forcing his arms and legs to fly about like a toy doll being dropped to the floor. But he felt them, he really felt them.

As he came to rest in a crumpled heap, his immediate reaction was to try and sit himself up, and to his surprise, he could. She had rushed around to his aid and was similarly elated that he was able to at least partially lift himself. Having checked that he was okay, no further injuries at least, she crawled around behind him, and wrapping her arms under his and around his chest, she dragged him, a few inches at a time back to the kerb stone and heaved him up onto the footpath. It was only when they got there that he realised that nobody else had stopped to help or assist. Passing cars had simply carried on their way, with no care for the fallen man. 'Fucking people!' he thought.

Being sure that he could manage to sit unassisted, she picked up the trolley and positioned it as though she intended to get him back on. He knew that she would never be able. He was little more than a dead weight, and he would need to be able to help, which was presently a little too much to ask. She told him what she was going to do, and he shook his head. '*No*' he managed to mutter, surprised at how legible it had been. *Just give me a few minutes*', at least that was what he had tried to say. She seemed to have grasped what he meant.

She had told him that time was precious and that the assailant would likely be gaining on them. She realised that the gun would have fallen from the bed and searched around them, but there was no sign of it, even in the road. Where could it be she asked? She was clearly agitated. He was able to ask her to help him to move, but those three words had come out not quite as clearly as he had hoped, though again she had understood him. Between the pair of them, they were able to organise moving him laterally across the floor, where he could prop himself against the side of the corner building.

'*It dropped*' he managed, '*back there, the gun*' and he pointed back down the way from which they had come. It had fallen when the bump had jolted him. Furious, she challenged him about why he had not said. He hadn't realised at the time, but regardless, he wasn't able to tell her anyway, other than perhaps to try and attract her attention in some way. She figured this was likely the case without interrogating him further. She moaned about it but told him to sit tight whilst she went to find the thing. There weren't that many people walking the streets, but surely someone would have seen it and then who knew what would have happened to it, and as she moved on in her search, he could hear the faint undertones of her comments about police or drug dealers. He rolled his eyes.

Several minutes seemed to pass and he decided to consult his band whilst he waited. 16:50. He could tell by the continued plummet from dusk to night that the hour was getting on. There was little more than two hours left that he had with her. Under any normal circumstance, if you knew you were going to die in two hours' time he thought, there were a million and one things they would rather be doing than what they faced in the coming couple of hours.

He checked the map to see how far away she was. She was moving, swiftly. He rolled along the map away from his location, hoping to see that Scarface would be a way off, but he wasn't, he was close, gaining on her. He felt helpless, still trapped in a body that had little motion. He longed to be able to rise to his feet and run towards her, but there was nothing other than minor movements in his lower limbs and he knew he had no power that would allow him to run. He became aware of a sharpness of pain in his right knee and shin, perhaps from the impact with the bumper of the vehicle only a couple of hours ago.

Shock ran though him at the sound of a single gunshot that echoed and reverberated off the buildings around, clearly having emanated from her whereabouts. Almost instinctively, he threw himself onto his side to look around the corner in hopes of discovering if it were she or the assailant that had fired. He pressed down against the floor, raising his shoulders, and lifting his head, he saw she was sprinting towards him. The ferocity with which she moved was overwhelming her ability to control it, she was about to go head over heels when a second shot of sound burst through the air.

She hit the floor, with no grace or dignity, and rolled somewhat uncomfortably, gathering herself back to her feet in a continuous motion, and tried to maintain her sprint. Down she went again, this time with no shot echoing around. She rolled to a stop, turned her head towards him, and once more raised herself to continue her advance, she was now less than 20 metres away, but he could not see her pursuer.

Dragging himself to a position where he could support his upper body against the wall yet still see in her direction, he called out with all his might for her to take cover. He was surprised how audible he had been, that she could notice.

Passing cars had all screeched to a halt at gunfire in the road. Scarface emerged into his view, he was gaining on her, only 30 metres or so beyond where she was now holed up in the doorway of the building against which he was resting.

'*Stay there*' he yelled again.

17:00

———

A round ricocheted off the masonry above her. Scarface moved further out into the road to give himself a better angle of aim around her cover. Another two shots sent brick dust ejecting from the wall over her shoulder. Still moving, Scarface now grabbed his weapon in two hands to stabilise his effectiveness. Helpless, he watched on, now full of fear and anticipation, unable to do anything to help. Another bout of panic that had continually plagued his very being since when he had first awoken, laying helpless, unmoving on the cold steel. And now, he was again unable to move. It was horrifying to be a bystander as she continued to be attacked.

The cacophony of three more shots rang out in rapid succession, although there was no flash from the muzzle of the firearm.

It seemed like slow motion as he watched Scarface crumple, the stature just dropping like a tower in a controlled demolition, caving in on itself.

His immediate thought was that she had fired back and been able to place the slugs on target, but she was still cowering in the corner of the doorway 20 yards up. He scanned around and noticed a man, pistol in hands, across the street, keeping it aimed on the now grounded body of their hunter. Who was this man? He was not one of them, his clothing told him so, unless they had changed. Were they simply the driver of the vehicle behind which they were partially covered? Thank God for the man, whoever they were.

She had noticed Scarface had fallen and she ran to the corner to meet him, keeping low as she advanced. She slid to his side like a baseball player trying to make the 'safe' call under duress. 'What the hell is going on' she uttered, though he was not sure if it was a question or a statement. 'We need to move' she said, mirroring his thoughts.

The unknown shooter had now advanced towards Scarface, who showed just a twitch of motion, indicating that the bullets had not been instantly fatal. The shooter kicked away the weapon that had dropped to the floor when Scarface had toppled, and was now using his phone, pressed between shoulder and head, presumably calling the emergency services. He looked over towards them, and quickly field stripped to parts the weapon that had rendered the other lifeless, placed the pieces on the floor and raised his hand to give them an 'all clear' signal with his thumb raised. The shooter motioned with his hand for them to come over, phone pressed to his head now in the other; but, still without the use of his legs was he, and she was evidently now in shock.

She had earlier coped with valour and courage in the face of such trauma, bringing retaliation to their attacker, but now it seemed, it had gotten the better of her. Perhaps this was the straw that broke the camel's back. Unlike earlier when there was urgent need to escape, perhaps now it was that she knew that Scarface was not going to pursue them anymore. Whatever it was, she had seemed to glaze over and was unresponsive.

The commotion was continually building in the street, as more and more onlookers of those in proximity had come to see what had happened. The inevitable crowd of phones in hand, filming the scene, which would doubtless be the swiftest and most widely reaching media report of this event. Each onlooker seemingly now feeding their online 'social' interactions to the world with the pictures of the wounded and the shooter. Several of them the star of their own show through their handheld gateway to the global media in which they took centre stage; the pair of gunmen in the background - one dead, one victorious - as they talked to their audience. Self-centred arseholes.

They needed to move, to get away from this commotion before the authorities came. He knew that if the police arrived and they were questioned, hell would freeze before they would get out, and meant there was no hope for either of them. Hope was lost now for her, the passing of time meant her predecessor was no more than a lifeless mannequin, posed in the place of their final falling when the poison had taken effect. But if they could both get away from here, despite the brutality of what was required, he knew that there was a possibility of saving himself. No such opportunity existed if they were detained for questioning. Moving on was all he could think of.

His legs, still regaining their feeling, remained to lack the strength to allow him to pick himself up. If he could actually get up, he was confident that he could stand without aid, though walking would likely remain problematic. Getting to his feet was the first hurdle. How queer a thought he pondered, that leaping metaphorical hurdles were his problem, when he could not even stand.

The dross of the crowed had grown and he was aware that several were directing their cameras towards them, and they too would now be visible evidence for the authorities as persons of interest in the events unfolding at the scene, which was undoubtedly being broadcast to the world. How quickly this caught up with them, with him, could easily spell despair. He pondered the reaction time of the Police. With reports of gunfire, they would not likely be more than a few minutes.

The satchel, now slung across his shoulder, had contained several more of the magic pills which had earlier allowed him some swift recovery. He knew not what chemical composition they contained, but they had been instrumental in staving off the earlier traumas his body had endured and allowed him to regain strength and vitality. The problem presently was how long ago he had previously popped the last dosage? Try as he may to remember, the last few hours had blended and merged. Had it been four hours? It must have been more, six perhaps? Regardless, he knew not what schedule one could continue to consume these mystical marvels without a significant knock-on implication on him through other side effects.

The concept of this gave way to the harsher outcome of imminent death if he could not get moving soon. The side effects of the tablets would likely be a far easier puzzle to solve than the grave. But how could he metabolize them faster? He threw two in, chewed them, grinding them as best as he could, and pushed the paste under his tongue hoping that the medicine would be absorbed into the blood faster this way. The taste was foul. The label on the bottle said 'take two every six hours'. It must have been at least that he thought and gulped, struggling to swallow the powdery mixture from his mouth.

The sound of sirens was now echoing off the buildings around them, disguising the direction from which the sound had emerged, but this was accompanied by the ever-growing thump of the whirling turbine of a helicopter. There was no time to lose. They needed to flee from this place. The ambulance trolley looked to be an attractive means to assist his motion. If he could prop himself against it, he may be able to use his legs to propel the thing like leaning heavy on a shopping trolley.

It was too far away for him to reach on his own. Taking her by the hand, which he held with a strong grip, *'The bed'* he called at her, *'grab the bed, we need to leave'*.

Still glazed over, she seemed to hesitate whilst she processed what he said. It took several seconds for her to realise what he wanted her to do. He pulled at her hand in the direction of the trolley, and she moved with it, jumped to her feet and retrieved the thing and brought it directly in front of him. He rolled to one side and placing his palms on the floor, raised his backside from the cold of the concrete, onto all-fours, his back to the bed. With hands now on the brickwork, he lifted his torso perpendicular, and found his balance was good. As he stood further and turned to grasp the trolley, he suddenly realised how little effort it had taken him to be on two feet. This was a blessing.

'I'm okay' he said, *'I think I can manage without this'*.

'Well, let's at least get a hundred metres with it, to see how you fair' she said, 'We can ditch it on the next corner'.

All too aware that the eyes of an unknown multitude were watching them from near and remote locations through the lens of mobile technologies, they were both alert to the fact that their escape from this scene and evading of the police, would not likely happen quickly enough without the use of a vehicle. They were 'on the run', only they could not run, or at least he could not. And what good would it serve either of them if she were to get away but not he? He knew that she had less than two hours ticking away on her life, being alone for this time was not something he wanted for her. And not being with her was now no longer any option, as she held the keys to his chains. If she got away, it was certain doom for he too. Howsoever they did it, they needed to stay together, and they needed to evade the law.

One foot in front of the other, it felt like he was learning to walk for the very first time, as he had seen his nephew do only a couple of years earlier. His sister had been so proud to share video clips of the infant now becoming a toddler, and by the time they had visited only a week later, he was amazed to see how advanced the youngster's tottering abilities had developed. He hoped the same for himself now. Onwards they moved, slow but sure, and being honest with himself, he was glad to have the trolley for support at first, yet with each passing step he was becoming more reliant on the use of his own legs. More good things.

Without warning, hunger struck him. It must have been a half a day since he had last eaten? Breakfast with pyjamas and the kid. His thoughts of food were momentarily interrupted as he considered where the young one would now be up to in his search of others; but the knot in his stomach from the need to pack it once more with sustenance, drove his desires once again. He remembered the food stuffs he packed into the satchel at the house of the rich man. As soon as they had gained some distance from the gunfight behind them, he would need to eat something. He wondered when she had last eaten? He still knew nothing of the details of her day, her telling of the story was only a skimming of the surface.

Yet silence befell them as they continued, even as he relinquished the trolley to continue on of his own accord, not a word was spoken. It was not an awkward silence, and neither of them felt compelled to talk, despite the circumstance and situations they had found themselves in over the last 20 something hours. On they moved.

It was sometime later that they reached a distance of around a quarter of a mile from the street scene carnage and he decided to take a break. Walking was slow, and though she supported him with his arm around her shoulders, and her arm around his waist, it was hard progress. His strength was lacking. The effects of the medicine were now starting to take effect, as he felt less tired, more energetic, but the strength did not match his vigour.

'I need a minute' he said, and sat down on a low brick wall.

'You holding up okay?' she asked, and he closed his eyes and nodded. He needed a drink. He really needed a drink! Something hard. He had acquired a taste for Single Malt Scotch Whiskies and a variety of dark rums; but right now, it was a thirst that needed quenching, not just a desire for alcoholic remedy to his mental and physical torment. He drove his fist into the satchel again and grabbed hold of a bottle. Ripping open the lid, he chugged it back, initially giving no regard as to whether she needed any, chivalry was lost at this point, but then he realised the error of his actions and offered her some.

As she took the bottle, he re-entered the sack, to pull out some snacks, and came upon the coffee flask he had filled from the rich man's kitchen where the body of the ogre lay on the slab of stone worktop. He felt some remorse for his 'friend' as he unscrewed the cap from the flask, the guy knew what was needed, but it was unattainable for him. The curly haired enchantress had stolen away with his remedy, safe from his giant meat hooks.

As he raised the flask to his lips, the smell of the coffee rose through his nostrils, causing a taste sensation before the liquid hit his mouth. He quickly spat it out. 'Cold' he said, as she looked at him in surprise. He re-screwed the lid and set the flask down, diving once more into the bag and retrieving more water. Almost another entire bottle gone in next to no time, and she was taking large mouthfuls of the bottle she held, clearly dropping all decorum of ladylike behaviour. She just came up for air between each swig, whilst he had downed it in one go.

Setting the bag on his lap, he opened it up to inspect what he had. Foil wrapped the cheese and ham rolls, and whilst these would probably be the best source of sustained nutrition for them, the concept reminded him too much of the giant's mutilated corpse on the counter. Cereal bars would do. He handed one to her, remembering now to be chivalrous, and peeled one open himself before taking a huge bite.

It tasted bland, and whilst this was probably nothing to do with the quality of the food itself, and more akin to his state of anguish, he ploughed on through the bar until he had swiftly consumed it and moved on to another, this time no chivalry.

The hour was progressing and he was conscious that in light of her remaining time being less than 90 minutes, they were here, in this random spot, eating and drinking as if death was not just around the corner. How could he approach this with her? What on earth could he possibly say to let her down gently? Was it even worthwhile?

He knew that it would be callous of him to simply ignore it and wait for the time. He loved her too much. He felt deflated and full of sorrow, that he had given up hope for her, but at this time, all hope was gone. Unless by some miracle, in the next hour or so, someone produced a magical cure for them all, she was a lost cause. How hollow that made him feel. What could he do about it? How could he move on with the next 90 minutes, knowing that death was knocking on her door? His mind toiled over a thousand possibilities, from coming clean out with the truth, to gentle revealing, to even plotting the sequence he may pursue in the minutes following her death to so grotesquely invading her, literally, as he would rummage through her innards for the element of hope that could remain for himself.

What a disgusting man he had become. Only 20 hours ago, he was waking, knowing not what was happening, a time where he would have considered himself a good man, loving, kind and caring. Yet now, less than a day later, he was a monster. His outward appearance likely resembled such in view of all he had been through, but the change in mentality, in his humanity even, had grown to new levels; or should that be stooped to new lows, he pondered? He knew that he had become something that he never thought possible. Through all of the events that had unfolded in the day that he had been granted, this 'one day to live', he had toiled with his conscience over whether he could take the life of another. Now the decision seemed out of his hands, but whilst he wasn't the one who would kill her, he was unable to prevent her death, and what's more, he would personally benefit from it. What a piece of shit. He beat himself up for it.

'Hey, hey, hey' she called out as he realised it had gone beyond a mental beating and he was repeatedly slamming the heel of his palm into the side of his head. He was so tired, so irate, so tortured, so aggrieved, he felt like he was no longer in control of himself, that his actions in that moment were a spontaneous autonomic response to his mindset.

She took hold of his hand and the warmth and softness that he knew so well, overcame him as she now cupped it in both of hers and drew it close, cradling it near to her chest. He broke down and cried.

'We're going to be okay' she said, with compassion in the voice, yet staring at him with an expression mixed of confusion and sadness.

'But we're not' he retorted, fighting for composure as the tears continued to flow. 'We will never be "okay" after this, ever again' and he paused for breath amongst the heaving of his chest through continued tears. 'Even if we both got out of this, we'd never be normal again, not with what I've been through' and he fought some more to find the air in his lungs to speak, his body too consumed by the physicality of crying. Clearly, she knew he had a point, her silence spoke louder than words. Yet the worst was still to come for her.

He found the act of getting back to his feet a difficult task. He began to move, and a stiffness set in throughout his whole body. She aided him to fully stand and supported him with an underhanded grasp on each of his, interlocking her fingers with him. His right hand, still bound in the swaddling bandages the medicine man had applied seemed to be in far better condition than he had anticipated back in that ambulance.

They stood face to face, though he was a good half a foot taller than she. They met each other in continued gaze as his sobbing was now receding. He lent in and kissed her, the softness of her usual voluptuous lips had paved way to a dry and firm texture, though her upper was still moist from swigging from the water bottle.

Passionately, he held his kiss with her for what seemed like a million years. When they eventually released their lock, he drew her in to him, engulfing her with his arms, and kissed her on the forehead, as she had to him only a short while ago. He held her close, knowing that time was almost gone, that he would never again have the opportunity to talk with her, laugh with her, cry with her; to go on holiday; out for a meal; enjoy the cinema or theatre; to be sexually intimate, or to share in the emotions of their wedding day and the family they had planned together. Once more he was overwhelmed, and the floodgates of his face reopened.

He glanced at the time on his wristband, the flick of the wrist replacing the small red '36' with the thumb sized screen indicating that it was now 17:47. Just over an hour of her 'day' remained. He would not let her final hour be overwhelmed by his tears. He fought them back once more, regaining composure, and with his arms still wrapped around her, he wiped his face with the same heel of the palm that had minutes ago been pounding the skull.

The embrace faded and they slowly drew apart, '*We must move on*' he said, and taking her hand in his, he drew the satchel up on to his shoulder again and began to plod on. They weaved through the streets, taking several turns but still heading in the same general direction, though there was no end goal in mind, they just continued to gain distance from the shooting gallery where the emergency responders would likely be scraping a dead man from the floor about now.

The glow of the streetlights cast that familiar warmth over the scene as they moved, sending shadows in multiple directions. It started to drizzle; the kind that gets one soaked without even noticing. The night chill was noticeable now that they were wet and with the adrenalin subsiding.

They rounded one more corner and he spotted a fast-food place ahead, the same chain as that in which he had sat with the ogre when he had learned all there was to know of this madness. How fitting a place to sit with her now and reveal what he may, still toiling with all the how's; how to, how much, how it happens. '*Lets head for some warmth and somewhere to rest*' he said, '*there's so much you need to know*'.

18:00

———

Heading for the door, he was surprised to see that the place was filled with people. It was a hive of activity. Of course it was, this was prime time for people to be gathering an evening meal, and evidently, it was a weekend. He had not considered this when the draw of the warmth and a place to sit had grabbed his attention moments earlier. Was it too late to back out now? Would they even find somewhere to sit? It looked like an ant farm, crawling with bodies busying about.

Looking over, she had showed no signs of hesitation, so they proceeded into the place. The noise seemed to drown him and fill his head so that he could not think clearly, a hundred voices all speaking at once, kids screaming, a gaggle of girls cackling, it was as though his head was in a vice slowly being squeezed. He focused his mind and they headed for the queue, where they stood in silence yet surrounded by chaos. They reached the front, and he ordered two burgers with fries and coffees. Crap, besides a few small coins in the pocket of this liberated jacket, he had no means to pay. Just two coffees then, and he scraped together what he had that just about covered the bill.

After a minute or so looking for a place to sit, all they could get was a pair of stools along a lengthy row, in among other customers tucking into their delectable delights. This was hardly the place to have a heart to heart, the final goodbye;

this would not be where he would see her for the last time. To swig the coffee and go was all he could think of.

As they sat, she began to tell him of more of her day. Familiar themes ran on through her dialogue, initially pondering, as he had, as to whether she had been dead yet somehow raised to life, and the leaving of the morgue. She told him of her interactions with several others in similar clothing to what she had awakened to find, some had been helpful, some had been aggressive. But in all that she had to say, she still knew so little of what he had come to learn.

He was conscious that to her, he would have appeared as being absent minded, glossy eyed and hollow. His mind was presently divided in two and running overtime processing both sides; one listening to what she had been through, the other pondering what he should say, what he should do, where they should go. The curse of a man gave difficulty to multitasking.

All around them, people sat and chatted, eating and laughing, getting on with their day. A pair of mothers with a handful of young children sat within a few feet of them, and it brought to his consciousness a future with her that he would never get to experience. This sobering thought was like a firecracker under his seat, and filled him with impetus to move, and a desire to get away from the playful children that so distorted his mind. His coffee had long gone, and he was nursing an empty cup. It seemed to him that she was likewise, so he invited that they should leave, and talk in greater peace than the tumult that surrounded them.

But first, he needed to use the bathroom. The bottle and a half of water was now being pressed through his renal system with the addition of the coffee he must have gulped down without realising. The signs in the place were not clear, but they both felt the need, so took the time. How ridiculous a waste of what would be some of her final minutes. As he stood at the urinal, he considered the amount of hours one wastes in their lifetime through expressing surplus materials from the body.

Several minutes later, they found themselves back out in the cold, though the sleet-like rain had now subsided to momentary micro-droplets with much less frequency. The night was now well set in, and the volume of footfall on the streets around them seemed to have dropped by more than 50% from the half hour or so earlier whence they had taken refuge and the fill of caffeine. Businesses were mostly closed, with only a few here and there showing signs of continued trade.

The constant turmoil of his mind felt like such a heavy burden that it seemed to tire and drain him. He was not sure quite how he had managed to come as far as he had, given the mental abuse he had faced from the toiling, toing and froing in his mind. As he looked about the others around them, faces seemed to at times be blank, free of any features at all, as though there were no eyes, no nose, no mouth; yet at other times were striking and as though each and every one of them was a face that he recognised, or at least was 'familiar' to him.

As they walked on, he listened as intently as he was able, fighting the urges in his mind to ponder the other half of his processing and focus solely on what she was telling him. He was determined and resolute in making her final half hour as much about her as possible. He knew that he had to expose her to the truth, but he wanted her discomfort to be only a few minutes at most. He could not bear the thought of her grappling with what he knew.

The streetlights and shadows cast across her face in waves as they moved, and he was captivated by her beauty each time he lifted his eyes from assessing the path ahead of him, still needing to be sure of his footing with every step.

She had never really needed make-up; the type of woman who exuded a natural radiance, with make-up being only used to 'highlight' on the odd occasions she would wear it. But now, her radiance was lost. The torment of her day had washed it from her, drained her of her natural flushing of the face, which though apparently still present, was now more akin to the chill of the air pinching at her skin given that it appeared somewhat patchy. Her eyes looked dark and hollow, as though she had aged ten years in as many hours.

The physical toll on her, whilst pretty incomparable to his own, was still showing its way through her features, but it was only he who would notice; to any passer-by, there would be no indication of the costs of this day on her face. It was only because he knew her contours in intimate detail that he could see it. Nothing a few days rest and some good wholesome meals would not restore.

As he pondered this, the gravity of what she was about to face hit him like a heavy-weight champion. There was only eternal rest for her now.

Could she rest eternally? He held his own opinions on what happens to a man after death. To him, this meat-sack in which he presently found his existence, was just a shell he inhabited; but now, considering the desecration of the exoskeleton of her soul that he would have to complete before his time ran out, he considered if such acts would prevent any eternal rest for her? Some people were superstitious about such matters.

She had continued her tale of her time since waking, in as much detail as she could recount. Eventually reaching the point where she had rounded a corner and spotted him. From her perspective, he could see how ridiculously careless he had behaved, stepping out onto a road without looking. No sooner than she had clapped her gaze upon him, and felt overwhelmed with a rush of relief, was she emotionally crushed to see him hit by the vehicle. The call for the emergency services, the perpetual wait until the paramedics arrived, all the while he was completely unresponsive. Save for the rising and falling of his chest, there was no indication he had survived the impact.

He checked the time. How quickly her clock was ticking; a mere 19 minutes remained.

They walked without intention, no goal, no destination; just walked. He was surprised at the renewal of physical form he had since an hour earlier where his legs were still faltering beneath him. Those pills really were magic. If he made it through the next few hours, he'd have to look into them more.

The rich man crossed his mind once again and giving part of his attention to her continued account, now running over the details of the last few hours when they had managed to be physically close even if mentally and emotionally, they were still so distant. He could imagine his pseudo-friend far from sober, somewhere between a state of attempted relaxation and attempted numbing of his mind and body from the 24 hours that brought him back to his own kitchen, then like a hunter, had gutted his prize.

On she went, her commentary like the narrative of a story he had himself experienced, with more rhetorical questions that mimicked those she had raised when Scarface had been felled. She was still none the wiser as to what was actually going on. 15 minutes was all she had left, a final quarter hour, in which she had to enjoy the rest of her life. But there was no enjoyment here.

He imagined again what they would do, in any other circumstance, if they were aware that they had only 15 minutes left to live; the calls he would make, the people that he'd want to speak with, or a final time that they could be intimate. Whatever he could have hoped for, it was far from *this*. The pain and anguish of losing her was already starting to settle on him. As much as she was still there stood beside him, she was as distant as she could ever be, a chasm far too wide to be crossed by mortal men.

Somewhat suddenly, he recognised the scenery about them. He was vague but he knew he had been to this place before, the facades of the buildings, the texture and contours, something about the place made him know he had traversed this street previously. Presently, he was side-tracked in trying to fathom when and why. And then he recalled....... The Hallway of Horrors was just around the corner!

How grotesque a picture that place had been less than a day earlier, and now he was here, pondering the same gruesome ending to the woman he claimed he loved. His only saving thought was that it was too late for him to do anything to save her now. He was perplexed by the visions around him that took his attention away from her. He directed their path away from the streets on which he had run with all his might before giving in, to vomit at the roadside in a mixture of disgust, distress and drained of energy. Now he was fighting back the urge to puke once more, but this time at the depravity of his own soul and reckoning.

He began to tell her of his encounters that day, skipping the darker details, but outlining them with a feel more akin to an early teen rated movie rather than the R-rated horror that he had experienced. What better place to start given the streets on which they had just walked being part of his earlier path. He explained following the map on his band and finding the butchered body, how he had followed the next dot, leading to a café where he watched as a woman in similar costume had been accosted by cops, and the arrival of the ogre who had provided him with much knowledge of what he had learned of their predicament.

It was all a sick joke. Some sort of social experiment or part of an elaborate plan by some wicked mastermind who had been the architect of their fate. Their tormentor was pulling their strings, causing a collision of characters from all walks of life, some with the desire to help, other with the desire to kill. He spoke in rhymes and riddles, keeping much of the revulsion as close to his chest as he could. This was not a hand he wished to deal if he could avoid it.

She gazed at him in wonder over the copy shop, the police station, how they had ever got away from there. He spoke of how he lost his friend and nearly himself in the collision, only to be rescued by the rich guy who patched him up. Thereafter, the bacon breakfast before leaving, PJ's and the kid. It was a whistle stop tour before he fine-tuned some of the elements that he concluded to reveal.

She too had received the cryptic clue telling her to find her predecessor. She had witnessed the 37 on Scarface's jacket, and he could see the cogs all click into place as he revealed that he had once worn a similar coat. 'He was after you' she exclaimed, as much of a question as it was a statement, and he could see deep in her eyes that she was putting the pieces together. What felt like an eternity later 'You're 36', followed by another long spell of silence, and then 'You found me!'

She seemed to once again be excited by this, some thought or impression that they had reached the end, they had 'made it'. The elation drew her face to a smile he knew he would never forget. Despite the depravity of what was yet to be said, it had caused him to smile with affection at her joyous place of heart. But his smile was short lived.

Less than five minutes left...

'It's not that easy' he managed, choking as his throat seemed to suddenly become thick, and fear came on his tone. He explained that there was reason they needed to find their predecessor; they had all been given something not only for themselves, but for those that followed. She seemed dumbfounded and befuddled as he explained that the ogre had not died at the wheel of the truck through the impact, but as a result of a poison that had been prescribed by the one who dominated their destiny.

This *day to live* that they had all been granted, came with conditions and consequences. There were no winners, only losers. Martyr or murderer, there were no other options. As Goliath had fallen, David had conquered – the ogre's death had been the only reason that the wealthy Samaritan had escaped, but given what they had all been through, there was only torment that followed. For those like the ogre who had not caught up with their predecessor, there was only one way out.

As he spoke, he could read the anxiety in her eyes and the fear on her face as she put the pieces of the puzzle together.

She was relieved that he had been able to find her, and maybe now that Scarface was no more, he was on the home straight, but she needed to find 34. She punched at her wristband, but the screen that now came to life was not the usual display he was accustomed to. White turned to black, and black turned to white, the screen almost pulsating as double digits counted down as seconds passed, 43, 42, 41.

He took her by the hand, drew her close to his chest and wrapped his other arm around her shoulders, and pressing his lips to her forehead again, he kissed her then held her tightly. Trying not to let his mind be conscious of the countdown, he knew there were only a handful of seconds left.

Tears began to fall.

19:00

His heart was beating far faster than natural rest. Though he had no concept of the rate per minute, he knew it was at least a couple of times per second and correlating that to the slippage of time meant the hour had definitely passed. Fear gripped him and he gripped her in equal force. He again felt as he had in the early moments, confused, scared, filled with terror.

He clung to her, still as she was, lifeless. Holding her tight to himself, with his cheek pressed to her forehead as he continued to cry. This time it was silent, without the heaving of his chest and the gasping for breath. He held her close as the drops ran down his face and on to her head.

She stroked his back.

She stroked his back!

She was still alive!

By now, at least two minutes after her hour had passed, but she had moved! Having felt his tears trickle onto her brow, she had stroked him to show her care and compassion towards his emotional unrest.

Stunned he drew back quickly and regarded her, puzzled, dumbstruck. He stared at her with a quizzical look, and she.... she just looked back, equally puzzled.

'*You're not dead!*'

Peering through her dilated pupils and into the recesses of her mind, he could see the wheels turning, trying to process why she was still stood there, and what on earth was going on.

She was not dead!

She drew up her arm and flicked her wrist. She flicked it again, and again. She shook it, vigorously, in every which way her arm could manage to turn, but there was no life to her wrist band. No screen appeared, just the thin green line, broken by a white expanse, and a small number he could not read but knew to be 35.

What did this mean?

For several minutes they stood, pondering the what, the why, the how. Was this indeed all a sick joke? Was she ever going to die? Were any of them? Had this been a twisted attempt to cause chaos, with no real danger of death? He remembered it had all been 'Chinese Whispers'!

They began to move on, walking and talking, each a mixture of emotions, perplexed and feeling overwhelmed by the uncertainty of the present moment. As they talked through their experiences with others, he started to piece it together.....

She was not dead....

Yet.

Goliath too had survived for some time after his band had expired. It wasn't long, perhaps a quarter hour, maybe 20 minutes. He knew that the ogre had slumped as he drove the truck, that ended in the overturned vehicle. To anyone else, they may have believed the crash itself was the reason the giant had died. Be he had seen it. He was sure of it.

Perhaps the poison is released when the timer runs out. Perhaps it is contained within some capsule that takes time to dissolve, roughly 24 hours, but not exact. Perhaps the chemical processing within the body takes time for the concoction to have lethal effects. Whatever it was, he was sure that his friend had succumbed to the poison prior to the impact that sent them spiralling.

And if this was so for the behemoth, surely it was for her also.

How much time did she have? It could surely be no more than a quarter hour passed the zero point on her timer. His own told him it had already been five and a half minutes. How quickly would her passing be? How long would they have together? Was it still possible he could save her if he were only able to find her cure?

Surely it was too late. There was no time at all. Even if the corpse of 34 was laying around the next corner, it would take too long to open their organs and discover the vial. How long would it even take for the contents to take effect and suppress the sting of whatever they had been given before it had lethal effect?

He realised they had not shared a word in some time. These were her last moments. Their last moments. The time was now to say all that they ever could, all they ever will. Though words could never convey their true feelings, they tried their best to verbalise what they needed. She seemed to realise without his telling her, that despite still being alive after the countdown had ended, this was not going to last. It was now a case of when, and she knew it would not be long.

She wanted him to be able to move on. How hard this was to hear in that moment. As troubled as he was, scared to be alone in the next few hours, it would be ongoing and ever after should he beat the beast within. He was angered and annoyed at her telling him to find someone else, to be happy and enjoy life without her.

'*Stop it*' he screamed '*Just stop*,' now face to face, gripping her shoulders, his fingertips like claws, thumbs pressing into the socket as he had intended to ensure she did not continue. '*Don't you realise how hard this is?*'

But as he spoke, she went limp. It was like a switch had just cut off all power and the lights went out. She was hollow. Held there only by the tightness of the grip he had exerted to arrest her attention. If he were to let go, she would be a heap on the ground. Panic drenched him like a tidal wave. A flood of chemicals filled his bloodstream, bringing on the autonomic reactions, increased heart rate, breathing, focus.

She was gone.

Still there in person, the hollow shell that remained was but a remnant of the love of his life. He felt lost. An incredible sinking sensation now befell him, pulling deep within. His gut wrenched as though the grasp of Death himself had taken hold of his core and began dragging him downwards to hell.

He wrapped his arms around the remnants of her, drew her to him, and embraced the warmth that would slowly ebb away. He felt as hollow inside as she was, unable to process what was happening, empty and devoid of thought.

Her weight seemed to be slowly increasing and he struggled to hold on. He put one arm beneath hers, through the armpit and around the back, yet he still struggled to support her weight. He gave up, and slowly lowered her to the floor, and then suddenly became conscious of his surroundings. He felt exposed.

The surge of adrenaline was still at its peak, and he now considered the potential onlookers, and any intervention this may bring, which in any other circumstance would not be unwanted; but right now, he longed for the ground to open and swallow them both.

He needed to be in the shadows, somewhere out of sight of the passersby and the general populus of the place. Traffic was still relatively constant, there were people all around, though not so busy that they were underfoot. He tried to pick her up, scooping her with one arm again under the armpit, and the other beneath the knees. Her mass seemed to have more than doubled, and his first attempt failed spectacularly. He cursed.

The second attempt was more successful, but as his own knees had extended, the lower lumber section of his back did not have the strength to make it a swift and simple movement. Like an Olympic weightlifter, he readjusted and jerked to full standing. For such a small frame, her weight was incredible, the lifeless mass seemed only to want to fall. He truly understood the term 'dead weight', but at the thought, a shiver ran from between his shoulders, up the neck and lingered around the base of his skull.

He took a step, but again had to readjust his grip. Supporting her sinking shell from slipping from his grasp was more difficult than he thought as he progressed onwards. It became more manageable with every step, as he gained the experience of the movements he would have to make. He needed to find somewhere to hide, somewhere out of sight, somewhere he could ultimately leave her, to be found, recovered and treated to the burial that she deserved, regardless of whether he would ever be able to save himself.

He threw up again in his mouth as he thought of what came before that. The debauchery of the butchery that was to come. It was only out of his respect for her that he did not allow the half-digested mashed up cereal bars mixed with the remains of the earlier bacon, egg and sausage sandwich from being ejected, which doubtless would have spewed all over the body suspended between his arms.

He quickly turned to a side street and progressed away from the more populated areas. He needed a back alley, behind some retail spaces, at this hour, when shops were mostly closed. A place where darkness was in full vail, and limited scope for people to be about; it was a tall ask, but he knew this was what he needed. How long before he could find such a place?

Having stopped for a few seconds every fifty or so steps to readjust and give his back some respite, his arms grew tired quicker than he imagined. How long could he continue he wondered. It had surely been at least a quarter hour since the lights out moment. That must have been ten to fifteen minutes after the countdown expired. Two and a half hours were all that remained, but at least he held in his arms the ability to prevent his own demise. All he had to do was find it. He threw up a little once more.

It dawned on him that since the Samaritan had escaped in his helicopter and having heard of his disappearance on the news broadcast, there had been no developments of his finding that had come to the forefront. Had the vial actually worked? This was yet one more unknown. The usual pragmatic and calculated approach he took to any conundrum, bore no resemblance to the processing of the events in which he found himself enthralled. His mind was awash with a thousand possibilities, and he had lost the clarity of mind to decipher which had more or less risk, opportunity, or reward.

Onward he moved, slowly, deliberately. The side streets were indeed less busy. His eyes were constantly scanning his surroundings, hoping to find a place to lay her, a temporary resting place, but also somewhere he could perform a makeshift surgery.

His progress was slow, he was not surprised. Despite the constant mental torture that he had experienced over the last 22 hours, his body had taken a significant toll. Only a couple of hours ago, he had been scooped up by paramedics and stuffed into an ambulance. The events that unravelled since that point had been the most surreal thing. It was not something that he could even conceive in his own mind, so unnatural these things would otherwise ordinarily be.

He eventually found an alley. From the mouth of it, he was reminded of the alley at which he had witnessed the hallway of horrors which had also induced vomiting. This was becoming a common theme.

Dark and dismal, this place seemed perfect for what was to come. It seemed only 50 metres or so long, leading to nowhere, a dead end. The only essence of light about the place was from that which echoed off the buildings, itself emanating from poor streetside lighting some five metres from the ground.

Barely three meters wide, there were some large industrial bins to the left around a third of the way along. Several doorways lined the alley, but these were nothing more than fire escapes from the buildings that boarded the blackness.

This was the perfect place to shelter her shell while he set about the gruesome task that lay ahead.

As he walked along the alley, there was broken glass all over, some of it crushed by the countless deliveries to these back doors of businesses, and other larger pieces that seemed as though the local vagabonds had used this place as a hangout, with bottles of cheap booze being carelessly discarded. Beside the bins seemed to at least offer some concealment from anyone that may pass the mouth of the alley, and the cast-off bottles here seemed a little less concentrated than elsewhere. The glistening glass looked like the starry vast expanse of the night sky as the shards reflected the minimal light that was present. It seemed to create a sullen black hole like effect in an area beside the other bins that made him believe that another such would ordinarily occupy this space, but for some reason was missing. At least he could kneel or sit here without too much problem.

He laid her down carefully. Her hair draped across his arm as he slowly withdrew it, trying not to let her head hit the ground to hard. He was in utter despair. He had just lost the love of his life, yet he could not even begin to mourn. He too would be done for in just over two hours, unless he now desecrated her body in a fleeting effort to save himself.

He collapsed from his knees to his backside and slumped himself against the wall weeping, trying to make sense of what he needed to do. He couldn't focus his thoughts enough to ponder the actions and began to play over in his mind scenes from their time together. He sobbed, though his face showed no emotion whatsoever. A blank emptiness with tears trickling.

The scenes and visions progressed to their last encounter before this day. Walking in the park, free from all this torment. The events thereafter played out in his mind in quick succession, until the moment he had been stood in a kitchen, watching the ogre be dissected. He needed to act similarly. He knew he needed to focus, there was a task at hand, and he had lost too much time sitting and sobbing. He needed to act in order to save himself. Had he picked up that Stanley knife from the Samaritan's home? He had rinsed off the blood and set it down on the worktop. He rummaged through the satchel, but it was not there. Damn.

He slowly got to his feet, with his consciousness now filled with questions as to how he will ever be able to get past the trauma of this day. As he began to search around for something sharp, some implement that could be a makeshift knife, he was consumed with endless questions of morality, and pondered whether he would one day likely find himself stood atop a bridge, or at the end of a noose, or swallowing a bottle of pills sometime after all this. Was life worth living now? Should he even bother?

He recalled how he had resolved to do all he could to escape this evil and to seek justice for those who have lost to this wicked and grim game of death. He could only do this if he himself escaped, and the resolve to do so was renewed within him.

Having found a piece of broken glass around four inches long and roughly resembling a blade, he believed this would be the best thing at hand to begin. Placing the satchel down on the floor, he stood over her, peering with pity as he pondered the manner in which to commence. Her eyes were wide open, and it seemed as though she was watching him. Getting on to his knees beside her, he put down the glass knife and tried to close the eyes like he had seen on TV. But it did not work like in the movies. Her lids just raised again, exposing her bloodshot eyes, exhausted from the exuberance of twenty-four hours of trauma.

He undid the button of her uniform trousers, pulled down the zipper and peeled open the front. He knew this was not a wide enough opening and was forced to begin to undress her waist, rolling the trousers over her buttocks which required some manhandling of the torso.

When eventually ready to proceed, he pushed from his mind the grotesqueness of the actions to come, took hold of the glass blade, and placing the tip around an inch below her navel, he began to put pressure downwards. Watching the depression of her abdomen under the pressure of the glass, he lost focus as the glass pierced the skin and blood started to emerge.

The tip broke off.

This caused him to retract his hand quickly, and at the same time, just like the giant, the corpse let out its final breath, vibrating the vocal cords as it did – it sounded like she had moaned. He near soiled himself and let out a scream of his own, reeling backwards before realising it was nothing more than the air in her lungs escaping the collapsing corpse.

The blade had broken only a shard and would be good for him to continue. He resumed his incision and found the resistance was much harder than he had anticipated. Cutting skin with glass was not as easy as it seemed, cutting muscle was even harder, but he had no time to search for a more suitable instrument. With difficulty he progressed.

Perhaps some mental disassociation, but he found his hands simply moved, without emotion or thought. Had his mind split from the trauma of what was happening; a second persona now taking charge, protecting the true personality from the horrors?

Having cut around six inches downwards towards the pubic bone, he made another incision at 90 degrees roughly halfway along, creating a makeshift + on her lower abdomen. It was far from perfect. Once long and deep enough cuts had been made, it was time to try to get inside. Again, it was much harder than he had thought. He could not simply peel back the skin and tissue as he had with her trousers. The bond beneath the fibres needed breaking and he continued to use the broken glass to aide him, which became increasingly difficult with his hands now blood soaked, causing the glass to slip in the grip of his fingers.

Shifting the glass to his non-dominant hand, bandaged and already blood soaked, he could keep it out the way; he then pressed his free fingertips together making a point with them and pressed into the hole he had created. He was disgusted to his deepest core at what he was doing, though it was almost as though it were an out of body experience. He felt not in control, it was just happening.

The textures within were not what he expected at all. He began to feel around, hoping to identify small intestines or organs. Wrist deep as he was, it seemed as though he could spend hours searching for this vial and never find it. Perhaps he wouldn't.

As that thought went through his head, the sound of a door crashing open echoed through the alleyway, accompanied by two voices talking, one of them clearly steeping out into the open.

He spun his head around and caught sight of a man, bin sacks in hand and a dirty apron covering his front.

'What the fuck!' screamed the man, realising that there was a body with his hand inside it.

The disassociation vanished in an instant and he found himself kneeling there wrist deep. His instinct kicked in. He quickly withdrew his hand, jumped to his feet, and began to run.

20:00

―――――

He broke into a sprint and rounded the corner from the direction he had entered when moments earlier laden down with her load. Unburdened, he was much spritelier on his feet, although that pain in his heel was returning with every strike it took on the pavement. His right hip and knee ached from the impact with the car that resulted in his unconsciousness only hours ago. His shoulder seemed to have also taken some shock with the impact that he had not noticed previously.

Though it felt like he was in full sprint, he knew the reality was far from it. This was little more than his natural pace on a Sunday morning jog. Hardly the swift escape from the scene, but he had now put several hundred meters between he and the bin bag wielding challenger. By now they would have realised she was dead, mutilated, likely murdered. And he, the blood-stained man who fled, was likely her killer.

What on earth could be done now?

She had his potion; she contained the liquid that would liberate him. Was it now lost? His jog became a plod as he continued. By now, the emergency services would have been called. Police and paramedics were likely already on their way. Was it possible he could get close again? Was it possible he could ever retrieve that vial? His body was surging chemicals, and he knew he was riding the wave for as long as he possibly could.

The thumping in his head disrupted his thoughts and he struggled to think of his next move. How on earth was he going to get hold of that vial? He had less than two hours to do it.

With hands so covered in blood, he would need to find somewhere to wash them. Being on the streets now was risky. If the bin bag man had given a description, they would doubtless be looking for someone fitting that image. But it had been dark. Could that man really have gotten a good representation from the fleeting moments he had been in his sight? It was not likely that his face had been catalogued with sufficient detail, but his clothing would surely be the giveaway. He knew he needed to ditch this coat, red as it was, like a beacon. The rain had all but ceased but it was far too cold out, despite the elevated core temperature from his attempt at running and the spike in chemicals coursing through his veins. He needed the coat to keep warm.

The inner lining was black. Under any lighting, it may be obvious that the coat was inside out, but in the dark of the night, he was confident it would throw an image of a black jacket rather than the obvious red of the outer skin. Now at a walking pace, he progressed with a limp at both legs, slowly but surely, marching onwards, as he stripped the coat from his arms, keeping hold of each cuff as he did, flipping it inside out. He turned the hood too and proceeded to put it back on. He hadn't thought about how to close it properly with the zipper and popper studs of the wind flap now on the inside. The zip was a struggle, but he managed to get the pieces engaged and draw it up to his sternum once he had given up trying to walk and act at the same time.

Stood still as he was, he took stock of his surroundings, and realised that he had moved along the same paths that he had taken with her a short while ago. Instinctively, he had returned the way that they had come. Every turn had been a mystery, but automatically he had followed his previous steps, and was now at the place they stopped for coffee, where the warmth had provided respite.

His bladder was pressing again from chugging of liquids he had earlier consumed. The coffee now fully processed was ready for release and he needed to relieve himself. One positive was that this place had a bathroom where he could also set to cleaning his hands. He looked at them and wept. The crimson stain was hers. His entire left hand was covered in traces of her exclusively and he could not see any of his own skin tone. It was a sickening thought. He wiped his tears using the bandage at the rear of his right palm, about the only place that wasn't soaked in red.

He needed to hide his hands if he were to enter this place, as people would become suspicious of a man covered in blood. He instinctively reached for the pockets, but his hands just slid along the fabric of the lining that was now on the outside. The pockets were within. Resolving to simply covering his hands with the sleeves until he reached the bathroom, he moved towards the doors with his fists clenched, and hoped that people didn't look on at the strangeness of a character with his coat reversed.

Through the doors, the overhead heater dried the air as he breathed, and a shiver passed through him as he transitioned into the blast of hot air. The sign hanging from the ceiling indicated that the restrooms were up a flight of stairs to the right, open and spiralling. He had visited them earlier and needed not the direction. The place was still busy enough that he would be relatively unnoticed, and he thought this a good sign as he slowly ascended, each step seeming to add an extra 5lbs to his weight. His hip, knee and heel made it more of a waddle than a walk as he passed by the seated diners, talking, gesticulating and laughing to one another, lost in their own worlds, oblivious to the awkward individual passing by.

Arriving at the toilets, he was perturbed by what seemed to be a constant flow of traffic. He could hardly wash his hands in full view of onlooking users of the facilities and he needed something less obvious. The signs indicated that the accessible toilet was located on the ground level, which no doubt was locked to prevent misuse. He had no choice but to proceed into the gents. The putrid smell of urine from countless users that had missed their mark gave a sour impression. He headed into one of the cubicles and closed and locked the door. It was far from clean, but he was limited for choice, the bowl was half full of the previous patron's release. The sight made him baulk. He hit the flush which got rid of the majority.

Grabbing a fist full of paper, he tried in vain to wipe the blood from his hands. The tissue turned pinkish but had little effect on actually removing anything from him. The coat came off and he hung it from a peg on the rear of the stall door. He flushed the bowl once more and it was at least free from the debris it had contained when he arrived. Peeling off the dressing from his right, he hit the flush again and shoved his hands into the stream of fresh water that crashed through the inlet from the cistern and rubbed them as thoroughly as he could. The sting to the open wound was sharp. It had been relatively successful, but he needed another round and waited for the cistern to refill.

At least one other person had come in and two more had gone out since he had entered the cubicle, and right now there was at least one person washing their hands at the basins. The noises emanating from the adjacent cubicle told him of another present, although evidently engaged for the next couple of minutes. He grimaced as he again plunged his hands into the flushing toilet and scrubbed as hard as he could. The flushing made him realise quite the discomfort his bladder was in despite only emptying a short while ago. Satisfied he had made a half decent job of removing the blood; he wiped his hands off again with tissue before relieving himself.

Hearing the hand drier fire into life outside the cubicle, he took the opportunity to get to the sink whilst there was likely no one else there. Grabbing the coat from the door hook, he pulled it open and the guy at the drier shot him a fleeting glance through the mirrors but returned their attention to their task. Having approached the sink, he tucked the coat between his legs and reached out for the soap to be automatically dispensed with his hand under the sensor. Had the other man looked, beyond question there would have been some concern at the state his hands were still in. His wound was not too bad, but he tried to avoid aggravating it.

As he scrubbed under hot water, with suds now acting, the blood came off much easier. His heart sank as he watched the pink water swirl down the drain, realising that he was literally washing her away.

Thoughts now turned to the vial once more. He had wasted over 20 minutes already; time he could not afford to lose. By now it was likely that police had arrived at the scene and an ambulance would not be far behind if not already there. Soon she would be moved. Where would they take her? A hospital seemed superfluous, although they may have a morgue, and as that thought went through his head, the horror of his awakening, entombed inside the cadaver cooler, came flooding back to him and filled him with the terror he had first encountered.

Unnerved by the remembering, he reviewed his hands, which had now had several rounds of soap and rinsing, and there was no obvious blood apart from under and around his fingernails which would need a brush to remove. He shook off the excess water and pushed them into the drier, watching the timer count down the 10 seconds of operation. As ever, they were never dry from the limited run time of the machine. Putting the coat over one arm, he opened the door and stepped out into the diner. Passing through, there were now less than half the volume of people than had been here not two hours ago. He was grateful of the fact, although these people cared not about the dishevelled man moseying through the place.

He checked his wrist, 20:28. Time was slipping away. How he wished for some magical powers to pause the passing. He could feel his life was ebbing away with every minute that slipped by. Descending the stairs, he headed for the door and passing under the heater for a final blast of warmth, he swung the coat onto himself trying to trap the heat. In doing so, he aggravated the perforation in his chest, still covered with a strip of duct tape in a makeshift bandage; boy did that hurt. His shoulder, dislocated in the early morning, was going to cause problems later on.

Needing to learn what had happened to her corpse, he knew that he must return to the place he had laid her and figure out what the authorities would be doing with her body. He had only 90 minutes to attempt to access it again. Was it likely that he could? As he moved on, he pondered the ways in which he may be able to approach her corpse if it were now surrounded by others. At very least, the bin bags man and whoever he had been speaking with, would be crowding around her, but there would doubtless be others now also about the place.

Had the bin bag man got a good enough view of his face to identify him? The red coat was probably all that he could confirm given the darkness of that alleyway. Would the inside-out jacket now pass under the same shadowy darkness to conceal that he was one in the same? He could pretend to be a physician that just happened to be passing by, perhaps that would get him close enough, though likely without ability to complete his internal exploration. Should there be paramedics at the place, he could tell them of their connection, she his fiancé, and hitch a ride, as she had tried, to wherever they would be taking her. Yet still, this would not give him access to resume rooting about her innards. Could he seek to harm them in order to access her? His life depended on getting hold of that vial.

He was stumped and the weight of the realisation was growing second by second. Was it the gravity of his lost hope, the pain of losing her, or the state of his physical distress that seemed to slow his movements, and drain him of the will to progress? He had come too far, and simply placing one foot in front of the other was all he could do for now. The rest will be figured out, flying by the seat of his pants, he would come up with something, anything.

But if he made some drastic decision to dive deep into her gut in full view of onlookers; even if he could find, retrieve and consume the contents of the tiny glass container; what good would it do? Such a sight in front of who knows who, would only end up with him in cuffs, and sentenced to a life in a true prison, more real than the one of his mind.

Could he perhaps explain it away? The police would surely know more of what had been happening. This strange 'cult', in their uniform of industrial garb, having committed countless atrocities would soon become known to have been victims of some deranged demon of their destiny, pushed against their will into a world of wickedness and iniquitous actions. Would they believe him? What would possibly happen if the truth became clear and the details of this vaudeville villain surfaced?

Should he be remanded for violating a dead body, would he possibly be vilified by the world once the details came to light? Would the truth result in him being processed and released? Would release be any better option than incarceration? Though he may not be physically detained behind bars, he would be incarcerated to the haunting that would never pass from his personality. His body, though broken, would heal. There will be lasting remnants, scars at least, that would serve as a permanent reminder of this day, but the emotional torment and torture would be unbearable.

His life had taken a drastic turn, and he was now alone forever. Even if he could save himself, she was lost to the ether. He prayed for her soul. Once more, despite his prior agnosticism, he now called out to a deity he had previously given no regard to. He stilled his heart and asked that she be taken care of, without memory of the day that had taken her, just eternal peace and endless joy. He would happily spend infinity in the underworld if it meant that she could be in a heavenly place.

He had ground to a halt. Subconsciously, as he had stilled his heart, he had stilled his body, dropped his head and had lost focus in his eyes. He came out of it with a start, and quickly raised his head to take stock of his surroundings. Nothing looked familiar. He had no idea where he was, or where he needed to get to. Was he completely lost? Perhaps to keep moving forwards would give him some recollection of certain features that he would regain his bearings.

He decided to check his map first. 20:44. Shit, this was not good. He navigated to the map and could see there was another close by. Too close, only 20 meters or so behind. Spinning around, there was a woman, late 40's, dark hair that appeared lighter at the roots, clearly greying but masked with a dye that was far overdue a top up. The clothing told all he needed. She was the new dot he had witnessed at his wrist.

'Is it you?' she called as she continued to approach, evidently studying her own band as she did.

He didn't respond, dazed by the presence of another. It had caught him completely off guard. How stupid had he been. At any moment one of them could have sneaked up on him. He had failed to even consider keeping an eye on where the others were for longer than he cared to think about.

'Is it you?' she asked again, 'Are you involved?'

He needed to respond, but he was still a little dumbstruck.

He knew this wasn't 37. Scarface had been gunned down hours ago. He had not stopped to contemplate what this meant, but his successor was already dead. He was no longer being pursued. If only he could grip that ampoule of antidote, he was in the clear.

'Hey you. It is you'. She was now only feet away.

'Err..... Yes, I'm the one you're looking for'. He could see 43 at her breast. Quick maths meant she was still new to this, only hours into her journey.

The newcomer asked him for help and began reeling off what he expected as a typical outpouring of someone new to this mania. He couldn't listen to it; he had zoned out before she got to any details whatsoever. He knew he had to interrupt.

Cutting her off mid-sentence, he explained that he did not want to be rude, but his time was almost up. He had little more than an hour left, but the finish was truly in sight. He invited her to walk with him as he moved on, and they could talk through what was happening and he could give her the knowledge that would save her life. She seemed elated.

It was as though to her this was something of a weird prank. Was she being punked, she had wondered. She had no idea what had happened to her, but had woken, like them all, in an abandoned morgue, got dressed into clothes that had been left out, almost as though they were for her directly. Once out on the streets, a slew of people, drove after drove, simply ignored her pleas for help, believing her to be demented or insane. Given her waking experience, she believed she had come back to life. For sure, she sounded insane.

She had found a police station, but like so many it was closed, a victim of the lack of funding and centralisation of local forces to command units. She had spoken with someone through a telephone intercom system, a desk clerk at the central command, but she too had believed the woman was deranged, or perhaps intoxicated, and refused to send help. Messages at her band had then spurred her to search her map, and she became intrigued by the other blue dots and attempted to locate them. That was how she had found him.

She knew nothing. How hard it would be for her to hear. He explained how he too had similar experiences, but that he had found the dots were people when he came across the mutilated carcass at the hallway of horrors. She seemed petrified. In brief detail he told of how he had interacted with several others that were all numbered participants in some twisted torment. A game of cat and mouse, where each player was equally both hunter and prey. She would need to simultaneously find 42, but also evade 44, who would be waking in just over an hour.

He had begun to recognise visages of the buildings around them and knew that he was close to where he had left his love. He pulled them to a stop.

'Look, I will tell you all you need to know. You won't like it. It will forever change who you are. But first, I need your help.'

Puzzled and taken aback, she stared at him with a furrowed brow. The light caught her eyes that were such a subtle pale brown, in the dim glow of the streetlights, had a yellow appearance.

'What? Tell me and I'll do it' she responded with eagerness to please. She still had hope and optimism in her heart. How drastically different she would feel by the coming morning.

Though he was clearly a good few years her junior, she seemed to him to be submissive to his lead and yearning to aid however she could. He told her that he expected that as they turned the next corner, there would likely be emergency services there, possibly police, but she needed to resist the urge to approach them and ask for their help. They would only consider her a lunatic, as others already had.

Instead, what she needed to do was stay composed, they would watch from a distance, and he expected to see that a body was being moved. She queried who, what, and why, but he simply told her that he was 36 and the body was 35. Without any graphic detail, he explained with simplified terms that he needed to retrieve something 35 had, but that she had been killed before he had been able. The woman had a thousand questions, but he responded to all with a vagueness that only invited further questioning. Time was of the essence, and he killed further questions for now.

Her help was needed to attempt to retrieve what he required. He told her only of the countdown they all had, and that he needed to get to 35 with little more than an hour to spare, and checking his wrist, his spare change was only three minutes. Fear and sinking feelings once more took hold. Was it all too much, too little, too late? This newcomer was yet to experience all he already had, of the terrifying haunting as she progressed through, meandering the madness she faced. He hoped she would not take the physical beating that he had. A woman of her size would likely not fare as well in vehicular impacts, both as passenger and pedestrian.

The hum of an engine grew, and as they rounded the corner, the brake lights of an ambulance went off, the taillights still lit. The driver had clearly begun to pull away. They were too late.

He tried to sprint, but his condition still would not allow it. A slow jog was as much as he could manage but he persisted, passing the alleyway where he had left her. The ambulance stopped at the far end of the road, not more than 50 metres ahead of him, indicating left to pull out.

It disappeared.

She was gone.

21:00

―――

Oblivious to the fact he had called out aloud, he came to a halt, as reality started sinking. Too tired to process all that this meant, he simply stood, slumped at the shoulders, head hanging. A tear gathered in the canthus of both eyes, yet before they could start to roll, an involuntary reaction caused him to eject more than a mouthful of whatever his stomach still contained. He bent at the waist and wretched out again.

The constant cacophony of the world seemed to fade slowly until all he could hear was the hammering of his own heart. It filled his ears with a rhythmical romp that at his rate of beats per minute was reminiscent of trance music of the latter years of the last century. An empty, hollow stare had beset him; his vision had all but faded anyway. Peripheral perception decreased to pinpricks that showed only of the fact there was something, though he failed any clarity of sight. Lacking both the ability and the mental capacity, visual perception was currently not a skill set he required.

Likewise, mental perception seemed to have disappeared too. He just stood there, lost.

He truly was lost now. Beyond not knowing where he physically was - what could he do, how could he retrieve his antidote - Hope was lost.

Thoughts began to dance in his mind, should he just keep walking forward, one step at a time, until he crossed out into the road ahead, and could get wiped out by a passing vehicle? If only he had a knife, he could slit his own wrists. If that gun had been stowed in his satchel, he could have eaten a bullet.

It seemed pointless to delay death any further. It was already en route, now less than an hour away and would soon be arriving at his station. The unwanted visitor would remove all chances of vengeance and retribution. What use is the final hour when there seemed no possibility of consuming the concoction that would defeat his demise? Perhaps this was as far as he could ever come. He begged for it to be done with already, for the Grim Reaper to swing their sickle and despatch him to the depths of the hell he deserved.

Gathering himself, he knew that as a final act of selfless good will, he could at least impart the knowledge he had gained to the yellow eyed contender that had arrived only moments before. Where was she now?

He turned but could not see her. Had she vanished? Maybe she had not come with him around that corner? Maybe as he broke into speed chasing the paramedics, she had considered him crazier than herself, and left him to behave like a dog, gnashing and barking as he bounded up the road. He could hear voices coming from the alleyway. There were several people there. Were they police? What about Mr Bin Bags? Could he show his face? Would he be recognised? Did that even matter now there was no prospect of denouement?

It would probably be best not to become involved in any remnants of the atrocious alleyway acts if he were to remain in any realistic control of his final fate. Even just answering questions at the scene would take far too long of his precious minutes. He imagined the bureaucracy that would ensue if he were taken to a police station for questioning and then died in their charge less than an hour from now. Surely, they would be used to dealing with the dead, but the paperwork alone seemed unfair on anyone that would have to process it.

Walking to the corner where the ambulance had vanished, he observed the busyness of a crossroads a quarter mile ahead. The stream of passing vehicles seemed relentless and those waiting to join, were held back by glowing red orbs for what must have been two minutes whilst he watched. He knew he would never have been able to cover that distance before the lights turned green to have caught up with the glorified meat wagon carting her away to the coroner.

Where was 43? The map would tell him. He checked his wrist and was disheartened to see that the screen was no longer occupied by the time, but his final count down.

51:52

51:51

51:50

Less than 50 minutes and he was done for.

The floating arrow now pointed in the direction of the atrocious alley. She must be there. A blue dot on the map confirmed it. He knew that once the time had run out on the bands of others, they stopped functioning as they once had, but did they still allow others to see the location of the wearer? Now that his love had been moved, the presence of a blue dot there could only be that of 43. He wished she would appear.

A horn sounded in the distance taking his attention back to the crossroads. Trying to observe, he could only make out the continuous flow, like a perennial stream, being fed from tributaries and side branches. Ever flowing, never ending. Hordes moving in their masses. An army of ants scurrying along.

She startled him when she spoke. He had been so engrossed and lost for thought, transfixed on the traffic, that he had failed to notice her approaching. She had gathered some details from the two witnesses and the uniformed response officers who awaited a crime scene investigator. A woman had been brutally murdered, massacred. She asked if it were he. Had he been the killer?

'What do you think of me?' he responded. *'I knew her, you know. Before all this, we were together'.*

A solitary droplet ran down, around his right nostril, and dripped from his upper lip. His head was hanging again.

'You want to say a last goodbye? I know where they've taken her. Come on' this newcomer proclaimed.

Perhaps this was it. He did not process what she said after that, instead his mind churned over the possibilities of getting close enough that he may attempt to attain the ace in the hole. He wondered if that was metaphorical or physical?

Perhaps he could profess to be her next-of-kin and seek to identify the body. Maybe they would allow him to be alone with her for a few minutes. Would that be enough? Could he find the solution, or was this just one more semblance of sanity? Would there even be time? 47:21, 20, 19....

As he considered his chances, she had continued to chat of the dishevelled terrible spectre, draped in a red cloak that one of the two minions had seen as it shot from sight leaving a dismembered damsel far beyond distress, swallowed by the eternal abyss. The man had thought the thing to be eating her, blood running from its mouth. Had the police taken this guy seriously? He pondered the reliability of eyewitness testimony considering how shockingly appalling Mr Bin Bags account had been; or was this metaphorical?

The police were now hunting the killer.

He hadn't even realised they were moving. Lost in his head, they had covered ground. The junction of the crossroads was now upon them, and it seemed to be a contest for the culinary connoisseurs. On every corner was a restaurant of different kinds. Oriental foods, seafoods, a posh pizzeria and a stylish steakhouse, which was the closest as they approached. A plan had hatched, and this was a helping hand, far better than fate, a destiny delivered.

She should wait for him a minute; he would only be a minute.

Leaving her at the roadside, he approached the door of the restaurant and slipped inside. Greeted by a maître d', he was hardly a vision of their usual clientele and attracted an unsavoury expression. Having apologised for his appearance, he explained that he had been knocked down hours earlier, on his way to meet friends in this restaurant. He wished to see if they were still here. He gave the first common name that came to mind, and having checked his reservation records, the maître d' instructed him to follow along before pointing out a table ahead. These were not his friends he explained, they must have already left. He thanked the man for his help, but he would be on his way.

Wanting to ensure that this broken body received the aid he needed, the greeter offered to call someone for him. He declined and again thanked them before leaving the place.

'But Sir, before you depart.... you're inside out' they said as they tugged at their own lapels to indicate what was meant.

He thanked them again and slipped out the door.

The man had been none the wiser. As they swathed through the restaurant, meandering through the mortals enjoying their morsels of pretentious proportions; he had discreetly swiped a serrated steak knife from one of the tables and tucked it into his sleeve. This would come in handy if he needed to make additional incisions in a short space of time. First, he needed to get access to the body of his beloved.

Stepping out into the cold, rain had resumed. The other had successfully hailed a taxi and called to him to get in as she climbed aboard through the far door. Approaching the cab, he checked his wrist, 39:17, 16, 15. Two thirds of an hour.

She had given instructions before he had embarked, and the vehicle began to move as soon as he closed the door. He wondered how the bill would be covered, but this was not his problem. He was grateful for the ride, and knew that without it, he did not stand a chance. This journey could potentially take all the time he had left as it is; equally it could also be only minutes until they reached the destination. He had no idea.

Driverless cars had been common for some time now, but he still felt uneasy whenever he used one. Nonetheless, there were no prying eyes or ears to listen to his tale, and he began to offload the sorry state of affairs that she had yet to face. He was just another link in the chain of Chinese whispers, no one truly knew all there was to know, save for the perverse puppeteer controlling them. Each had been given one day to live. Many had fallen, few had escaped.

Having witnessed a true David and Goliath moment, the death of his giant friend had meant victory for the wealthy wanderer. This had confirmed to him that the unthinkable was inescapable. Details of his day were met with disbelief and horror as she intently hung on his words. She was now the one to toil with the morality of the human condition. Could she take the life of another to save herself? Could she then knowingly allow another to die so that she could live?

This would weigh heavy on her soul for the twenty some hours she had yet to endure.

He had barely got to retelling the Scarface showdown when the ride pulled into the hospital drop off zone. The rest of his tale would have to wait. She confirmed this was the place. As the car came to a stop, he was already half out of the door.

Turning, he found she had leaned across the back seat, and she wished him her very best. She had her own demons to face now and could waste no time whilst he attempted to dodge death. He bid his own well wishes and closed the door. Through the window, he could see she was inspecting her band as the whirr of the electric motors whipped the car away. He could not wait and watch. He too had no time to lose. Death does not discriminate. It marched on him; he could hear the footsteps.

There seemed to be a slew of people leaving the place, many of whom wore typical tunics that told of their service to the Hippocratic oath. Could any of them do anything to save him? It was not likely. The exodus of employees meant it was likely that a shift change had just occurred. A handover of about half an hour was to be expected; surely it was around 9:30 now? Did he have but a mere half hour left?

27:27, 26, 25, 24

Approaching the main reception desk, the clerk immediately attempted to direct him to the Accident & Emergency section having seen the condition he was in. Waddling from the agony of the injuries, although no longer aware of the pain; temporarily suppressed by the succinct position he was presently upon. His face bruised, swollen in parts; clothing soiled and scruffy, an unkempt image befitting a vagrant that told the tale of several incidents and injuries. A&E was where he may get to, once he had retrieved his remedy.

He apologised for his disordered appearance for the second time in this closing countdown. Explaining that his partner had been picked up by ambulance and brought here a half hour ago, the clerk asked for the name. He gave it, though doubted they had her recorded; she had passed before the paramedics had arrived. The look that washed over the clerk's face showed an instant compassion and acceptance for his ratty form and they told him where he could find the coroner's office.

The typical smell of the hospital stung his nostrils. Chemicals and crappy meals, the hallways were awash with pungent odours. The signage was simple to follow, but the stairwell was difficult to manage. He had not considered how lowering himself only a few inches at a time, could have stressed the muscular skeletal system so savagely as he descended to the 'sub-ground' level. He should have taken the lift.

Butterflies were filling his belly. It was a feeling he had not had in a long time. Anxious excitement, a little nervous and terrified, with joy and jubilation in small doses, mixed in a concoction with alarm and panic adding a balance of light and dark. The yin and yang, opposite but interlaced. Inseparable and interpenetrating, an unnatural equilibrium of positive and negative, the perpetuating forces spiralling, growing. But as the old proverb provides, these butterflies will create hurricanes.

He had less than 20 minutes on hand. Surely this was not enough.

There was no one at the desk as he arrived at the correct place. In fact, there was not a soul to be seen. How apt, in the depths where the deceased are deposited, the place was as dead as they were. A set of double doors lead through into the department, and remarkably, there was no form of lock whatsoever preventing him from passing through. Would passing from life to death be as simple and painless he pondered? It was almost unbelievable that he was able to go through room after room without hindrance.

After less than a couple of minutes, he had found the body cooler. His day had started in such a place as this, and now it was ending here, almost identical to where he had escaped from the cold metal tomb that had held him captive until the manipulator of the Machiavellian had woken him for his bidding.

The doors stood in a four by three format. He wondered how he would be able to see those in the upper row without the use of some form of step. He'd start at the bottom. Most of the doors were marked, a small card dropped into a Perspex pocket that told of the occupant's name and insignificant other details. He checked each one, name after name, knowing that the staff would have no way of identifying her, it seemed useless anyway.

Three of the bank had no tags at all. He opened the first and the mist of the chilled air rolled out as it collided with the warmth of the regular atmosphere. The rolling tray revealed itself as the mist thinned. It was vacant of possession. He closed the door.

The next indeed held a resident, a thick black body bag of rubberised material encased what appeared to be someone much larger than himself, so certainly not her. He used the open aperture as a foot ledge to reach the upper row and cracked open the final untagged tomb. How on earth do the porters lift the dead to these carcass cabinets? He tugged at the tray, but it did not roll out.

The dense cold air spilled over the lip of the opening and cleared, where he could then see the locking catches on the tray bed. He could reach them both from the ground and was able to get the thing to slide. Another body bag stuffed with some unlucky soul. Climbing on the doorway of the middle row once more, he positioned himself that he could pull down the zipper, but composed himself before he did.

Anticipation grew and the butterflies had now all been crushed by the knotting in his core. If this was her, he feared he would have another involuntary ejection of munched and mulched remains. His entire digestive system seemed to move within him making it even worse.

The zipper was held in place with some form of plastic tag. He could not read what is said from this angle, it looked like a number, could it say 35? Could this really be her? Lacking any other information, perhaps they had tagged her with an identity based only by the number on her clothing.

Trying to break it off, it was too strong to snap, and simply stretched slightly as he twisted and turned. Supporting his weight with his elbows, he slipped his fingers into the cuff of his jacket and retrieved the knife he had earlier pilfered from the pretentious restaurant, then leaning over, taking the tag in one hand, cut it from the loop holding the zipper in place.

BH

The tag read BH. He wondered what that were, until turning it over, the all too familiar symbol gave it away. Bio-Hazard! Had he already been exposed to something he should not of? His face had been only inches away. He was glad he had not breached the zip and quickly got down, pushed the drawer back inside and closed the hatch.

She was not here.

He moved into the corridor and could hear voices in a room not 15 feet away. Rather than returning the knife to the sleeve, he turned the coat the right way and pulling it back on, placed the knife into a pocket. Small square windows in the swinging doors allowed him to see some surgeon and his lackey performing what looked like an impromptu operation on a stark-naked patient. An autopsy was in progress.

Another naked body occupied another gurney off to the side, that looked to have already undergone the process from the way the midsection appeared; its torso having been open from sternum to cervix.

A birthmark on her hip made him sink deep within.

He rattled at the doors as he tried to enter the room. Why was this the one door that was not unlocked?

His clanging of the door had alerted the living occupants; heck he could have woken the dead. Reacting to his presence, the shocked surgeon told him he could not be there and needed to leave.

'That's my fiancée' he called, but the surgeon cared not. The exchange continued, but there was no faltering in the position of the physician, who's companion was now on a call as the coroner shouted that security was on the way. Shit. How could he be this close, but yet so far?

He was determined to get in that room, and he thumped his fist against the glass several times to no effect other than further his injuries. It hadn't even cracked. Reinforced with a wire mesh running through it, there was no way he would squeeze himself in even if he could break it. It was far too small.

Determination had besieged him. He cared not for the physical or emotional wellbeing of those on the other side as he continued like a rabid animal, attacking the door. He was going to get in. Some form of a magnetic lock held it at the top. The bottom could move more independently, a good inch or so as he beat against it. He dropped to the floor and filled the width of the hallway with his body stretched out, arms up, hands on one side, feet against the door. His memory flashed with the scene from 24 hours earlier, when in similar actions, he had forced open the cadaver cooler that had contained him.

He kicked. He kicked again. It was futile. He was not going to get in with the force of his body alone. He needed some implement, some form of battering ram. A scan of his surroundings showed a fire extinguisher at the end of the hallway. Its colour told of its dry powder contents, but this mattered not to his intended use. Just as she had used such a thing to escape from the scarred aggressor, he would use this to escape the antagonist of anarchy and be free from this demonic day.

Having retrieved it he struck the door several times, causing it to begin to split and crack.

This was it.

Continuing to hammer, the split grew, and he knew it would be only a few more strikes before he could get inside. The nurse was screaming and cowering in the corner. The forensic examiner was trying to shield her, placing himself and several trolleys of apparatus between the doorway and themselves, pleading with him to stop.

The door at the end of the hallway sprang open and a portly patrolman of short stature in a guard's uniform shouted at him to freeze. He was too cliché. Porky was brandishing a bright yellow taser pointed in his direction, and instructed him to get on the floor, face down, hands behind his head.

His wrist showed seconds over seven minutes left as he glanced at it before taking inspiration from his deceased damsel's earlier actions, pulling the pin and activating the extinguisher in the direction of the sentry. Filling the hallway with a cloud of white powder, he charged the man, slamming the canister into him and driving him backwards like a front row prop, sending him on to his backside and falling on top. Recovering himself, he began to run. He was actually running. The physical ailments could not hold him back as he burst into a sprint, smashing through a door into yet another hallway. Would there be more pursuers?

He followed the glowing green signs that told of the quickest way out, intended to direct in the dark to any emergency exits. This was the fastest he had moved all day. He lost balance more than once and putting out a hand to the wall, managed to stop from falling.

The exit was now in sight, a basic push bar mechanism was all that prevented his escape. A few more steps and he would be outside.

The door burst open without any hassle and the cold of the air struck his throat as he inhaled as much oxygen as he could to fuel his muscles that continued to propel him at an unrivalled pace. Rounding the corner of the building, the expanse of the car park was mostly vacant, there were few visitors at this hour. The emptiness left fewer places to hide from the pursuing patrolmen that doubtless wouldn't be too far behind. He weaved through the parked cars, crouching somewhat to evade detection should anyone be looking. A quick inspection suggested there was no one immediately able to cause imminent issue.

His pace had slowed, the toll of the sprint caught up with him. His legs tired within seconds to the point he could no longer stand. Like a sack of potatoes, he thudded to the ground. Slumped against the side of a vehicle, his head swirling from the exhaustion of all that he had endured. He sat to ponder his final moments.

Was this all he could amount to?

What use had been the day that he'd lived? He had been given one day to make a difference, and he was no closer now than a day ago.

He felt like a failure.

Chewing the cud of the situation, he considered the distorted day that had been plunged upon him. He recalled the six honest serving men that Kipling had coined so well.

What?

This was simple, he had lived it, at least he believed it so. Though in processing his ending endeavours, the second-hand information seemed crazy considering what had transpired. Was this really what was happening? Had it been true?

Why?

That was the question that required the most complex of answers. He would never know.

When?

It mattered not the time from when he had disappeared to when he had awakened. Only his 'day' had been of importance, and now he was at an end.

How?

This brought as many questions as 'what'. The meticulous planning and preparation that the puppet master must have partaken, was immeasurable. The taking of who knows how many people, the storage of all those bodies, under the influence of some drug to keep them in a state of suspense. The carefully measured poisons that would kill with near perfect timing. The planting of antidotes inside them all.

This was a feat of unimaginable precision.

What if they all got it wrong? Had the cycle of passing on parcels of information perpetuated a spiralling suffering? Was it really possible that all of these players had each been given a potion so different from the next that only their predecessor could save them? That really would be something. Surely not.

What then of the wickedness he had witnessed? Had the participants of this perverseness taken it upon themselves to be so violent and vile? Perhaps the melancholy of man had twisted what should have been into something so deranged. Was there a way that they each could have helped one another to prevent the poison from action? Information could be all that was supposed to be shared between any one of them and their predecessor.

Could their predecessor have meant to inform them how to save themselves?

If each had ingested an ingot of treasure for their own rescue, perhaps all they ever needed was to pass the potion and consume the contents?

If so, within him was the means to have prevented it all. To drink the vial was all he needed. But it was too late. His band showed less than a minute, the entire screen now consumed by descending digits, pulsating as he had earlier witnessed - 51, 50, 49.

The poison would soon take hold, he knew from witnessing the demise of both his girl and the giant, he had maybe fifteen minutes at best. What use was this time? Even with a laxative agent, surely, he could not pass the vial in time?

But maybe he could get his hands on it!

He would die shortly, or he could die trying. He removed the knife from his pocket and then with his battered hand struggling with the zip, opened the jacket. Lifting his shirt, he placed the tip of blade to the skin. It depressed a little as it had on her only two hours ago. He would have to inquire of his intestines within himself. Could he really manage to do that without passing out? Would the pain be too much for him to reach inside and rummage around? He was out of other options. He had to at least try.

Fifteen minutes at best. It was do or die, just as Goliath had told!

Checking the band one final time.

06

05

04

03

With a deep inhale, he pushed the blade in.

Don't miss out!

Visit the website below and you can sign up to receive emails whenever Brendan Kage publishes a new book. There's no charge and no obligation.

https://books2read.com/r/B-A-MBWWD-QVTJG

BOOKS 2 READ

Connecting independent readers to independent writers.

BV - #0245 - 210725 - C0 - 203/127/21 - PB - 9781068283314 - Gloss Lamination